Praise For *Unspeakable Things*

"Set in Lilydale, Minnesota, in the 1980s . . . the suspense never wavers in this page-turner."

—*Publishers Weekly*

"The atmospheric suspense novel is haunting because it's narrated from the point of view of a thirteen-year-old, an age that should be more innocent but often isn't. Even more chilling, it's based on real-life incidents. Lourey may be known for comic capers (*March of Crimes*), but this tense novel combines the best of a coming-of-age story with suspense and an unforgettable young narrator."

—*Library Journal* (starred review)

"Part suspense, part coming-of-age, Jess Lourey's *Unspeakable Things* is a story of creeping dread, about childhood when you know the monster under your bed is real. A novel that clings to you long after the last page."

—Lori Rader-Day, Edgar Award–nominated author of *Under a Dark Sky*

"A noose of a novel that tightens by inches. The squirming tension comes from every direction—including the ones that are supposed to be safe. I felt complicit as I read, as if at any moment I stopped I would be abandoning Cassie, alone, in the dark, straining to listen and fearing to hear."

—Marcus Sakey, bestselling author of *Brilliance*

"*Unspeakable Things* is an absolutely riveting novel about the poisonous secrets buried deep in towns and families. Jess Lourey has created a story that will chill you to the bone and a main character who will break your heart wide open."

—Lou Berney, Edgar Award–winning author of *November Road*

"Prolific mystery writer Lourey tells of a matriarchal clan of witches joining forces against age-old evil . . . The novel is tightly plotted, and Lourey shines when depicting relationships—romantic ones as well as tangled links between Catalains . . . Lourey emphasizes the ties that bind in spite of secrets and resentment."

—*Kirkus Reviews*

"Lourey expertly concocts a Gothic fusion of long-held secrets, melancholy, and resolve . . . Exquisitely written in naturally flowing, expressive language, the book delves into the special relationships between sisters, and mothers and daughters."

—*Publishers Weekly*

PRAISE FOR *SALEM'S CIPHER*

"A fast-paced, sometimes brutal thriller reminiscent of Dan Brown's *The Da Vinci Code*."

—*Booklist* (starred review)

"[A] hair-raising thrill ride."

—*Library Journal* (starred review)

"The fascinating historical information combined with a story line ripped from the headlines will hook conspiracy theorists and action addicts alike."

—*Kirkus Reviews*

"Fans of *The Da Vinci Code* are going to love this book . . . one of my favorite reads of 2016."

—*Crimespree Magazine*

"This suspenseful tale has something for absolutely everyone to enjoy."
—*Suspense Magazine*

PRAISE FOR *MERCY'S CHASE*

"An immersive voice, an intriguing story, a wonderful character—highly recommended!"
—Lee Child, #1 *New York Times* bestselling author

"Both a sweeping adventure and race-against-time thriller, *Mercy's Chase* is fascinating, fierce, and brimming with heart—just like its heroine, Salem Wiley."
—Meg Gardiner, author of *Into the Black Nowhere*

"Action-packed, great writing taut with suspense, an appealing main character to root for—who could ask for anything more?"
—Buried Under Books

PRAISE FOR *MAY DAY*

"Jess Lourey writes about a small-town assistant librarian, but this is no genteel traditional mystery. Mira James likes guys in a big way, likes booze, and isn't afraid of motorcycles. She flees a dead-end job and a dead-end boyfriend in Minneapolis and ends up in Battle Lake, a little town with plenty of dirty secrets. The first-person narrative in *May Day* is fresh, the characters quirky. Minnesota has many fine crime writers, and Jess Lourey has just entered their ranks!"
—Ellen Hart, award-winning author of the Jane Lawless and Sophie Greenway series

"This trade paperback packed a punch . . . I loved it from the get-go!"
—*Tulsa World*

"What a romp this is! I found myself laughing out loud . . ."
—*Crimespree Magazine*

"Mira digs up a closetful of dirty secrets, including sex parties, cross-dressing, and blackmail, on her way to exposing the killer. Lourey's debut has a likable heroine and surfeit of sass."
—*Kirkus Reviews*

PRAISE FOR *REWRITE YOUR LIFE: DISCOVER YOUR TRUTH THROUGH THE HEALING POWER OF FICTION*

"Interweaving practical advice with stories and insights garnered in her own writing journey, Jessica Lourey offers a step-by-step guide for writers struggling to create fiction from their life experiences. But this book isn't just about writing. It's also about the power of stories to transform those who write them. I know of no other guide that delivers on its promise with such honesty, simplicity, and beauty."
—William Kent Krueger, *New York Times* bestselling author of the Cork O'Connor Series and *Ordinary Grace*

BLOODLINE

BLOODLINE

JESS LOUREY

THOMAS & MERCER

Published by Thomas & Mercer, Seattle

www.apub.com

Amazon, the Amazon logo, and Thomas & Mercer are trademarks of Amazon.com, Inc., or its affiliates.

ISBN-13: 9781542016315
ISBN-10: 1542016312

Cover design by Caroline Teagle Johnson

Printed in the United States of America

To Amanda, who's the real deal

AUTHOR'S NOTE

On September 5, 1944, six-year-old Victor John "Jackie" Theel of Paynesville, Minnesota, walked to his first day of morning kindergarten wearing a blue sailor suit with a square-cut collar. The matching long pants were secured at the waist, a safety pin replacing the back button. Towheaded Jackie sported new black shoes and a fresh scratch below his right eye. His older brother held his hand on the walk. At lunch, Jackie's teacher allowed him to leave school despite instructions otherwise from his mother.

He never made it home.

Soon after Jackie left school, a woman claimed to have seen a boy weeping as he walked along Highway 23 on the other side of town. A group of teenagers testified that they spotted something similar later that day. The Civil Air Patrol was brought in for search and rescue. A bloodhound tracked Jackie's route, wandering from the school to the nearby Crow River, before losing his scent. Other leads were followed, but Jackie was never found.

Mrs. Harold Theel, Jackie's mother, stated in an interview conducted a year after her son disappeared that she had "several theories" about what happened to Jackie but couldn't prove any of them. The most chilling statement in response to Jackie's disappearance came from Sheriff Art McIntee, local lead in the 1944 investigation, who had this to say about Paynesville: "[T]here is something in the community we haven't figured out."

But outside Paynesville—my hometown—the world moved on.

In 2016, in response to developments in another abduction with Paynesville roots, Kare 11 News reached out to the Minnesota Bureau of Criminal Apprehension for an update on Jackie's then decades-old case. The BCA claimed to have never investigated it. In addition, the Stearns County Sheriff's Office had purged all pre-1960s reports.

There was no official record of Jackie's disappearance to be found.

However, Jackie's mom never gave up on finding her son. She had kept tucked in her Bible the original BCA circular, which featured his case number—32719—above a photo of Jackie wearing his sailor suit and smiling shyly.

Bloodline was inspired in part by Jackie's story and the mystery that still surrounds it.

PART I

A woman's scream wakes me.

I whip my head and—*hunh*—pain ricochets, a blistering agony. My skin's been peeled off, my bones scraped clean.

Breathe.

Where's the pain coming from?

Everywhere.

Move slowly.

Blink. Blink again.

I'm lying down.

The room. I recognize it. Crown molding. Walls painted lemon. A dresser and next to it a vanity, both in matching oak. The heat is oppressive, the air thick as wool. And the smell. Sweet Jesus. It's turgid and salty, the rank odor of a heaving animal, cornered, at the end of the hunt.

Get out.

I try to move, but my legs are strapped down.

Or paralyzed.

My breath catches—*lord please no*—and even that tiny movement amplifies the stabbing torment, but (*the struggle makes me weep*) . . . I can move my toes. At least I think I can. I must see to believe. I raise my head just enough, swallowing against the brown-green waves of nausea, my eyelids flapping to hold the pain at bay.

I cling to consciousness, promising myself that I am *me*, that I know things.

I'm Joan Harken. I'm a reporter.

My neck trembles with the effort of holding up my head. Triple images condense to double, and then the vertigo passes, and I can see. A leg pokes outside the bed coverings, a slab of white against the blue-and-red quilt.

My leg. Toes wiggling.

I'm not paralyzed.

This smallest sip of relief is immediately swamped by a sudden clarion panic.

Something's missing.

The missing is crucial, I know this in my scraped-raw bones, but what is it?

My head drops onto the pillow, skin fish-clammy. I must check the contours of my body, locate the absence. I drag my other leg, the one still tucked under the quilt, a few inches to the side, and the scratch of sheets against flesh assures me.

I have two legs.

I struggle my arms out from beneath the blanket, hold them up, study them as if they belong to someone else. They're unmarked despite the deep ache at their centers. I wave my fingers, a magician about to perform a trick. They work.

I probe my head. It's tender, logy but unmarked.

Good. I need my head.

A wheeze, a sort of laugh, hikes my chest, but the motion sets cold worms of nausea squirming across my flesh. I must move slowly, or I'll black out.

Gently, inch by inch, my hands slip beneath the quilt and travel south.

They find my breasts. Swollen and aching. Damp.

Intact.

Except . . . their peculiar pain licks at something, sharp and bloody.

What is it?

Farther south. My hands don't want to go there, they're hot with pushback, but a morbid *need to know* forces them.

They reach my stomach.

It's soft, quaggy.

Empty.

My baby is no longer inside.

That's when I understand.

I am the woman screaming.

CHAPTER 1

Minnesota, 1968

"They're going to love you, Joanie."

I smile at my fiancé, grab his hand. Pray that he's right. It's been so sudden, this move. My editors had passed me over for the promotion. That same day, Dr. King was murdered in Memphis, where he'd traveled to march peacefully for the rights of mostly Negro sanitation workers.

The nation descended into chaos.

In DC, marines guarded the Capitol steps with machine guns while buildings were torched. Baltimore's protests overwhelmed the National Guard. Paratroopers and artillerymen were called in. Cincinnati fell under siege, and Chicago's West Side burned. Decades of festering tension, fueled by black poverty and racism and war resistance, exploded to the surface.

Getting mugged had been the final kick.

Let's move to Lilydale. Deck's words the night of the mugging were soothing, his face bright. He held me as I cried, releasing me only to clean my wounds. *We'll be sheltered there, safe from the world. Promise. You won't believe how perfect it is.*

I didn't agree right away, not by a long shot, but then he mentioned preserving his life by avoiding the draft—his dad was the head of the county draft board and had the power to save Deck from Vietnam; he was also mayor of Lilydale, a postcard-perfect town as Deck described it, nestled two and a half hours northwest of Minneapolis—and what could I say?

I'm sitting on one leg as I grip Deck's hand, perched in the Chevelle's passenger seat, hurtling toward my new home, a place I've never been. My cat is curled on my lap, and with my free hand, I'm caressing the itchy stab wounds through my pantyhose. Leftovers from the mugging. They're angry red scabs, halfway to healed. They weren't deep, and if not for them, and for Deck's reaction, the mugging would have already faded into the shadows of my mind. Why dwell on what you can't change?

Deck was shocked, though, horrified, swore that strangers didn't assault women in his hometown. Lilydale was peaceful, friendly. Everyone knew everyone, looked out for one another. The world outside might scream and swirl like a tornado, but Lilydale floated in a bubble, outside of time, as safe as a smile. The town even had a newspaper, Deck said. The *Lilydale Gazette*. I might finally get my byline.

Yes, I said, finally convinced. *Yes, please.*

It wasn't just the byline. After a childhood of moving from one city to another, the idea of settling down with Deck, of *belonging*, well, it suddenly sounded all right. We packed up our tiny apartment within days, and here we are, humming along the road to a new life. The skyscrapers and stores of Minneapolis almost immediately gave way to lonely swaths of prairie, only the occasional farm to give scale to the emptiness.

I've never lived outside a city. Driven through the countryside, to be sure, but never with the intention of making it my home.

The specter of permanence makes the landscape as welcoming as the moon.

I squash that thought, rubbing one of the wounds so hard the scab cracks, leaking crayon-red blood into my pantyhose.

I chose this.

Deck's tapping his fingers along to "I Can See for Miles." The radio's been blotchy the last half an hour, but the music is clear as water now. I wish it weren't. The Who unsettle me. They're all sneaky drums and sharp guitar. Particularly this song. It's too near the bone because I truly *can* see for miles. There's not a building in sight, not even a barn, just the forever grass.

"Nowhere to hide," I say, stroking Slow Henry, the cat purring in my lap.

Deck's fingers freeze. "What?"

I grin and toss my head, but I'm seeing Frances. My mom. She's bright-eyed in the memory, years before the cancer fishhooked her. We're moving, maybe from Seattle to San Francisco? I can't line them all up. Sometimes we didn't stay long enough to enroll me in a school.

"I love this," Mom's saying as we pull into New Town, its skyline reminding me of a castle rampart.

"Seeing a city for the first time?" I ask. My hair's in pigtails, so I'm younger than thirteen, the age that annoyance gave way to a warm fizzing when a boy strutted by. That buzz ignited a whole parade of changes. Hair brushed a hundred strokes before bed, until it gleamed, until I was as glossy as a horse, and no way was I going to hide that power in little-girl pigtails. Cheeks pinched and lips licked when I might be *seen*. My own strut, awkward and unnoticed.

Mom lights a cigarette. The gritty, elegant smell soothes me. Always has.

"Nah," she says, taking a deep suck. "Not *seeing* a city."

I'm studying her profile. I scored her nose. The rest of my features—brown eyes, brown hair, sharp cheekbones—must be from my dad, though I don't remember what he looked like. I don't even recall his name, though I bet she'd tell me if I asked. But what'd be the point? I've been told he was worthless, a petty criminal, and that was enough.

She blows out the smoke. I lean into it.

"*Being* in a big city is what I love. Those long, empty stretches of road between? No good. Nowhere to hide. Small towns are even worse. Might as well tattoo a bull's-eye on your back. Give me tall buildings and a crowd of strangers any day of the week."

Nowhere to hide.

My mother was given to drama. It grew worse right at the end. I wonder what Deck would have thought of her. We met two weeks after she died. I lean forward to nuzzle my face in Slow Henry's lush Creamsicle fur. He smells like dust.

"Are we close?" I ask Deck.

"Close as a whisper," he says, tipping his head toward the windshield. His fingers are tapping again.

I turn down the radio and squint. We passed through the last town ten miles back. It was little more than a cross street with a filling station. Ahead, black sentinel trees have popped up, swallowing the road, a thick forest of pine and oak as out of place as an overnight carnival on this flat plate of earth. There's a sign, though, a billboard offering big, looping words.

Slow Henry stretches in my lap, gunning his motor. I pet him absentmindedly, struggling to read the message. It takes several moments of tires thrumming on pavement before we're close enough.

LILYDALE
COME HOME FOREVER

The promise is surrounded by white flowers.

Lilies, of course.

Before I can process the words, we've zoomed past the sign and pierced the dark watchman woods, a pop as we push through the skin of my past life, past the trees jutting like swords, and emerge into a new world, bright and solid.

I'm holding my breath, have been since the sign, a child's game to survive a tunnel.

Hold it 'til the end and make a wish!

I release the breath through my nose, craning to stare behind us. The trees look different on this side. Tire-swing ready. I face front. We're at Lilydale's edge. I'm relieved to see it's significantly larger than the villages we've passed through. Houses, clean and tight, immaculate squares of lawn, shops including a real estate office, a barber, a filling station selling unleaded for thirty-two cents a gallon, a clot of kids biking down side streets, lobbing jokes, women in pretty spring frocks strolling in twos, laughing.

It's everything Deck promised and more.

The rocky knot between my shoulder blades relaxes, finally. I crank down my window and inhale the scent of fresh lilacs.

Slow Henry swats at a lock of my hair stirred by the breeze, and I smile.

It's a fairy tale, a storybook land. Even the sun seems to be shining brighter.

The prickling worry I've nurtured on the drive, the paranoia as the towns grew smaller and the prairie hungrier, it all flows away. *Nowhere to hide, my ass.* I squeeze Deck's hand, the other resting on my belly. The baby is barely showing, the tiny swelling easily hidden beneath a loose blouse.

Deck squeezes back. "What is it, darling?"

"I believe I may be the luckiest girl in the world," I say.

The sun chooses that moment to slide behind the clouds, a gloomy wink, almost as if it hears me.

CHAPTER 2

It's unsettling how much Deck and his father look alike.

That's what wallops me when I lay eyes on his parents for the first time.

Deck resembles a crew-cut Jerry Lewis from *Three on a Couch* enough to get stopped by girls on the street. His dad is nearly a twin other than the gray stippling his hair and the pooching at his belly. A senior Jerry Lewis standing next to his wife. Her brown-silver hair is enormous, a tortoiseshell comb holding the towering haystack in place, two well-chosen tendrils loose, one on each side, curling in front of her ears. She's wearing a crisp summer dress, one she's clearly ironed and starched. Her perfection makes me feel filthy in comparison, even from a distance, even from inside a car.

They're waiting—Mr. and Mrs. Ronald Schmidt—outside a pretty little white craftsman with blue shutters when we pull up. Ronald's arm is tossed around Barbara's shoulder. She's holding a covered Corning Ware dish, a flick of desperation in her wide-set eyes. Our new house is on Mill Street, a short residential lane just off Lilydale's downtown. The entire avenue is lined with oak and maple trees, a slice of apple pie straight out of the '50s.

I lick dry lips and smooth my dress, rumpled and covered in cat hair from the drive. Deck I love. Same with the town; I'm going to *make* myself feel it. Meeting parents, though? Never been my game. I'm having a hard time drawing a full breath.

"You ready, baby?" Deck asks, cranking the car into park.

He's being thoughtful. He's so eager to go to his parents that he's trembling. I'm struck anew by how handsome he is, how uncomplicated his love. I like that about him, that he isn't slick and quick. It's a breath of fresh air after the fast-talking guys I've been with. Plus, he's the best damn kisser.

"Ready as rice," I say, my voice hitching.

He lands a peck on my cheek. "This is your home now, Joanie. And my parents are your family. You can relax and settle down for the first time in your life."

"Deck, I'm fine," I say. "Go on. I'm just gonna grab Slow Henry."

Deck's out of the car before the sentence leaves my mouth. I pretend to reach down, into the footwell where Slow Henry hopped when the car jerked to a stop, but I'm watching Barbara openly sob as she sets the hot dish on the sidewalk and clamps her arms around her son. Minneapolis is only two and a half hours away. Why haven't they visited in the nearly year Deck and I have been together?

My cheeks flame as I realize Ronald is watching me watch Barbara, expressionless.

Is the jealousy spelled out on my face? *He gets a mother* and *a father.* I duck all the way down, out of sight, making the situation impossibly worse. I should have just waved. *All's fine here! Just a normal person thinking normal thoughts.*

I learned that trick in my fifth high school. Always smile. Agree. Be invisible when you can, friendly when they spot you. But then a spike of self-anger surprises me. *I'm not that girl anymore. I'm a grown woman. A reporter. I have a fiancé and a baby on the way.*

I take a breath. Lift Slow Henry, who doesn't let anyone but me hold him. Wish I had a drink, just a nip to grind down the edges. It's not only parents. Meeting new people period has always been difficult.

I'm afraid they'll see right through me, recognize that hiding beneath the prim clothes and proper makeup is a feral girl wearing hand-me-downs, never staying put long enough to make friends, certain everyone knows some trick of getting along that she doesn't. Rooming with Libby and Ursula in college was the first time in my life I had girlfriends.

Then along came Deck, sweeping me off my feet and, ten months later, out of Minneapolis.

I step out of the car tentatively.

This is not a speed that Ronald acknowledges.

"Our new daughter!" he booms, charging toward me with arms outstretched. It's a relief that his voice at least is very different from Deck's. Deck has an ordinary voice, slightly nasal. When Ronald speaks, it sounds like footsteps in gravel. Right before he embraces me, his glance lingers on the faded bruises at my neck and face long enough that I wonder if I've forgotten to apply foundation to them. Deck and I agreed that we'd never tell anyone but Ursula about the mugging.

It's one of the gifts of, once again, moving away from almost everyone I know.

Before I grow too self-conscious, I'm girded by Ronald's chain-link arms, his menthol scent reminding me of my mom. I'm surprised by the push of tears, which I blink back. *The pregnancy is making me moody.*

Ronald allows room in the hug for Slow Henry, who I'm cradling.

I'm not used to being held like this and don't know how long to stay put. My ear is pressed to Ronald's chest, so I count his heartbeats. They're strong and steady. I reach fourteen before he releases me and steps back, grinning widely, and indicates his wife.

"This is Barbara."

I smile at the woman clinging to Deck like she's afraid he'll otherwise float away, a precious peach balloon released by mistake and forever.

"So nice to meet you," I say, pointing at the dish on the ground. "Can I help you with that?"

How they knew exactly when we'd arrive is beyond me. I stifle a funeral giggle at the image of them standing in this spot for hours, Ronald glancing at his silver wristwatch, Barbara gripping her hot dish and wearing that desperate expression.

"Thank you, but I have it," Barbara says, lips curving shyly. She lets go of Deck—I startle when he stays put, solid, not a balloon after all—to grab the Corning Ware before disappearing inside the house.

The craftsman was Barbara and Ronald's home for decades. They grew up in Lilydale, bought it when they married, raised Deck here, and then relocated to a small rambler half a block up a few years ago, trying with no luck to rent the craftsman.

When Deck told them we'd be moving to Lilydale, they offered us their first house.

I asked Deck why they'd gone through the trouble of moving to find themselves living on the end of the same street. He said they'd been hoping for years he'd return to Lilydale and had saved his childhood home for him.

Well, they've gotten their wish.

I turn to Ronald. "Thank you for letting us stay here."

"Stay here? It's your home!" he exclaims.

I suspect he exclaims many things. He's one of those men. My journalism professor was like that. Owned every room he walked into. All the girls wanted him. He selected a sophomore from Illinois. I would watch her approach him after class, whisper and flirt, a mix of jealousy and awe crackling under my skin. Imagine, being *that* comfortable with yourself, *that* sure of the love you're due.

I excuse myself to check out the new house.

Deck's old house.

"Dad and I'll be inside in a minute," Deck calls to me as I walk away. "I need to dig out my briefcase. Show yourself around."

His briefcase is behind the driver's seat. I tucked it there myself and then pointed it out before we left Minneapolis. He must be giving me a chance to settle in before our "helpers" arrive. He warned me before we pulled out of the Cities that there'd be a large welcoming party soon after we showed up.

"Your high school friends?" I'd asked.

His eyes slid sideways. Of course not. They'd be off at war.

Deck has managed to avoid the draft so far, but if we'd stayed in Minneapolis, it would have been only a matter of time. It's a mercy that the move happened so quickly.

Almost before I had regrets.

I step inside the house. Slow Henry jumps out of my arms with a squawk and sets off to explore. The interior smells musty, like there was water in the basement at one time. The windows are closed. When I lean in to open the nearest, I discover it's painted shut. Deck'll have to fix that. I glide from the front den to the kitchen and am childishly excited to spot a newish refrigerator and a dishwasher, in matching avocado! I've never lived in a house in my life, always apartments.

"Isn't the kitchen lovely?" Barbara asks. She's sliding the dish she's brought into the oven. "We purchased the new appliances when we moved out. They've been waiting for Deck ever since. Please, make yourself at home."

I smile and continue my tour. Opening doors, I discover a pantry, a dirt basement that I have no intention of ever visiting (show me someone who's not afraid of dirt basements, and I'll show you a person not right in the head), and a connection to the dining room. I step into the pantry, running my fingers along the shelves. They hold a generous stock of staples. Flour, sugar, canned carrots and peas. Tucked in the back I discover a half-full bottle of crème de menthe, absinthe-green and sticky.

I can hear Barbara puttering in the kitchen, running water. I unscrew the cap, inhale the syrupy toothpaste smell, and take a swig. The warmth melts into my blood.

Thank you, sweet liquor.

I have no intention of following in my mom's footsteps (she'd enjoyed a shot of brandy every night before bed when pregnant with me—good for *my* development and *her* rest, she'd said), but boy, do I need the courage right now. I take another long pull, swishing it around my teeth, then screw the cap back on, return the bottle to the shelf, and glide into the dining room.

My mood picks up even more when I spot the photos of Deck nailed to the wall, starting with him at age five or six and ending with his high school graduation. I straighten the frame holding an image of him wearing his mortarboard, grinning, and feel my heart swell. Opposite the photos is a lovely built-in sideboard and cabinets, one of them stacked with china. I walk over and rest my cheek against the leaded glass of the cabinet nearest me, soothed by its coolness.

This is my new home.

Minneapolis is my history, Lilydale my present and future.

I am happy, safe.

A shuffling behind me tells me someone has entered the room. I peel away from the cabinet to spot Deck crouched by the dining room table, his back to me. He's setting down our knickknack box.

Staring at his back, I'm overwhelmed by a love so strong I nearly weep with it.

Ten months ago, Deck introduced himself at the 620 Club, a bar I frequented every Friday night after work with some of the women in the typing pool. It's located near the *Minneapolis Star*'s Downtown East offices, and it's always packed with newspaper people, local sports stars, and businessmen, all vying for a spot at the men's-only Round Table. That's where all the real Minneapolis action happens. Deck stood out in that crowd, buttoned up with a buzz cut, not my type at all. In fact, when I first spotted him, I thought *Ken Doll* and kept looking.

But he made his way over, laid down a line so corny I couldn't help but laugh (*If I could rearrange the alphabet, I'd put U and I together*), and bought me a brandy Alexander. He was so adoring, hanging on my every word, that I agreed to meet him for coffee the next morning. We've been together ever since. Life's a gas, right?

"Darling, I love it here," I say to him, my voice low and husky as I kneel behind him and snake my hands around his waist. "And I'm looking forward to loving *you* here."

When he doesn't respond, I rub his chest, then move one hand suggestively lower. It's terribly naughty—his mom is in the other room—but the liquor has me feeling loose, and wasn't Deck the one who told me to relax?

He places his hands over mine, firmly, stands, and turns.

It's not Deck I'm caressing.

It's Ronald.

CHAPTER 3

Shame explodes across my skin.

Ronald is saying all the things people are supposed to say in this situation (*no harm, could have happened to anyone, I'm so glad*—Barbara and I *are so glad*—*that you love it here*), but I can only gargle in response. I back away, hands held in front, palms out, until I hit the wall and spin, see the stairs (*escape*), and run up them, breath ragged. I duck inside the first room I hit and slide to the floor.

Great job, Joan. For your encore, maybe you could walk in on Barbara on the toilet.

My cheeks are hot, probably scarlet. I glance around. Might as well get used to this room, as I'm never leaving it. Looks like the master bedroom. It's fully wallpapered, the pattern red-and-gold flowers, so loud it hurts my ears. A fresh breeze spooks the curtain, itself a clashing floral pattern.

This must have been Deck's parents' bedroom.

If Ronald follows me into here, I might as well commit hari-kari now and get it over with.

When after several calming breaths he doesn't appear, my shame gives way to anger. Why didn't he stop me sooner? Before I opened my mouth and reached for his zipper, for God's sake.

But that's not fair. He was probably as shocked as me.

My eyes begin itching, and I notice something in this room smells oversweet, like fruit gone bad. I stand and walk to the window, the deep pine-green carpeting swallowing my footsteps. The window is open only an inch, and despite all my strength, I can't open it any farther. I kneel to gasp at the air like a fish in a bucket.

While the warm May breeze clears my nose, I focus on the house next door. It's a near copy of this one—a craftsman, only in reverse colors, blue with white shutters. And the bedroom I'm staring into doesn't have wallpaper but is laid out identically, sheets draped over the furniture.

Huh. Two empty houses next to each other. Probably haunted. I snort. That's silly. I saw a single poster for *Rosemary's Baby* before we left Minneapolis, and now I'm imagining demons and conspiracies in this sweet little town when I've just proven myself the most dangerous thing on wheels.

Having arrived not even an hour ago, I've already groped the mayor. *You're just tired from all the packing. Plus, nerves. Settle down already.*

A brush at my ankle makes me jump out of my hair.

"Slow Henry!" I scoop him up, chiding myself for being so excitable. "You're lucky my knife bites are nearly all better, you old codger, or I'd be crying right now."

The sudden bustle and clamor of voices downstairs tells me the welcoming committee has arrived. I peek inside the other rooms—a spare bedroom, a bathroom, a large linen closet—then pop into the bathroom, finger-combing my hair and pinching my cheeks for color. No point in delaying the inevitable.

If Ronald's a gentleman, he won't mention my mortifying mistake.

In fact, I'm going to decide it never happened.

"Come on, you," I say to Slow Henry.

I toss a parting glance at the house next door, noticing its window is open the exact height as mine. I shiver and squeeze Slow Henry tighter, making my way to the main floor.

The dining room seems to have shrunk, jammed as it is with strangers, all of them eagerly watching me descend, a hungry nest clamoring as its food drops down. My gut grows slimy.

"There she is!" a large man booms from the bottom of the stairs, his voice so loud that Slow Henry yowls and leaps out of my arms. The man is square-jawed, one of the biggest humans I've ever seen, the size and build of a grizzly bear. "Ronald and Barbara's new daughter-in-law!"

"Mr. Brody," Deck cautions, appearing beside the man.

Before I can figure out the joke, Mr. Brody wraps me in a hug that steals my breath.

"My name's Clan," he says, still too loud. "Clan Brody. We live right next door."

Engulfed in his arms, I think about the empty house I just peeked inside, the one with sheets draped over the furniture. He must mean the other next door.

"You'll have to tell my wife, Catherine, if you need anything," he continues. "She's in charge of Lilydale's welcoming committee."

"Nice to meet you," I murmur into his shirt.

They sure like their hugs in Lilydale.

"Oh, let her go, Clan," I hear. I'm released to face a woman with a sharp, broad face. She looks familiar.

"I'm Catherine," she says, holding out her hand.

When I clasp it, I realize she doesn't look like anyone I know. Rather, she's a dead ringer for the mother captured in Dorothea Lange's iconic Depression-era photo, the one of a woman sitting grimly on the edge of a tent, covered with her dirty, tired-looking children. *Migrant Mother.* That's the photo's name.

Clan the Brody Bear and Catherine the Migrant Mother.

"My turn," I hear.

Catherine releases my hand. Another man moves in to embrace me, but he makes it short, a quick squeeze before stepping back. He's wearing browline glasses, striking against his tight, narrow face.

"Mr. Schramel," Deck says respectfully, gripping the man's hand before turning to the woman with mouse-colored hair standing next to him. "Mrs. Schramel."

Another casserole, I think, noting her acorn-shaped covered Pyrex dish with a matching acorn-patterned towel wrapped around its bottom and handles. But then I catch myself being ungenerous. It's a reflex, something I do as protection when I'm overwhelmed. Here I am judging these lovely people—Deck's family and friends—when they're bringing me food and welcome.

"Mildred," she says, ducking her fuzzy brown head.

Browline Schramel and Mildred the Mouse.

It's what I do to organize the chaos of the world: create characters out of the people I meet and turn those characters into stories. But there are too many new faces coming at me. Browline Schramel and Mildred the Mouse step aside, and I find myself in the arms of a police officer, still in uniform.

"Amory Bauer," he says, "chief of police. And this is my wife, Rue."

If I were to pick two people in the crowded den less likely to be a couple, it would be Amory and Rue. She's tiny and birdlike. Her neck twitches, and her eyes behind her glasses dart everywhere. Amory, however, is a mountain of a man, even larger than Clan in girth but not height. He was handsome once, I can tell from the pale blue of his eyes and the silver streaking his ink-black hair. He's carrying forty extra pounds, though, most of it inner tubing his stomach. His smile, while dashing, has an arrogant tilt.

My mother never liked police officers. Said they couldn't be trusted, not one of them.

Amory Mountain and Birdie Rue.

"Last but not least," Ronald says, pushing a wheelchair to the front of the receiving line. (*That's what this is. A receiving line.*) The man in the wheelchair is hunched and trembling.

"Pleased to meet you," I say, hands stiff at my side. Should I crouch so I'm at his eye level? I hate myself for not knowing how to speak to someone in his condition. I dearly hope I'm not making him uncomfortable.

"Did you hear that, Stanley?" A woman appears next to him, patting his hand, gazing at him lovingly before winking at me. "This is Deck's girl. She says she's pleased to meet you."

Stanley doesn't make a noise, but he drags his rocking head upward for a moment. A bulbous nose shades thin lips. I think I spot a flash of something smart in his rheumy brown eyes, but the light promptly fades.

The woman holds out her hand. "I'm Dorothy. Dorothy Lily."

Despite being petite, she carries herself in a way that suggests authority. She's wearing a smart red pantsuit, the flower-shaped, enameled white locket at her neck her only jewelry. I self-consciously straighten my posture. "Joan. So nice of you to drop by."

"So nice of you to move in," she says, her smile distant but warm. "It's been too long since we had young blood on Mill Street."

Startled, I glance around the room. The guests are snacking on Ritz crackers and deviled eggs brought by I don't know who, the men drinking beers like they've visited here before. I suppose they have. "You all live on Mill Street?"

She nods, and something slips in her face. It's gone so quickly that I almost believe I imagined it, like Stanley's flash of intelligence. "Most of our lives. I tell you what, I wouldn't mind moving south, at least for the winter, but with Stanley's condition, travel is out of the question."

Sad Stanley and Saint Dorothy, the Lovely Lilies of Lilydale.

"I'm so sorry," I murmur, unsure whether it's the proper response. "Will you excuse me?"

I suddenly, desperately, want to return to the grungy little one-bedroom Minneapolis apartment Deck and I shared for the last six months. Just me, him, and Slow Henry, tucking into eggs and toast in our kitchen nook, watching Sunday television on our drooping couch, making love like we invented it in our tiny bedroom.

Deck, catching my eye across the space, seems to read my mind. He smiles, his dimples lighting up the room.

I paste on a matching grin. I will make the best of this.

For Deck.

For the baby.

CHAPTER 4

"They really all live on Mill Street?"

Deck's perched on the edge of our bed, which one of our neighbors set up and made for us, sheets, pillowcases, bedspread and all. (*Who makes someone else's bed?*) After meeting what seemed like the whole town, I spent the rest of the afternoon in the kitchen, accepting hot dishes and feeling stunned, like a cricket dropped into a beehive.

I'm exhausted to my core.

"My parents, plus the eight who were here right away," Deck says.

"Some of the people who came later seemed nervous," I say, remembering the way the non–Mill Streeters seemed to be staring at Ronald for approval. Come to think of it, the whole welcome party was like some sort of royal gathering, with the highborn first and the commoners allowed after.

Deck chuckles. "Probably because you were hosting the most important families in town. The latecomers were ass-kissers. I didn't know half of them. They just showed up to get in good with my dad and Amory, mark my word." He pats the open spot next to him. "Come to bed?"

I drop my nightgown over my shoulders. "I have to brush my teeth first."

"Isn't it nice, having a bathroom right off the bedroom?"

"I won't remember all their names."

The lie gives me a fizz of pleasure.

The people I've met today are locked in my treasure chest, their names my rubies and sapphires. And I finally have space to spin their stories. *Clan the Brody Bear hibernates in his cave while Catherine the Migrant Mother hunts to feed her starving children. Browline Schramel and Mildred the Mouse live in someone's cupboard, like the Borrowers. Amory Mountain and Birdie Rue solve crimes. She's the brains, he's the brawn. Sad Stanley and Saint Dorothy, the Lovely Lilies of Lilydale, embark on a romantic adventure, one where they realize Stanley really can walk. They simultaneously inherit a million dollars, which they use to open a wheelchair factory for orphans.*

Deck sighs. He doesn't like this game, but he'll play it. "You *know* you never forget a name, Joanie. You're just tired. You'll recall my mom and dad, of course. Clan and Catherine Brody live next door. Clan's employed at Dad's insurance company, where I'll be working, too. Teddy Schramel with the glasses is an engineer at the phone company. His wife is Mildred. Amory Bauer is the police chief. His wife's name escapes me at the moment because I guess I'm tired, too."

Birdie Rue.

"Stanley's in the wheelchair. That's new. He's a direct descendant of the original founders of Lilydale, you know, practically royalty here back in the day. His wife is Dorothy, and that's it for the Mill Streeters. The others who showed up live in town, but not on this street."

I duck into the bathroom and then step out, gripping a toothbrush with a pearl of toothpaste gleaming on it. "But the person who owns the newspaper never dropped by?"

"Joanie, you know I would have told you if he did."

"It's just that I need a job, Deck. I have to write." This is true. If I don't get all the stories I carry in my head out on paper, they turn on me, like an infected sliver just beneath the skin. I've been that way for as long as I can remember.

I return to the bathroom, run water over the toothpaste, and start brushing. *Clan the Brody Bear needs insurance to survive the winter, and Catherine the Migrant Mother won't sell it to him. Browline Schramel and Mildred the Mouse live inside a telephone, one that Browline Schramel is always tinkering with.*

"I know you have to write, baby. Come to bed?"

"What did Stanley do before . . . before he retired?" I ask around a mouthful of toothpaste.

"Attorney."

Sad Stanley earns a million dollars in the case of a lifetime, and he and Saint Dorothy donate the money to crippled children.

I brush all my teeth for another full minute, rinse, spit, wash my toothbrush, drop it into the holder, and pad into our bedroom. "I wish we could fast-forward to being done, being settled in, everyone knowing about the baby," I say, pulling my thoughts back. "I want to be on the other side of all this, where everyone's happy."

He's suddenly studying the wallpaper as if it's a love note.

I don't know why he's acting uncomfortable, but he is. I change the subject. "Why do you think the house looks empty next door?"

His head jerks, as if I've woken him. "The green house? I told you. That's the Brodys'. Clan and Catherine."

"No, the other one." I drift to the window, which someone has closed. I tap the glass, indicating the white-shuttered craftsman on the other side of our driveway. I can see by the shadowy streetlight that the window mirroring ours has also been closed. Guess nobody in this town likes fresh air.

Deck appears behind me, our images a warped version of *American Gothic* reflected back at us. "That's Dorothy and Stan's. I suppose they don't need the second floor now that Stan's in that wheelchair."

I nod, let him wrap his arms around me. He's nuzzling my hair, whispering how much he loves me, when a face appears in the opposite window. I scream and yank the curtains shut.

"What is it?" Deck asks, releasing me.

"Dorothy," I say, my heartbeat clobbering my veins. "She was staring at us from that empty room."

Deck's brow creases. "You sure? That doesn't seem right." He flicks off our bedroom light and returns to the window, pulling the curtain to peek at the edge and then sliding it all the way open. "See? No one there. Probably only your reflection."

"Maybe," I say, peering out. Except I still feel the jolt, electric, like I've licked a battery. I close the curtains again, with finality.

Then I remember. "Why did Clan Brody call me Ronald and Barbara's daughter-in-law?"

I'm hoping Deck will explain it away as a poor joke, an overfamiliarity meant to put me at ease. The pained look on his face tells me otherwise.

"You told them we're married!"

"Eloped," Deck says, wrapping me in a hug that mimics his father's from earlier, only smaller. (*Not just his father's hug. All the men embraced me.*)

"It'll make it easier once our baby starts showing," he's saying. "Trust me, my parents and their friends are good people, the best, but they're still in the dark ages on some things. They'd flip if they thought you were pregnant and unmarried."

He pulls back and grins his charming grin. "Besides, it wasn't really a lie because we'll be married soon enough. In the meanwhile, I did what was best. Those bohunks wouldn't accept a bastard."

The word is too sharp. "Deck!"

"You know what I mean. It's only for a bit. As soon as we're settled, we'll be married, and think of all the money we'll save by actually eloping." He smiles again, wider, hoping I'll fall for it.

I just might. I want to ask him *why* we're not married already, know I should, but I can't bring myself to do it.

Yet.

Instead, I close my eyes, trying on his words. The two of us, forever joined. I inhale deeply. I can't envision us with an actual child, have hardly felt pregnant other than that invasive doctor's visit.

"Doesn't it feel great to be here, baby?" he asks, kissing my forehead. "Safe, with family? Away from the draft, and the mugging?"

And just like that, he's awoken the memory I meant to forget.

CHAPTER 5

I'd stopped by the Red Owl grocery near our apartment, full of self-pity because I hadn't been promoted (*hadn't even been considered, if I'm being honest*), with instructions to pick up Tang for Deck.

I grabbed some milk and bread, too, paid for my groceries, and took a shortcut through the alley. The sun was sinking behind clouds, the alley shadowed, but there was no safer city than Minneapolis—I swear to God that's what I was thinking. The temperature dropped the moment I stepped between the buildings, driving a shudder up my spine.

Someone's walking on your grave, my mom used to say about such a shiver.

"Excuse me."

I turned toward the voice, the hairs at the back of my neck vibrating in alarm. The man had appeared from a cross alley. He was disheveled, breathing like he was winded. A rankness, pungent like sour milk, radiated off him.

"Yes?" My pulse grew thick at my wrists, but I wasn't scared, not yet. It was a few minutes after 5:00 p.m. and still light out. Our apartment was around the corner and a block to the right. There would be other people on the main street. I was jittery only because I'd been thinking of my grave when he popped out.

The man shambled closer.

I covered my nose, discreetly so as not to offend him.

The echo of two people talking, laughing, careened around the corner on the far end of the alley and bounced toward us.

"Do you have a light?" he asked, holding out a pack of cigarettes.

I breathed a sigh. I'd been more scared than I'd admitted. He only wanted help with his smoke. And now that he'd stepped out of the shadows, I could see that he was actually reasonably dressed, average size, his tan suit and porkpie hat several seasons out of style but presentable. He was still panting like he'd run to get here, his hooked nose dripping with exertion or the cooling temperatures. The rotten smell I'd initially associated with him—powdery sour—was surely coming from the nearby garbage bins.

I smiled and set down my grocery bag before tugging my purse off my shoulder. "You're in luck. I don't smoke anymore, but my best friend, Ursula, talked me into a quick puff the other day and gave me her lighter—" were the last words out of my mouth before he shoved me against the brick, slamming my head against the wall with such force that shooting lights exploded behind my eyes.

There wasn't time to scream.

The bone side of his arm pinned my neck, the tip of a wicked-looking hunting knife resting between my eyes. I blinked to make sense of it, to erase the double and triple view until it settled into a single blade. I'd never been attacked before, not so much as slapped.

I tried to swallow, but his arm didn't allow for it.

None of this made sense.

The echo of laughter on the street seemed to grow closer and then fade.

He leaned in. "I'm going to hurt you."

No shit, I thought before a crazy idea lit up my brain, a ridiculous image of me telling the editor who'd passed me over for a promotion that I'd finally landed a scoop: my own mugging. But was that what this was? A mugging? I blinked some more, the pain at the back of my skull exploding in red mushroom clouds. My eyelids were the only part of my body that seemed to be working.

I opened my mouth to yell for help. Only an ugly grunt escaped.

He scowled, and I spotted something green between his front teeth. I was too terrified to look into his eyes.

Think. There must be something I can do.

But my head was empty, wiped clean by terror. The blankness endured as he released me and I dropped to the grubby pavement, landing hard on my knees and soiling a new dress, but somehow I was grateful because *I could finally breathe*, jagged and deep, past the bruised, fragile chicken bones of my throat.

But there was no reprieve. He wrenched my head back, ripping out a clump of hair, and then struck me so hard across the cheek that I was blinded.

That was when I first thought of the baby.

And I resented it.

It was just a flash, the awful emotion—*I have to protect two of us and it might cost me my life*—so brief that I immediately buried it. My sight returned in silver bursts. I heard a wheezing exhalation and realized it was me. My attacker smacked me again on the other cheek before shifting behind me, his moves quick and certain.

I was on bended knee. I cried out as one ankle was punctured, and then the other. The long, wicked hunting knife. *He's stabbing my ankles.* The sharpness of the pain woke me up. I scurried back against the brick, away from him, drew my knees to my chest on instinct, and huddled in the shadow of a rancid-smelling trash bin.

"Take my purse," I croaked, holding it out. "There's money in there. I won't yell. Take it and go. I swear I won't tell on you."

I closed my eyes to demonstrate.

I see nothing.

He snatched my purse from my hand.

I whimpered. My eyes spasmed with the force of holding them shut. I promised myself that I would be true to my word, I'd be a good girl, I wouldn't tell a soul, if only he'd leave me, let me be. But a soft thump at my feet forced my eyes open. My cheeks were already swelling, I could see them in the bottom of my field of vision, and blood made my ankles sticky.

No more than two minutes had passed since I'd left the grocery store.

The hook-nosed man was holding my wallet and had tossed the purse at my feet. His brown felt porkpie hat, even more outdated than his suit, rested on his head, unbothered. I focused on that detail.

"You holler, I'll kill you."

I put my hands over my mouth. *I say nothing.* Except I felt a scream rising, a burning howl that wouldn't stop once it started. *Mom, help me* was the shape it took, but she'd been dead for months. I swallowed against it, but it fought back.

"I mean it," he said. "You count to five hundred, and then you can leave. You tell anyone, I'll find you. I swear it."

He walked backward the way I'd entered the alley, toward the Red Owl, threading his way down the narrow walkway. I forced my neck to turn, made myself look away from him, to stare into the side alley he'd appeared from. My eyes grew dry, and still I didn't blink.

Neither did I count.

I remained motionless, frozen in something like stasis, not wanting to face what'd just happened. The stifled scream was lodged sideways in my throat.

I don't know how long I would have remained there, stunned and bleeding, if the alley cat hadn't slunk out from behind a trash bin, rubbing against the unmolested part of my leg, purring.

He was orange and white.

I watched him from a great distance.

He looked soft.

Real.

I scooped him up and ran all the way to my apartment.

Where I found Deck. He held me, cleaned my wounds, promised he'd take me somewhere safe, said I could keep the cat, chuckled when I named him Slow Henry because he'd saved me, but late.

That's why I agreed to move to Lilydale, to restore the delicate fabric the mugger had shredded, that quivering cloth that made me believe I might not be as whole as other people, but at least I'd be safe in my own body.

I had no choice.

The lemon-yellow room.

My mouth snaps shut, lips sewn, teeth bolted. I do not want any-one to hear my screams, to come running. It wouldn't be safe. *They* aren't safe.

Was it just the one scream, the one that woke me? I close my eyes, measure my breath. Ragged but steady.

Listen.

I do. No floorboard creaks, no footsteps.

Think.

The effort feels like rusty nails dragging through my brain.

I am Joan Harken. I am a reporter. My baby is gone.

I weave something real from those three thoughts, summoning them from the fog, giving them shape and power (*I am Joan Harken. I am a reporter. My baby is gone*), until they are as solid as the bed I'm lying on.

Whose bed?

Yes, the room. I recognize it. I've been here before, inside these bright walls. Slept here? Visited? Remembering this bedroom is vital.

The knowledge is almost there, but when I try to squeeze, it escapes like a slippery silver fish between my fingers. I can't concentrate enough to hold it, not over the driving primal drumbeat of . . .

I am Joan Harken. I am a reporter. My baby is gone.

It doesn't make a difference where I am.

I have to save my baby.

I'm overcome by a desperate thirst, and my breasts are so swollen with milk that the flesh threatens to split, and it doesn't matter because I finally understand what I must do.

I begin to sit up, slowly, but even that small effort is too much. I fall back into the pillow, my world narrowing to a pinhole, one thought echoing down.

Don't scream this time. You don't want them to come.

CHAPTER 6

I'm whistling as I look around the sparkling interior of the Schmidt house.

Our house.

In the almost week since we moved to Lilydale, I've scoured the interior from top to bottom, with the exception of the dirt basement I still can't bring myself to enter. The lovely avocado-colored Amana fridge required only a soapy scrub down and a crisp orange box of Arm & Hammer to freshen it up. Once I stripped the horrible flowered contact paper from the oak cupboards and scoured their fronts, they suddenly appeared modern, gleaming against the white countertops. I couldn't do much with the mustard-yellow linoleum, cracked at the edges and worn in high-traffic areas, but a coat of tangerine paint on the walls and the white lace curtains I discovered in a box in the corner of the attic have brightened the room immeasurably. Plus, the paint killed the musty odor I first noticed upon entering the house.

I also bought a can of paint remover at the downtown Ace Hardware and discovered, to my boundless delight, glorious maple crown molding in the dining room beneath the rust-colored paint that has covered it since the '40s, according to Deck. He encourages my puttering. I love that he doesn't mind me overhauling his childhood home, though he drew the line at me removing the hideous red-and-gold wallpaper in our bedroom.

He'll come around.

In the meantime, I have plenty enough work to do chiseling through the paint sealing the windows shut and airing out the upstairs. I wouldn't mind a full bathroom on the second floor—ours has only a sink and toilet—and once I'm working full-time at the newspaper, we should be able to afford it.

When I mention this to Deck, he frowns. "But you're working constantly," he says, indicating the dining room, which does look beautiful with the newly revealed crown molding.

His expression throws me off. I take his hand across the table, fumbling to explain something I assumed was a given. "When we decided to move here, you said I'd be able to work at the paper. I was full-time when we lived in Minneapolis."

We're eating dinner, one of a dozen casseroles that's been dropped off since we moved in. Our freezer is at capacity, yet the women keep showing up with their hot dishes, like Lilydale is a regular old Mayfield and I'm June Cleaver. I've named this one Soothing Stomach Stew: rice, hamburger, onion, and cream of mushroom soup, all stirred together beneath a crushed potato chip topping. A few nights ago, we ate a nearly identical hot dish topped with cheese.

Deck cradles my hand. "Sure, but you didn't have a baby then. Keeping a home is its own job. I've never seen you work so hard. Now let's stop talking about the newspaper for tonight. I'm tired."

He said the same thing last night and the night before. But I swallow the spike of resentment right along with the salty hot dish, both of them thudding in my belly. I smile to mask my discomfort and try a different tack. I must relax him so I can convince him to let me work. I didn't need his approval in Minneapolis, but here . . . he's made clear the paper won't hire me without his and Ronald's endorsement. Said that's just how small towns work.

"I had a lovely conversation with Dorothy next door," I lie, smiling even wider, so wide that my lips creak. "Such a gracious lady."

Deck's shoulders relax. Good. I can come at this sideways. "I so much love living here," I continue. "It's everything you promised, so calm."

Here it comes, the question that will allow me to lead him back to talking about the newspaper. "Why, I bet there hasn't been a single crime ever committed here, not a dangerous one, just like you promised, not one that would put a reporter in danger. Has there been?"

His face puckers for a moment and then relaxes. "I suppose the Paulie Aandeg kidnapping is the closest thing to news we've had."

The room shrinks and my breath expands. I didn't expect such a powerful answer. *A real story.* "Paulie Aandeg?"

"He disappeared on his first day of kindergarten."

"When was that?"

He glances at his wristwatch as if it might tell the story. "Decades ago."

Disappointment settles like a gray scarf over my shoulders. Any story there has already been told. "They never found him?"

"Never," Deck says, patting my hand. "But don't you worry. There's always news to cover, and Dad and I'll get you a spot at the *Gazette* real soon."

"Thanks, honey," I say, pinning a smile on my face. But Deck is staring at his hot dish, his expression tight again, and I find myself wondering what made him move away from Lilydale in the first place.

CHAPTER 7

The next day, I hop right back on the house-overhaul wagon, tackling something I've been putting off since we moved in: the garden. I don't know a weed from a wisteria, but I decide to begin by trimming the gawky shrubs lining the front walkway. They scratch me every time I come and go through the front door. While I'm at first intimidated by the project, once I track down a dull pruning clipper in the garage and begin snipping, I find I genuinely enjoy the work. The May sun is warm on my bare shoulders, and the sweet purple-honey smell of lilacs floats through the neighborhood.

I even find myself humming.

Ursula would flip her wig if she saw me now. As domestic as Aunt Bee.

My college roommate and best friend in the world was miserable when I told her I was moving, said it'd be the end of me, that I'd become a baby machine. Today, working in the earth and shined on by the sun, I can think of worse things.

I trot out the aqua-colored mower Ronald dropped off and trim our tiny yard. Without deciding to, I realize I'm making up stories for the infant, surely no larger than a peach pit in my belly. *Beautiful Baby helping his momma to work, growing strong in her tummy. We're going to be best friends, aren't we?*

I'm delighted by the positive feelings.

I didn't plan to get pregnant, didn't expect to keep it once I found out I was, almost didn't tell Deck. But in the end, I spilled. It was something my mom had hammered into me one night: a good woman is a responsible woman.

When she told me that, we were in my favorite apartment in all our travels, a one-bedroom over Ralph's Diner. Mom waited tables just below. I could pop down for an icy-cold Coke and french fries whenever I wanted, on the house.

"A perk of being the prettiest girl in town and the daughter of my best waitress," Ralph would say with a wink.

We lived there four months, but then Ralph showed up at our door, just up the stairs, his face tight with worry, voice low and urgent, but I still heard it. "I got a call from the IRS, Frances. They said there's something off with your information, that I might be audited because of it. I'm sure it's just a mistake, I told 'em. I'm telling you the same thing. What say we get this straightened out?"

Mom smiled, patted his arm. Frances Harken was a beautiful woman. A chocolate-eyed redhead, she styled her hair just like Rita Hayworth. Got whistled at all the time. "Don't worry, Ralph. I'll dig out the paperwork and get it to you tomorrow. That okay?"

His relief was comical. "Sure it is, Frances. We'll get it all straightened out tomorrow."

She'd started packing before his footsteps reached the bottom floor.

"Mom?" I'd been on the couch, doing homework. I didn't want to move, didn't want to leave the icy Cokes and the french fries and being the prettiest girl in town.

"We don't have a choice this time, Joan," she said, her voice wavering. "Ralph's a stand-up man, and I'm not going to get him in trouble. A good woman is a responsible woman."

Well, I'd been neither good nor responsible the night I'd gotten pregnant, so I decided to start by coming clean to Deck.

"I'm late."

By that time, he and I already lived together. I don't think I would have taken that leap so soon—I'd never lived with a man—if Mom hadn't died a few short months earlier, a bottle redhead by that time but still so beautiful, even as the cancer gobbled her up from the lungs out.

Deck's building was past its prime, his apartment a faded one-bedroom. Still, I'd moved in, and despite its shabbiness, I grew to love it because it was ours. My favorite place in the world was the breakfast nook off the kitchen, just big enough for a chipped table and two garage-sale chairs. Every Saturday morning, we shared our coffee there, smiling at each other over steaming cups, planning our day just like an honest-to-god couple.

That's where we were when I decided to spill the beans about the late period. I appreciated that he didn't crack a low-hanging joke, didn't waste time with, "What do you mean, late? Breakfast just started."

He didn't propose, either, not right there on the spot. I didn't think I would have wanted that. Well, I was okay that he didn't. I was a modern woman, after all.

Instead, his eyes tightened at the corners. It reminded me of his expression when he was talking about his boss, who regularly cheated him out of commissions, except this time his eyes were squeezed because he was happy.

"You're sure?" he asked.

I nodded. "I think so. You don't need to worry, though. Ursula knows someone who can take care of it. It doesn't need to be a big deal at all. Just a bump in the road, easily corrected."

Ursula had had two abortions. She said it was no worse than a bad period. If I didn't think too hard about it, I wasn't terrified at all. Not even sad.

"A bump in the road?" Deck asked. His voice was rising. I thought he was about to yell, but instead a laugh erupted from his mouth, a guffaw so immense it bounced off the walls and echoed through my ears. "The Gobbler!"

It took me a few seconds. When I got it, I smiled, and the smile turned to laughter to match Deck's. The Gobbler. Deck'd squired me away to the themed hotel one state over the month before. The Gobbler was shaped like a turkey—he said that wasn't unusual for Wisconsin— and the rooms contained wall-to-wall shag carpeting, heart-shaped beds, and mirrors nailed to the ceiling. I hadn't been able to stop giggling at the cheesy place. Deck had other plans, though, plans that involved champagne and chocolate-covered strawberries and a passion so combustible that I'd forgotten to remind him to wear a condom.

"We're gonna have a baby," Deck said, the laugh gone, his jaw rock solid.

"I guess we are," I replied. It's what he wanted.

And here I am, living in postcard-perfect Lilydale, finally at peace with that decision. Not just at peace. *Thrilled.* The smell of cut grass, the warmth of the sun on my skin, the feeling of tending to my home for my baby. It's overpowering. The sense of satisfaction is so strong that I want to share it with someone.

I'll bring Deck lunch. Surely he'll have half an hour to eat with his "wife" and hear her blather about yard work. I smile at the joke. Deck and I've taken to calling ourselves Mister and Missus when we're alone, laughing at the idea of it, at the thought of the harmless wool we're pulling over the town's eyes.

A shower is in order before I embark on the ten-minute walk downtown. Once clean, I towel off and wander upstairs to don a short-sleeve white blouse with a Peter Pan collar and grape-colored cotton knit capris. I decide to leave my hair in its ponytail. I've wanted to cut it short ever since I spotted Mia Farrow's scandalous pixie cut on the front cover of last August's *Vogue.* The courage has never found me, though, and Lilydale certainly isn't the place to adopt a statement hairstyle.

I head out toward Schmidt Insurance, which is nestled in the middle of Lilydale's busiest street—I chuckle at the thought of any place in

Lilydale being considered *busy*—with Little John's bar anchoring one corner and Tuck's Cafe the other.

I stroll up Belmont to River Street, the sunburn sinking a pleasant tightness into my flesh. Deck likes it when my skin browns. At the corner of James Street and Augusta, I pause to glance left at the Creamery, the largest building in Lilydale. It's a buzzing concrete factory that processes all of Stearns County's milk. Deck was proud when he told me, as if he were the one singlehandedly transforming raw dairy into neat, square cartons of milk.

A soft smile creases my cheeks.

Men. Needing to feel important.

I'm nearly across Augusta when I glance at the Creamery one more time. From this angle, I spot a small crowd gathered at the edge of the railroad tracks. They remind me of a cluster of sugar ants on a crumb. I want to ferry Deck's sandwiches to him before they turn in the heat, but my reporter's instincts (*when will Ronald set up my interview at the paper?*) propel me toward the group. It's such an odd place to gather, especially for folks dressed for business. What are they all staring at? Something on the ground.

I itch for a pad of paper and a pencil. The ache of not working, of not telling stories, is sudden and strong. The emotion catches me off guard and dilutes the domestic bliss I was about to share with Deck. I suddenly feel queasy, a lotus-eater who should have been doing real work. Deck has allowed me a subscription to two newspapers—the *Minneapolis Star* and the *New York Times*—so I can stay abreast of world affairs, but I've been so busy painting and cleaning and building my nest that I've hardly opened them except to spread on the floor and catch the paint drips.

If I'm honest, it's not just that I've been busy remodeling. Lilydale is so soothing, so *apart* from the world. Race riots. War. Strikes. It's somehow rude to invite all that ugliness here by reading my newspapers.

The slow pace has even lulled me into letting Deck control my career rather than simply taking care of it myself.

What the hell?

Well, I'm waking up now. Whatever everyone is staring at, it's directly on the train tracks, not alongside. Their legs part enough that I can see a flash of muscled, mangled red. I catch a whiff of something gamy.

The smell raises the baby hairs on the back of my neck.

CHAPTER 8

A woman separates herself from the edge of the crowd just when I can almost make out what they're circling.

"Joan!"

I recognize her from the first night I arrived—*tuna noodle hot dish and crème de menthe squares*—but the group of people staring silently at the ground has shaken me.

"Mildred Schramel," she says, accurately reading my face. "Teddy and I live down Mill Street from you, near the school. He works for the telephone company."

Browline Schramel and Mildred the Mouse, living inside a telephone. I'm ashamed of myself for forgetting her name, even for a moment. That's never happened to me before. I hope my smile is polite. "Of course. I haven't wandered in your direction yet."

Deck's been encouraging me to get out, but other than necessary errands, I've kept to myself, just like I did in Minneapolis. I shake off my unease and point at the backs of the crowd ten feet away, their bodies clustered too tightly for me to see what they're peering at. A dead animal, judging by the smell, but why in God's name would they all be circled around it like that, just staring? "What's happened here?"

Mildred's lips stretch but her eyes are doll-flat. "Just a poor dog hit by a train."

My stomach does a tumble. There must be a dozen people gawping at it. Not doing anything, simply staring. I crane my neck, trying to get a better look around Mildred, through the crowd's legs. I catch my second glimpse of raw red, but also blue cloth.

Oh no. Not a stray. A dog someone loved enough to smarten up with a bandanna.

Mildred moves to block my limited view, her hands dropping on my shoulders. "This isn't for a city lady to see." Her eyes drop to my waist. "Especially in your condition."

My condition?

The truth drives home like a punch. *My pregnancy.*

Mildred knows. This drab woman I've met only once before knows my private business. How? My hand instinctively travels to my stomach, a gesture that Mildred misinterprets and rewards with a warm smile.

Not so good at reading facial expressions now, are you, Mildred.

❖

"But you said . . ."

"Said what?" I demand. I'm in the break room at Deck's office, and I don't like the daggers in my voice.

"That you'd like people to know." He appears genuinely distressed. "You said it that first night we moved in. In the bedroom."

The billowing sheets of anger make it difficult to see the truth of what he's saying, but then I remember my words. *I wish we could fast-forward to being done, being settled in, everyone knowing about the baby.* But how to explain that I'd wanted him to hold me and tell me everything would be all right, not wrest away my fragile control?

He must see the capitulation on my face. "It's not like the city, baby," he coos. "Here the women think being pregnant is a good thing."

"Deck!"

His expression is pained as he unwraps his second sandwich—ham, onions, and Miracle Whip on white bread, his favorite. The waxed paper makes a rustling sound. "People were bound to find out sooner than later," he's saying. "You look great, you really do, Joanie, but you're gonna start showing any day now. If we don't tell anyone before then, it looks like we're either hiding something or like it was an accident."

"But it *was* an accident!" I wring my hands.

"I'm afraid this is all my fault."

Ronald's unexpected voice from behind shocks me. My heart pounds, but I keep it cool on the surface. I won't show him that I'm startled, will calm myself before I turn to face him. I've always been a cool head when angry. A stoic, everyone says. I'd be surprised if any Schmidt Insurance employees even noticed my rage when I came through the door, anyone except Deck. I had smiled at Becky (*Blonde Becky, a receptionist as beautiful as a butterfly, she'd fall to the earth if she stopped smiling*), nodded at the four men working behind desks. I recognized only one, the giant Clan Brody, as I took a seat in the break room, sitting primly until Deck finished a meeting in Ronald's office.

I didn't let loose until we were alone.

Thought we were alone.

"I was the one who blabbed the good news," Ronald continues from behind me, where he opened the door and slipped in as quietly as a snake. "You have to understand how a small town works. We're a big family here. You don't keep secrets from family."

I'm trying to hang on to my calm, but my hands are shaking beneath the table. I cannot unring this bell, and the powerlessness is unnerving. Deck is staring at his sandwich, the ham leering out like a tongue from the pillowy slice of bread. He's leaving me to address Ronald alone.

Very well. I swivel in my seat and stand to face Deck's father.

I'm shocked to see from his expression that he thinks he's teasing me, that we're all in on a big, harmless joke, that it doesn't matter a whit that I wanted a job and identity before I become a mother in everyone's eyes. When he holds out his arms, I'm so caught off guard that I walk toward them.

"We're so happy for you and Deck," he says, wrapping me in his embrace. I stiffen when he buries his face into my hair, but I don't pull away. With a Ronald hug, I'm learning, retreating simply isn't an option. "Children are a heritage from the Lord, offspring a reward from Him." He chuckles, his laugh as gritty as his voice. "Guess the Schmidts have planted our stake in your real estate."

I take three full breaths before Ronald releases me. I don't know about any of my body being real estate, but I can't see any options. *Be invisible when you can, harmless if they spot you.* "Yes," I say, patting my hair. "Deck and I are very happy."

"You bet you are. Nothing greater in this world than a child. Barbara and I've been meaning to have the two of you over to celebrate ever since Deck told us the news. I'll let her set that up with you." He twists his arm to pull his wristwatch into view. "You should get going."

I bristle. "Excuse me?"

Ronald ignores my question, glancing at my stomach, then Deck. "You have to understand—in my generation, pregnant women didn't work."

I swell, soaking up anger like a towel dropped in water. *Screw having a cool head.* Before I can sound off, though, Ronald raises his hand, laughing more deeply this time.

"Now, hold your horses before you lay into me. I was about to say that I understand you and Deck are from a different generation than me and Barbara. Deck told me you want to work, and I admire that. You want to contribute. I *understand* that. You women these days," he says, shaking his head, smiling like he can't believe what he's about to say, "cooking for your husbands, cleaning, raising children, *and* working. If only we could build an army of you!"

Deck nods, finally abandoning his second sandwich to stand next to me. "Joanie is an incredible girl."

"That's what I told Dennis Roth over at the *Gazette*," Ronald says, going serious. "It's no big-city newspaper, but they do solid reporting. Now be a good daughter and head on over. He's expecting you."

❖

I put Dennis Roth at fifty, and he is the skinniest man I have ever laid eyes on, his fingers nearly as long as my feet, his translucent green eyes wide beneath unruly red hair. I don't know what's in the Lilydale water, but between slender Dennis and giant Clan, this town could staff its own traveling sideshow.

When Dennis leaves his desk to greet me, he unfurls more than stands.

Dennis the Daddy Longlegs, dispatching the news.

"Mr. Schmidt speaks highly of you," he says.

I wonder why the formality and whether he's referring to Ronald or Deck. Ronald, I suppose. Dennis almost sounds afraid of Deck's dad, but maybe that's just the way he speaks.

"Thank you. I'm sorry I didn't stop by earlier." I don't know why I'm apologizing, except that it's habit.

Dennis indicates the chair in front of his desk and reclaims his own seat after I take mine. "My grandfather founded the *Gazette* in 1867, a decade after Johann Lily platted the town," he says, stone-faced. "I'm pleased to say it's grown since then."

I can't tell if he has a sense of humor. I passed only one other employee coming in, a woman who I'd also put in her fifties, her hair tight and short and seemingly cut with the same pruning shears I used on my bushes earlier this morning. She appeared to be sleeping when I arrived, surrounded by stacks of the *Lilydale Gazette* leaning precariously, some with dates over a year old. The sound of the front door closing caused her eyes to snap open, like a robot who'd been activated. She studied me top to bottom and then jabbed her thumb toward a single office in the back.

Dennis's.

There's a closed door in the rear of it, which I assume leads to a bathroom, and an open one that I guess leads to the research and records room. Although, given the hurricane state of the main room, I can't imagine what sort of archives they keep.

"Journalism is an important business," I say. Best to stick to vague facts until I can get a bead on him.

"Indeed." Dennis steeples his elegant fingers and rests his chin on them. "Your father-in-law says you need a job."

"I have a journalism degree from the University of Minnesota, and I'm an experienced reporter," I say, not correcting his reference to Ronald as my father-in-law any more than I'd corrected Ronald calling me daughter. Pick your battles.

Dennis nods. "You can start today."

My heart leaps. "Really?"

"I trust Mr. Schmidt. If he says you can do the job, you can. We need someone to cover tonight's elementary school music program."

The weight of the world settles onto my shoulders. For a brief moment, I thought I'd finally land my byline. At the *Minneapolis Star*, they'd confined me and the other female reporter to the Women's News section. No bylines allowed there, just soothing stories of weddings and fashion and food. The handful of big stories I'd broken on my own, I'd had to hand off.

"You're not interested?" Dennis asks.

My expression must be telling the whole story. I force a smile. "I'm delighted."

He drums his chin, long fingers scuttling like a praying mantis across his skin. "There are only two of us here. You met Mrs. Roth at the front desk. She handles the administrative duties and types up the occasional piece. I write the articles and edit. We're a small-town paper, and there's no hierarchy here. Whoever's free takes what comes in. Right now, it's the school program."

His newly kind tone warms me, resetting the whole interview, if that's what you'd call this. "I'm thrilled, really. I was going a bit stir-crazy without work. Well, work outside of the house. This'll give me a chance to see more of the town. To meet more of the folks."

Dennis's eyes grow hooded. "And for them to meet you. You're the talk of Lilydale. We don't get much new blood here."

CHAPTER 9

I spend the afternoon immersing myself in Lilydale's businesses, determined to meet the locals head-on. It's the most uncomfortable thing I've ever done, but if it's necessary to do my new job, I'll do it. At Tuck's Cafe, I order banana cream pie and coffee and ask the waitress about her day. Inside Morrell's Ace Hardware, I ask for paint recommendations to touch up my exterior house trim, something I have no intention of doing. I check in on our mail forwarding at the post office, fill out a form to update my driver's license address at the county office.

Afterward, I stroll to Ben Franklin. I've stopped by there before, but this time I talk to the employees, feigning interest in the arts-and-crafts supplies they sell, selecting a new raspberry lipstick from their cosmetics department, exclaiming over their large display of penny candy behind the glass case, admiring the rack of enameled pins.

I've hated every moment of it, exposing myself like this, becoming visible and open to judgment. I feel not only naked but *skinned*. My mom was right about small towns, but here I am, trapped in one, dependent on the goodwill of these people to keep my new job.

The anxiety I feel causes me to do the most awful thing.

When the Ben Franklin clerk is called to the front counter, I slip a cloisonné pineapple brooch into my front pocket. It would cost $1.99 to buy. I have the money in my purse, and if anyone sees me, all the goodwill I've been building will be gone. Forever. I dip my hand in to stroke the brooch, running my thumb across the surface. I hate myself for stealing, but I need it. Just the thought of putting it back on the rack makes me feel like spiders are crawling across my scalp.

I'll return it later, I tell myself.

That's what I always tell myself.

The very first piece of jewelry I stole was at a five-and-dime where my mom worked, a store very much like the Lilydale Ben Franklin. We were living in San Diego, though not by the ocean, and I must have been old enough for school because I remember practicing cursive behind the five-and-dime counter and the smell of fat and waxy crayons when Mom would let me color.

I loved watching her as she worked. She was so pretty, so sure of herself. Men would stop at the counter to ask about perfume for a sister or jewelry for a mother. Mom would help them, or at least I thought she did, except they kept coming back. It didn't take me long to figure out they were there for her. Some of them even screwed up the courage to ask her out, but she always turned them down.

"It's just you and me, squirt, always," she said once, turning to cup my chin after a particularly insistent man demanded she go to the movies with him.

It swelled my heart to hear her say that, to see the tears in her dark-brown eyes, tears that proved she loved me more than anything. I wanted to pay that back. I saw my opportunity the next week, when a female customer approached her.

"I need something truly special," she said. "A beautiful piece of jewelry."

The customer's voice, ragged and wet, made me look up from the flappy-eared puppy I was coloring. Her face was swollen. Mom already had her hand on the woman's. She was like that, my mom.

"Of course," Mom said. Even I knew that the five-and-dime didn't have anything real nice, but Mom didn't say that, didn't look twice at the woman's shabby coat, just treated her like she was the most important person in the store. "What did you have in mind?"

"My husband left me," the woman said, though Mom hadn't asked. "Do you have anything gold?"

Mom squeezed the woman's hand and then ducked under the counter. She used the key at her wrist to unlock a cabinet, then came out with a scarlet box. I sucked in my breath and held very still, worried that if they remembered I was there, they wouldn't let me see what was inside the gorgeous velvet box.

Mom lifted the lid and took out a necklace. She held it up, a pea-size pearl dangling off a delicate gold chain. "Every woman should have pearls," Mom said, "to remind ourselves that grit under pressure becomes beauty."

The woman clapped her hand over her mouth, her tears flowing freely. She paid for the necklace, counting out part of her money in coins, and had Mom clasp it around her neck before she left the store.

When Mom took her cigarette break, I slid open that cabinet. She'd forgotten to lock it. Inside I found three more scarlet boxes. I took one for my mom because she deserved it, that's what I told myself, but when I presented it to her the next morning, wrapped in the puppy page I'd colored, her face went slack.

"Joan, where'd you get this?"

I wanted to tell her that I took it because I loved her, because she never got nice things from anyone, because I didn't want her ever to leave me. But I couldn't utter a word.

She made me return the necklace and apologize to her boss for stealing it. I remember his beetled brows, his angry red mouth, but I don't recall if he fired her or if she decided to move on her own. We were in a new city by the end of the week.

I kept stealing, right up until Mom died. It had always been little things that no one would miss, baubles that I could afford more often than not but that I was compelled to take. After Mom's funeral, though, the shame of it became louder than the compulsion.

At least until today in the Ben Franklin.

If I'm caught with the cloisonné pineapple, I'll say it was an accident.

When I pay for the raspberry lipstick, my hands so sweaty with guilt and exhilaration that I fumble the coins, I drop two dollars into the Lilydale Community Fundraiser jar, a penance for the brooch I can't bear to pay for or return. Then I bumble to the next store, heart still fluttering, feeling watched, as if everyone knows what I've done. To calm myself, I wander the aisles of Wally's as if I have nothing but time, selecting a package of chopped ham and another of bologna before filling my basket with American cheese slices, a rainbow variety of Jell-O, and a red-and-white checked box of Lipton Onion Soup Mix.

Everyone I speak with makes a point of telling me how Lilydale is the best place to live. The town council gathered donations to build the nursing home so no elderly people would be on the street, according to the stocker at Wally's. There's money put aside to cover health-care costs or missed work should any citizen need it, says the cashier. I wouldn't believe it if I weren't hearing the stories from the mouths of locals.

Lilydale is Eden.

The cloisonné pineapple burns when I hear these tales.

Three hours into my mission, I'm exhausted inside and out. I decide not to venture inside the police department to reintroduce myself to Amory Mountain, this time as the *Gazette*'s newest reporter. Maybe this pregnancy is taking its toll, but I simply lack the energy. I need to get the lunch meat into the refrigerator anyway.

A glance at my watch tells me it's nearly six. Deck is likely frustrated, already home and having discovered he has to fend for himself for supper. If I hurry, I can whip up some leftovers and give him a quick shoulder rub before I head off to cover my first Lilydale story. I find myself humming as I make my way home and then smile when I remember that's how I left late this morning: humming.

I even wave at Clan the Brody Bear and Catherine the Migrant Mother when I see them pull out of their driveway. I have yet to see Catherine smile, but Clan gives me a big grin and a salute.

"Deck?" I call when I step inside our house, admiring the trimmed bushes on my way in. "Sorry about dinner not being ready, honey. But I think you'll be happy to hear what I've been up to today."

The house's silence is heavy. Not even Slow Henry greets me.

Gritty eyes. Paste in mouth. Agony.

Blink.

The lemon-yellow room. Nothing's changed.

The light.

I tug out my arm—*is it moving more easily?*—and wipe crust from my eyes. Yes, the light filtering through the curtains is different. It's later in the day. The heat is still intense, though, if anything hotter than before. I am being cooked alive.

The smell of sour and blood turns my stomach. I lift the sheets—I can definitely move more easily now—and spot blood between my legs. I press on the sanitary pad that's been secured to my underwear. It's warm and engorged. Soon it will leak onto the white sheets. My breasts are already overflowing, yellowish milk trickling down their sides.

I am Joan Harken. I am a reporter. My baby is gone.

The beat is back, bracing. I welcome it. It reminds me of my mission. Get out of this bed and find my child. It doesn't matter what room this is or who put me here. It makes no difference what's happened to me at all. All that counts is that I hold my infant, feed him, release the agonizing pressure on my breasts, smell his hair, count his fingers and toes.

A sob expands in my throat, but I swallow it.

You didn't scream. Good job.

An oven-heated breeze flutters the curtains and brings with it the muted sound of voices. Laughter? I lift my head and hold my breath, listening for a baby's cry. I don't hear it. For the first time, though, I notice this room has three doors.

A closet.

A bathroom.

An *exit*.

I know this with certainty, even though I can't grasp anything else about the lemon-colored room. I will crawl to the bathroom. Clean myself. Pray for clothes. Because something is telling me that I must appear sane and composed.

It's my only chance.

CHAPTER 10

"Deck?"

I stroll through to the backyard. Maybe he's grilling, though I haven't smelled it. "Honey?"

Nothing. I peek into the kitchen and spot his note on the fridge, affixed with a Schmidt Insurance magnet shaped like a house, the logo "We're Family" above Deck's contact information.

Heard you'd be working tonight, it reads. *Going to an evening meeting with Dad.*

I remove the magnet and crumple the note, admiring the fridge again. It's so sleek and modern. I put away the groceries before pouring a glass of milk and making myself a tuna salad sandwich, giving Slow Henry—who's been tomcatting somewhere but shows up once I open the tuna can—the leftovers plus fresh water. Thank god the pregnancy hasn't affected my appetite. No morning, afternoon, or evening sickness for me.

Once I clean up the kitchen, I'm overcome by the craving for a cigarette.

Ursula sneaked a pack and her favorite lighter into my purse the day I told her I was moving. "Your Lilydale survival kit," she called it.

We were out for lunch at the Dayton's Sky Room in downtown Minneapolis. The clatter of forks and knives on china provided a pleasant percussion as we were led to our table, the smell of fresh-baked popovers and roasting meat making my mouth water. Ursula had wanted to dine at the Men's Oak Grill, which we could technically now visit without a male chaperone, but the single time I ate there with Deck, I found its dark wood paneling and enormous stone fireplace suffocating. The Dayton's Sky Room was my preferred lunch restaurant, the perfect blend of fancy and welcoming.

I told her about moving to Lilydale as soon as we were seated. She about swallowed her own tongue and then immediately tried to talk me out of it.

"If you have that kid there," she said, pointing at my belly, "you'll never leave. That's how small towns work. They trap you, making you pop out one kid after another until the day you die."

I flushed. "I'm not a breeder cow!"

Ursula tapped a cigarette out of the pack and drew it to her lips. "Really? I seem to remember someone hating kids in college, swearing she'd never have one."

I stared out the window to the ground twelve stories below. People flowed like quicksilver across the streets. I loved Minneapolis. It had a hundred good restaurants, the lakes, shopping, just enough to keep a person busy without overwhelming them. "I wish Libby was here."

Ursula's mouth grew tight. She snapped open the rhinestone-encased lighter and spun the wheel, staring into the flame as she inhaled. "Me too."

"Remember that great Halloween party? Where you dressed up like Eleanor Roosevelt?"

She tossed me the oddest look. I kept the smile perched on my face. The party was one of my favorite memories. I had a framed photo from the evening on my desk at the *Star*. It featured me, Ursula, and Libby dressed for Halloween.

Libby, wearing a bomber jacket and flight goggles, was supposed to be Amelia Earhart. Ursula camouflaged herself to resemble a prim Eleanor Roosevelt complete with wavy hair and a floral dress. I was supposed to be Natalie Wood as Marjorie Morningstar but ended up looking like me wearing more makeup. Only one person guessed who I was impersonating, but it didn't matter because that evening, the three of us laughed until our bellies ached, an emotion perfectly captured in the photograph: three young women tumbled into each other, bright-eyed and open-mouthed, the world at our feet.

"I remember that night," she said, the words sounding like sand in her mouth.

My smile slipped. Ursula was in a mood. I couldn't account for it.

"Hillbillies," she murmured, glaring outside.

At first I thought she meant the tiny people streaming below, but then she continued. "Each and every person in Lilydale is a hillbilly, I guarantee it. It's a good thing you're not moving. The best thing." She lowered her voice to a mock whisper. "They're probably rat-fucking Nixon supporters."

I threw my head back and laughed. That's why she was acting so odd. She didn't want me to move.

Smiling a satisfied grin, Ursula held out the cigarette pack. "Now, show me you're your own woman and have a smoke."

She ended up giving me the whole pack along with her rhinestone lighter, and now seems like the perfect time to crack them both out. I reach under the kitchen sink, where I hid them, and make my way to the back steps. I sit down and light the cigarette, eyes closing in ecstasy as I draw in the silky smoke, enjoying the sweet relaxation in my shoulders.

"I wouldn't have taken you for a smoker."

My eyes fly open, and I leap off the back steps. "Mrs. Lily. I didn't see you."

She's wearing gardening gloves, but her hair is perfect, the lily-shaped locket glittering at her neck, her dress ironed, wearing pumps wildly ill-suited for outdoor work. Her mouth folds into a slow smile.

"Just doing some outdoor work. Stanley used to take care of all of that, but he isn't able to any longer."

Saint Dorothy must tend to her kingdom after her king, Sad Stanley, is paralyzed by an evil ogre.

"I can help you," I say immediately, stabbing out the cigarette. I mean it. She shouldn't have to do all that messy gardening herself. She must be in her sixties, and besides, she looks too precious to work outdoors.

Her smile widens. She tugs off one of her gloves. With her bare hand, she reaches over to touch my hair, pushing a lock behind my ear. It's an oddly personal gesture, unsettling and soothing at the same time, and it brings to mind her staring at me across our yards the first night I arrived. "You're such a pretty girl. I used to be attractive, you know."

"Mrs. Lily—"

She gives a little tug to my hair, stopping my words. "Now now, no need for false compliments. I'm getting old, and that's the truth of it. And don't mind me. I've always been a jealous one. I tell you what, though. I couldn't be happier to have a baby in the neighborhood." Her gaze lingers on my belly before returning to my face.

She chuckles at my expression. "Small-town gossip is quite a thing, I suppose you wanted to be the one to tell us all first? I certainly would have."

A warmth fills my chest, unexpected gratitude at being understood. "Well, it's out now."

She pulls her glove back on. "I suppose it is. Now to that," she says, pointing at the cigarette stubbed out on the steps. (I'd give up my left ear to make it disappear.) "We won't tell Deck about it. He's never liked women smoking. We must have at least one or two of our own secrets, mustn't we?" With a wink, she turns on her heel and walks back into her house.

The cigarette isn't completely out, the acrid smoke crawling up my nostrils. A realization makes me shudder. Dorothy wasn't outside when

I came home, either in her front or backyard. And why would she need to wear gardening gloves inside her house?

Ronald's words from earlier today return.

You have to understand how a small town works. We're a family here. You don't keep secrets from family.

I spear my cigarette into the ground, dousing it once and for all, and make my way inside.

CHAPTER 11

Lilydale's school reminds me of every elementary school I've ever attended. It has the gray lockers, poured-concrete floors, and the slightly fishy, salty smell of a million school lunches. Being within its walls is surprisingly comforting.

The stroll here was wonderful, the evening lovely, cool but clear, ripe with joyful conversation as clusters of townsfolk file toward the school. The principal greets me at the door. I'm still tuckered from my earlier goodwill tour and so forgo introducing myself, instead walking in with what I hope is an "I belong here" gait. I follow the crowds past the lockers, the classroom doors taped with names and construction-paper cutouts, until I reach the gym. The bleachers are crowded with beaming families.

That'll be me and Deck one day, I think, studying them. *Parents coming to watch their children in a school production.* I scan the crowd, searching for other pregnant women. I don't spot any, but I notice that everyone here seems to look alike, probably because they're all dressed similarly. I suppose that's true of most small towns. Humans tend to prefer blending in with the herd.

I stroke my stomach. *Hey, Beautiful Baby. Ready for your first concert?*

A gale of laughter catches my attention. A group of people—a woman and children—stand on the edge of the bleachers, probably a family, Mexican by the look of them.

"The Gomezes. Too many kids, if you ask me."

I swivel. The woman at my side appears to be approximately my age, her brown hair curled into the tight bouffant similar to how Mrs. Lily wears her hair. The yarn-strung name tag at her neck reads "Miss Colivan, 4th grade."

"That must be common in a farming community," I say. I thought I'd spotted quite a few large families in the bleachers. "You're a teacher here?"

The woman nods curtly. "Fourth grade. You're Joan Schmidt."

I flinch but allow Deck's last name to stick. "Yes. Joan . . . Schmidt."

The teacher raises an eyebrow but doesn't comment. "I graduated with Deck. He was quite popular. We were all so happy to hear he was moving back. This is his home."

An irrational needle of jealousy pokes me near the base of my spine. "I'm here as a journalist for the *Gazette*." It's a ten-dollar word for a nickel job, but Miss Colivan has me defensive. "Any comments you'd like to make about the music program?"

She beams at the mass of kids horsing around on the gym floor, all of them dressed in their Sunday best. "Only that the children have worked very hard. The theme is the Beatles. Each grade will sing one of their songs, and then they'll all come together for 'Yellow Submarine.'"

"That actually sounds nice," I say before I can stop myself.

Miss Colivan grimaces. "We have culture here, you know. We're more of a family than a school. The students spent all week painting the submarine. Our janitor mounted it on wheels. The older children will guide it out at the finale. It will be quite something."

More of the Lilydale spirit I've been hearing about all day. I murmur something vaguely supportive (I hope), my glance pulled by the Gomez family moving toward the bleachers. I spot a child in the group I didn't notice before. He's small, prekindergarten if I have to guess, and he's so gorgeous that he steals my breath away.

"That's Angel," Miss Colivan says. "A boy shouldn't be that pretty. He'll get snatched right up."

I suck in my breath, turning to stare at her. "Like Paulie Aandeg?"

Her eyes are sparkling, but I can't read her expression. "That was decades ago."

"Deck told me about it," I say, too smugly. Why do I feel the need to remind her that he's mine?

"I wasn't born yet, of course, but I don't remember hearing that he was a particularly pretty child, not like Angel," Miss Colivan continues, as if she didn't hear me. "Paulie was wearing a proper little sailor suit when he was snatched, that much I do remember hearing."

My hand goes back to my stomach. I can't help it. "That poor family."

"Rumor was the mother did it. A drinker. *Shoplifter*," she says, with special emphasis on the last word.

The warm *thump-thump* in my veins freezes. She can't possibly know about the cloisonné pineapple brooch I left back at the house. "Why would a mother steal her own child?"

Miss Colivan seems to notice my outfit for the first time. I'm wearing a lavender-colored knee-length sheath with pantyhose and black kitten heels. Her eyes narrow. "I love that dress."

"Thank you," I say, inwardly relaxing. I make a mental note to ask Dennis Roth about the Paulie Aandeg case. He must have something in the archives. There's likely no story there, but now I'm curious. "I purchased it at Dayton's. In Minneapolis."

She perches her chin on her thumb, the picture of reflection. "You know what would go great with that? One of the new cloisonné brooches that just arrived at Ben Franklin. They're lovely. You should check them out next time you're downtown."

My mouth turns dry as dust. I can't make a sound to save my soul, and it doesn't matter, because she's flashed me a blinding grin and trotted off to the sidelines. The concert is about to begin.

Cruel Miss Colivan, dipping girls' braids in the glue pot.

She wasn't in the store when I stole the brooch. Was she? Impossible. Her mentioning it is the wildest of coincidences. I steady my breath and claim a spot on the bleachers, but I feel like I'm balancing on marbles the whole way. Miss Colivan has unsettled me, and if I don't put her out of my mind, I won't get what I need for this article.

Through sheer force of will, I manage to concentrate on the concert.

The evening is a mixed bag. The children butcher every song, but they're beaming with pride and sing with so much heart. My neck is prickling constantly during the show, like I'm being watched, but when I turn to see who's staring, everyone is focused on the stage and the children. Still, one time I catch Miss Colivan pointing in my direction before leaning toward a fellow teacher to whisper something.

That's when I realize I've felt watched the whole time I've been in this town, above and beyond what I'd expect as a newcomer. I shudder. Am I imagining it?

After the program, I gather quotes from parents and pose the children to snap some photos with the camera Dennis has lent me.

If only Ursula could see me now.

She would hate how I'm backsliding into a hausfrau reporter, right on the heels of transforming into a just plain hausfrau.

At least I'm finally looking forward to my baby being born, I decide on the walk home.

When I reach the house and discover that Deck has not yet returned, I'm too tired to go to sleep. Though the thought of a cocktail is as appetizing as swallowing a raw egg, I crave adult interaction after that terrible run-in with Miss Colivan. I write my own note, slip it under the magnet for Deck to find, pet Slow Henry, and hoof it to Little John's Pub.

Time to meet Lilydale's nightlife.

CHAPTER 12

Little John's reminds me of the 620 Club in Minneapolis, where I first met Deck, minus the perpetually turning plastic turkey on a spit that is the 620's showcase. Both bars are dim and murky, with thick currents of smoke lending the spaces an underwater feel. My eyes take a moment to adjust, inflating my other senses. I smell Aqua Velva and cigarettes and the sour lick of spilled cocktails. The conversation drops when I step into the bar, and it sounds like I'm being stared at, and then the door closes behind me and my eyes adjust and everyone in the bar is doing what people in bars do.

Elbows on the counter, talking to one another.

The *click clack* of a pair shooting a game of pool.

Men in shirtsleeves arguing across tables, their drinks sweating.

A handful of couples, the women coarse, their hair bound under kerchiefs, the men with dirty hands and wide smiles. Someone stands in a dark corner, his back to me. For a crazy second, it looks like he's licking the wall, but then he turns, a lighter illuminating his face followed by the orange ember of a drawn cigarette, before he returns to shadow.

Pulse thudding in my wrists, I have a moment to decide between sitting at the bar or a table. Any more time taken and I'll be making a spectacle of myself.

I select the bar because it's the nearest. My legs quiver on the way to the stool. I tell myself it's nerves. It's never easy being the new person. I crave an icy-cold Tab and good conversation, but ordering pop in this establishment will surely only call more unwanted attention to me. "Tom Collins, please."

The bartender, a small man with a face like a withered apple, studies me for so long that I think he's going to demand identification. I still occasionally got carded in Minneapolis, but I never imagined it would happen here. The thought, oddly, makes me feel extra small. Like I don't belong. I mean, I know I'm *new* to town, but something about the prospect of being carded right now feels like more than my ego can handle.

When the bartender opens his mouth, I discover it's even worse.

"How about lemonade, Mrs. Schmidt?"

I shrink to the size of a cockroach. "Pardon me?"

"I could pour you a refreshing glass of lemonade. It'll be better for you."

The bar has gone quiet but for the haunting strains of "Ode to Billie Joe" drifting out of the jukebox.

Ursula, Libby, and I used to catch *Candid Camera* together on Sunday nights, but I know I'm not being recorded, not having a prank played on me. The bartender is visibly uncomfortable. I glance down the bar at the men staring back at me, their expressions inscrutable. Honestly, I would have preferred a lemonade, but there's more at stake.

"Is everyone else having lemonade?" My voice jelly-wobbles.

"It's just, ma'am . . . your condition."

The second time today I've heard that. A fever starts in my chest and fires up my neck, torching my cheeks. I don't know who or what my anger would have burned if a woman around my age didn't pop behind the bar, grab a collins glass, and start mixing a drink as if it's the most normal thing in the world.

Judging by the apron at her waist, it is.

"I've got this, Albert," she says, smiling at the bartender. Her over-bite and dimples give her a playful, childlike appearance. "Ladies waiting on ladies. That's how it should be, eh?"

Albert grunts and walks to the other end of the bar. The waitress laughs, a deep chuckle that counterbalances her dimples.

"I'm Regina." She offers me her hand.

Rescue Regina, saving ladies in distress and smelling of verbena.

I shake her hand, realize my own is trembling.

She leans in so she can talk without everyone overhearing. "Small towns. Everyone knows your business. What're you gonna do?"

Regina suddenly reminds me of my mother so much that my heart twists. I don't trust myself to hold the drink she's offering, so I indicate the bar. She sets the Tom Collins in front of me.

"Are you going to get in trouble for serving me?" I ask, my voice chalky.

Regina rests one hand on the bar, the other on her hip. Now that she's in front of me, I can see that she's in her midtwenties, a few years younger than my twenty-eight. "Maybe. There's worse trouble to come if we don't stand up for each other, though. Since when does someone else get to decide what you drink?"

"I'm pregnant." Here it feels like admitting to leprosy, or murder. My mouth is dry, but I can't bring my lips to the straw to drink.

"I'm Canadian," Regina says.

It takes the joke a moment to settle. It's not particularly funny, but Regina's effort relaxes me enough that I can finally take a sip. The crisp bite of gin unlocks my jaw. "How'd you end up here?"

"I was on the road with my boyfriend. Boy*fiend*, I now call him. We traveled as far south as Lilydale. We ran short on scratch, so the ding-a-ling ditched me. I got a gig here, an apartment." She points to the ceiling. "Upstairs from my job. Convenient. It's as good a place as any until I figure out my next move." She plants her elbows on the bar and drops her chin into her hands. "If you ever want to stop by and hang, I work nearly every day, and your money's good with me."

I smile as it dawns on me that I'm looking at the first thing about Lilydale that Ursula would approve of. I won't have any more of my drink—I didn't want it in the first place—but I'll be damned if I'll let my discomfort push me out.

CHAPTER 13

Which is how I wake up Saturday morning with a job, a friend, and an orange-and-white-striped ball of fur purring on my chest. "Slow Henry, you know you're not supposed to be in bed."

He pretends not to hear. I scratch him in the sweet spot behind his ear.

"Small-town life suits you," I say. "Maybe we can grow fat and glossy together."

I slip my hand under my nightgown, sliding it along my warm belly. The sip of last night's Tom Collins doesn't seem to have harmed anything, other than giving me a case of near-immediate heartburn. I'm four days shy of five months pregnant, and my pants still fit.

Soon they won't, though. The thought turns my throat greasy.

Morning sickness?

No, it's something else, one of the attacks that started at Mom's funeral. The first one, I thought I was dying but was too embarrassed to tell anyone, so I ran into the bathroom to hide until it passed. I recognize them now by the way they make the air go thick and slanted, until I can't seem to fit it down my throat. It's like I'm being buried alive and I need to run or hide or jump out of my own skin, but I can't escape them no matter what I do.

I shove the quilt off, Slow Henry with it.

He howls.

I feel terrible, but if I don't get some fresh air immediately, I'm going to vomit.

I race to the window, scrabbling at the wood. I must crack it. *Now.* I need air or I'll die. The window is stuck. In my desperation, I peel back two fingernails trying to pry it open. The pain is breathtaking.

"Joanie? Let me help you with that."

I spin, plastering myself to the wall.

Deck sets a tray down on the bed. He strolls over to the window. Unlocks it. Slides it open. The rush of morning-cool May air kisses my skin. Warbling birdsong and the distant thrum of cars drift inside. My heartbeat is no longer the loudest sound in the room.

Deck studies me, his expression perplexed. "Are you okay, honey?"

I nod. Swallow. Point at the tray. "You made breakfast?"

Deck smiles, runs his hand through his thick, dark hair. He's so damn good-looking. "Your favorite. French toast and bacon. Coffee with whitener."

I push sweaty hair out of my eyes. Smooth the front of my night-gown. Swallow again. The nausea has passed. "Thank you. Do I have to eat it here?" My lips catch on my teeth. "Because I don't want to mess up the sheets."

It's uncharitable, I know. He obviously wanted to bring me breakfast in bed. I need to escape this room, though, and some animal part of me understands I must do it calmly, to not alert Deck to the depth of the discomfort I've just experienced. I haven't told him about the attacks. I don't want him to think I'm losing my mind.

His expression slips. He turns from me, picking up the tray and walking out the door. "Let's eat in the nook you like so much," he calls over his shoulder.

I glance around the room, clenching and then releasing my hands to get blood circulating. I toss the quilt back on the bed, plump the pillows. Then I drop on my knees and peek under the bed. Slow Henry is hiding there, pouting and licking his paw, glaring at me. I stretch to pet him.

"Sorry, buddy. A momentary lapse of reason."

When I pad downstairs, I see Deck has a tablecloth—a sheet, actually; we don't own tablecloths—spread across the kitchen's built-in breakfast table. I've been begging him to eat there since we moved, but he hasn't wanted to. He was fine doing it in our Minneapolis apartment, but not in his childhood home. His mother taught him that meals involve family, and with only two seats, the nook doesn't have enough room.

I beam. Eating in the cozy alcove is the perfect antidote to what just happened upstairs. "You sure?"

Deck pats the bench next to him. "Yeah. It was unreasonable not to use this space. You were right. It's comfy."

I scooch next to him and sniff the food. It's gone cold and so doesn't have much scent. I see he's left all the dirty dishes on the counter, the ingredients he used to make the breakfast out and open. "This looks delicious."

He rubs my back while I douse the french toast in amber-colored syrup.

"You're not having any?" I ask.

"I already ate." He hadn't been home when I returned from Little John's last night. I assume his meeting was a success.

"I have so much to catch you up on," I say after I swallow my first bite. "I was at the school last night. Covering the music concert for the paper."

He nods.

"My first article, Deck! It was wonderful." I take a sip of my watery coffee. "Mostly wonderful. I met Miss Colivan."

Deck's mouth quirks. "And?"

"And do you remember her? Because she sure remembers you." I open my mouth for another bite. A lapel pin on the table catches my eye as the rubbery french toast passes my lips. I point at it and talk around the mouthful. "What's that?"

Deck's still rubbing my back. With his free hand, he picks up the pin. It's the size of a quarter, flower-shaped—the exact shape of Dorothy Lily's locket—a white background with a red embossed capital *M* on its face. I lean closer. That's not exactly right. The two top points of the *M* extend longer than they should.

"It's a capital *V*," Deck is saying, "on top of a small capital *M*. That's what I was told, anyhow."

"What's it stand for?"

"Something in Latin, I think. The group is called the Fathers and Mothers. What's Latin for that?"

Something slide-bumps inside my rib cage. "Pater and Mater, I think? Like paternity and maternity?"

"That's not it, then." Deck rubs his thumb over the insignia. Exactly like I rubbed the pineapple brooch when I first pocketed it. "Doesn't really matter. What's important is that the Fathers and Mothers is *the* in-group in town. I bet I landed a dozen new clients at last night's meeting."

"Deck, that's great!" My happiness is real. "I wouldn't have thought there'd be that much new business in a place this size. Everyone would already have insurance, you know? I should probably join the Fathers and Mothers myself, now that I'm working for the newspaper. When's the next meeting?"

He sets the pin down. "You're not going to like this."

Slide-bump.

"The Fathers is for men. No women allowed. But men aren't admitted in the Mothers, either, so it all evens out."

"What?"

He pulls his hand from my back, turns so he's facing rather than touching me. "It's a small town. What're you gonna do? The good news is that they host monthly mingles where all the men and women get together."

"The women cook, I suppose?"

He laughs. "Probably. Don't worry, darling. I'll do the cooking. Just like I did for you this morning. We'll shake them up from the inside."

His laugh is warm and inviting. I'm not ready to give in yet, though. "What if you lose business by 'shaking things up'? If they run this town, they're not going to like change."

"Nobody likes change, not at first. May I?"

He hovers his hand near my belly. I nod. He cups the curve just visible through my nightgown. "I see where they get the saying 'a bun in the oven.'"

"Deck!" I swat him, but playfully. "You're supposed to tell me I've never been more beautiful."

"You haven't," he says, suddenly serious. He traces my cheek with the back of his finger. "Joanie, don't think I don't see what you've given up to move here with me, to keep me out of the war. To start a new life where you don't know anyone. To have my baby. Gawd . . ."

He chokes on his next words. I'm shocked. I've never seen him emotional.

I toss my arms around him. "I love you, honey," I say.

"I love you, too." He kisses me on the mouth. I'm ashamed of my morning-breakfast breath. He doesn't seem to mind. The kiss goes deeper, searching, and I feel a pleasant warmth flowing through my blood, pulsing between my legs. We haven't made love nearly as much since I've been pregnant. I miss it.

He's pulling back to kiss my neck, a move that electrifies me. I tilt my head to give him access. Instead, he tugs my face back and rests his nose on mine, our eyelashes nearly touching. "I need to ask a favor."

"Yeah?" I've forgotten about my morning queasiness, the french toast, living in a small town. I just want *him*.

He clears his throat, his expression going soft. "I want to make lots of money, enough that we can buy a bigger house. A house that's all ours. I'm going to shake up the Fathers and the Mothers, I promise you that, but there's one area they won't budge on, and that's pregnant women drinking in public."

His words are ice water. I pull back, slowly, my fingers arching into claws.

"Word reached the meeting last night that you were out at Little John's."

My surge of rage is perfectly counterbalanced by a sense of impotence, leaving me nothing but numb. "But Deck—" I start. He cuts me off before I can tell him that I didn't even want to drink, barely choked down a sip before the heartburn kicked in.

"I know what you're going to say. It's your body, your choice. I agree with you, and I'll tell the world that."

The conversation is spinning so far away from me I can't even see where to get in. *I didn't want to drink. I only wanted to socialize.*

But Deck doesn't notice my struggle. He's gone back to fingering the lapel pin. "There's a doctor in town that everyone loves. Dr. Krause. The Mothers say he's the best. A real ace."

The words that finally manage to plop out are ugly, childish. "You said no Mothers were allowed at the meeting."

Deck's eyes flick to me, then return to the pin. "A few Mothers dropped by at the end to clean up. You caused quite a buzz, popping up in Little John's last night without me. Got the whole town talking." He chuckles. "The Mothers suggested that you see Dr. Krause, get his opinion on how a pregnant woman should conduct herself.

I figure, if he says drinking while pregnant is fine, then that'll shut everyone up."

I clip every word before I release it. I'm not even sure what I'm fighting for, but I'm desperate to be right about something. "And if he doesn't?"

"Then we'll both stop drinking in public. We'll save it for home, just the two of us."

The numbness hasn't receded.

"Please, Joanie? It's only for a few more months."

I twitch. He takes it for agreement. He stands, kissing the top of my head. "You're the best. The absolute bee's knees. I have to get going. Dad and I are looking at a property south of town. They need home insurance. Could be a big deal. Might go hunting after that."

He grabs his wallet and keys and is out the door before I can ask him when he took up hunting.

CHAPTER 14

After I shower, I find a handwritten note threaded into my typewriter's platen.

Baby, you are the earth, sun, and moon to me.

It's the fourth note I've discovered since Deck left. One was taped to the milk inside the fridge, another written on a square of toilet paper still on the roll—that one made me smile, grudgingly—a third coiled in the elf's-shoe twist of our toothpaste. All the notes say the same thing, essentially: Deck loves me and is always thinking of me.

The edges of my anger melt. I *do* need to find a doctor in Lilydale, after all. Might as well be one who comes highly recommended. Besides, it's so silly, how this escalated. I simply wanted to get out of the house last night. I'd be fine never having another drink in my life.

I make a silent pledge to call Dr. Krause first thing Monday morning.

That's also the deadline for the article I'm turning in to Dennis, but I see no reason to wait. I prop up the notebook that I brought to last night's concert, scanning my neat shorthand. With luck, the camera holds four or five good photos. Personally, I hope Dennis chooses the one featuring the student-made yellow submarine, a painted plywood cutout as large as a car. It had required several kids to wheel it out, and their pride glowed on their faces.

I click on the radio for background noise and begin typing.

We All Live in a Lilydale Dream

The radio drama that I flipped on is interrupted with another Vietnam story, this one about American troubles at Kham Duc. During an evacuation, there wasn't enough room in the helicopters for Chinese soldiers battling alongside the American boys. I think about those miserable men left behind, fighting a strange war with no end. I'm ashamed at how easy it is to tune out their pain, halfway across the world and me in this sleepy little town, but that's exactly what I do when I snap off the radio. A person can sit with only so much bad news.

Then I pause, bite my lip, and type my very first byline, a happy flush warming my cheeks.

By Joan Harken

May 11, 1968

Lilydale Elementary School's Spring Musical program was a hit! The May 10 extravaganza featured music by The Beatles with each grade, kindergarten through fourth, presenting one song. Miss Colivan, fourth grade teacher, told the packed gym that "we wanted a modern presentation, something children and parents alike could enjoy." The song list:

Kindergarten: "Twist and Shout"

First Grade: "I'm Only Sleeping"

Second Grade: "I'm Happy Just to Dance with You"

Third Grade: "She Loves You"

Fourth Grade: "I Want to Hold Your Hand"

Everyone certainly seemed to be having a wonderful time. A crowd of at least 400 people gathered to hear the sweet songs of youth. The grand finale featured all 243 children singing "Yellow Submarine," while some of the older students wheeled out the submarine they'd created in their Arts & Crafts class. If the evening concert was any indication, the future of Lilydale is in bright hands.

The relief is immediate. A story out rather than in.

I review my writing. "Twist and Shout" isn't technically a Beatles song, but I don't think this article is the place to mention that. The rest holds up. Edward R. Murrow doesn't need to stop the presses, but I'm satisfied. I zip the paper out of the typewriter, slide it into my portfolio, nuzzle Slow Henry, and pad to the bathroom. I brush my teeth, apply makeup, and scan the article one more time. I still like it. It's more Women's News than hard-hitting journalism, but it's a start.

And my name is on it.

I pat my head. My hair is not quite set from this morning's hot shower. I know what I could do while I wait for it to dry, but *hell*. I don't want to. My feet drag as I walk to the phone, my lungs heavy. I pick up the handset and dial.

Ursula answers on the third ring. "Hello?"

"Hey, it's me."

"Joan. What the *hell?* Why haven't you called before? I've been worried sick about you. I nearly drove to Lilydale, knocking door to door, asking who'd taken my Joanie."

I laugh, a dry sound. "I'm sorry. I should've called sooner. I've been so busy setting up house." I wait for her criticism. None comes, so I continue. "I got a job at the paper."

"That's good news," she says. I can hear the pouting, but she's not committed to it. Ursula never stays angry for long. "So, are they all hillbillies?"

I chuckle into the phone, but it morphs into a sob.

"Joan, what's wrong?"

I'm not exactly sure what's set me off—hearing a friendly voice?—but suddenly it's all too much. "I'm sorry, Ursula. I let the town do a number on me. Lilydale is everything you predicted, and worse."

"Tell me everything."

The stories begin to disgorge themselves: all the men hugging me, Dorothy peeping into my bedroom the first night we moved in, Deck telling everyone we're married and that I'm pregnant, not being allowed to apply for a job until Ronald gave me the green light, all those people staring at the dead dog by the railroad track, Miss Colivan knowing about the brooch I stole, the Fathers and Mothers running the town, that I can't drink. Ursula doesn't say a word, not even when I pause to catch my breath. "Ursula, I have to get out of Lilydale. I think they're following me. Everyone. Tracking me." I didn't know I believed that until I've said it out loud. It feels good to finally get it out there.

She's still silent on the other end. A car putters past outside my home, well below the speed limit. Someone else watching me?

She finally speaks. "Joan, you stole something from the Ben Franklin?"

Her tone—like she's talking a child off a tantrum—clangs my warning bell. I try to reel it back in. "Not exactly," I say. "I just didn't have enough money to pay for it. I'll bring it back. And I was kidding about the last part. No one's tracking me. You were the one who said small towns are so weird, that's all."

My blood's turned to sludge. She's taking too long to respond.

Finally: "Joanie, I'm worried about you. If you could hear yourself on this phone call, you'd be worried, too." She's silent for several more beats. When her voice returns, it's barely a whisper. "You remember Halloween 1962?"

I smile softly, immediately relaxing. I run over the rosary beads of my memory. The photograph, the one that sat on my desk at the *Star* and is now a centerpiece in my living room. Libby as Amelia Earhart. Ursula Eleanor Roosevelt. Me Natalie Wood. Three young women tumbled into each other, bright-eyed and open-mouthed, the world at our feet.

"Yeah, of course. It was a marvelous evening. One of the best." I'm so relieved she's changing the subject, isn't going to scold me about my wild imagination.

"Tell me what you remember about it."

That's easy. I was just thinking about it the other day. I remember it as clear as a movie.

I'd been staring into my mirror, glum, realizing that dressing like Natalie Wood had been stupid. Probably no one at the party had seen *Marjorie Morningstar*.

But then in swung Ursula, and she squealed when she took in my makeup and flipped hair. "Joan, you look marvelous!"

I grinned. "No, you do. Eleanor Roosevelt has never been more spectacular."

Ursula strutted into my bedroom and twirled, her then boyfriend, Todd, a few steps behind. I'd long been jealous of their relationship, but I couldn't find fault in his perfect depiction of FDR. This Halloween was going to blow everyone's mind.

"Before the polio," Todd said, catching my glance at his legs. "And you're Marjorie Morningstar, of course. The only question is: From the book or the movie?"

I didn't know there had been a book. I smiled and fluffed my hair flirtatiously to cover. "I'm just glad you know who I am."

"Libby," Ursula said, bringing the conversation full circle. "Have you seen her today?"

I noticed for the first time the worry lines creasing Ursula's eyes and mouth, all but erased by her heavy makeup. "She's not in her room?"

Ursula turned to plant a long, wet kiss on Todd. "That oughta hold you over. Now be a good lad and skip to the party next door. We'll meet you there in a minute."

Once he was out of earshot, Ursula grabbed my hand and marched me down the hall. Our three-bedroom Southeast Como walk-up had been a dream come true when we'd stumbled onto it between our freshman and sophomore years. The apartment was far enough from campus to feel grown-up, close enough that it wasn't a hassle to grab a bus to classes. Plus, we each had our own bedroom.

We'd made a vow to stay there until we graduated.

Now in our senior year, we'd held to it.

Ursula pounded on Libby's door.

"I don't know why you need me for this," I said, my stomach growing slippery. Libby had been distant lately. Her new boyfriend was a biology major, a nice enough guy, but he demanded all Libby's time.

"Because I think she's in there but ignoring me," Ursula said, raising her voice so that Libby could hear. "If you're with me, I can tell her that her roommates are waiting for her and not be lying."

"Go away!" Libby hollered from inside.

Ursula turned the knob and stepped into the room, me following at her heels.

Libby was a melted puddle atop her batik bedspread.

"What is it?" I asked, dropping next to her.

Ursula gently stroked Libby's hair. "Yeah, baby, why aren't you getting ready for the party?"

Libby sat up. Her face was puffy from crying. I assumed her biology-major boyfriend must have dumped her. So positive was I that was the problem that when Libby said, "The rabbit died," I initially glanced around the room, searching for a pet.

Then I understood. Libby was pregnant.

Ursula bundled her in a hug, and I piled on.

"We'll figure it out, darling, don't you worry," Ursula said.

"Yes," I agreed. "We'll get this taken care of. Don't you fret a bit."

It took another ten minutes to calm Libby down, twenty more to stuff her into her Amelia Earhart costume. By the time the photograph was snapped of us later that evening, we were three women tumbled into each other, bright-eyed and open-mouthed with laughter, and I'd all but forgotten about Libby's crisis. Ursula knew a person who knew a person, and it would be taken care of. Just a bump in the road.

"Like getting your tonsils out," she'd said.

Ursula's real-time question pulls me back into the moment. "And then what?" she asks.

Something sharp pierces the cottony fog of memory. When Slow Henry tries to rub against my ankles, I pull away, twisting the phone cord between my fingers. "What do you mean?"

"Joanie," she says softly. "You have to stop making up your stories. You spin everything better or worse than it is. You know what happened to Libby that night. After the party."

CHAPTER 15

"I know," I say, defiantly, tugging on the phone cord. Of course I remember, if I make myself. But where's the point in that? That's something my mom taught me.

Remember the good, only the good. Don't borrow trouble from the past.

A headache is beginning to bear down on my temples, clamping my head and squeezing. I need to get off the phone.

"I'm sorry, Ursula. I haven't been the same since Mom died." It's unfair to use my mother like this, but I can't bear to have Ursula doubt me. "I haven't been the same since. Then the move, and the pregnancy. It's a lot, is all."

"I know, Joan." Her voice is so relieved. "That'd be a lot for anyone. I'm so glad you see that it's temporary, that it'll pass. Do you have a good doctor in Lilydale?"

"The best," I lie. It's harmless, something I say to make her feel better. It'll be true enough soon, in any case, if Deck is right about Dr. Krause.

"All right, then." She talks cheerily for a few more minutes, telling me about the Ansafone her boyfriend's just bought for her so she'll never miss another of his calls, the far-out party she attended last week, the new dress she's going to buy. I'm so tired when we finally hang up.

I lean my head against the window, but it's too warm, absorbing the heat of the day. I need to get out of this house.

Slow Henry follows me to the bathroom, mewing for my attention as I remove my hair rollers, watching the curls stretch and snap back. I apply my new raspberry lipstick, blot it on a tissue and then pop my lips to set it, throw on some mascara, grab the concert article I wrote for the *Gazette*, and then glide out into the day, feeling a weight lift the minute I step into the sunshine.

The simple, happy sounds of small-town life buzz in my ear. A chorus of lawnmowers trimming yards, neighbors calling to each other across fences, the hum of cars traveling at a safe speed. I breathe deeply as I make my way downtown. Ursula was right. I completely overreacted about Lilydale. I was an unreasonable baby. I won't let that happen again. The air smells fresh and green, like just-cut grass. The dress I chose hides my pregnancy, not that it matters. The whole town knows, and I still landed the job at the newspaper. For all the lack of privacy in Lilydale, I doubt I would have been able to say the same had I stayed at the *Minneapolis Star*.

The *Gazette*'s offices are across from Schmidt Insurance. I didn't bother to notice the building next door to the *Gazette* when I went for my interview yesterday. Or rather, I did, and wrote it off as empty. I overlooked the white insignia embedded in the granite keystone because it didn't mean anything to me. Today I recognize it as the same symbol as on Deck's lapel pin, a large capital *V* held in the divot of a small capital *M*.

I press my face to the glass of the front door. A circle of folding chairs dominates the center of the room, and a dark chunk of wood, possibly an out-of-place wet bar, is shoved against the back wall. It reminds me of a lonely community center or church basement. Deck has clearly overestimated the Fathers and Mothers' influence. Definitely nothing to get bent out of shape about.

I walk next door. The *Gazette*'s offices are closed. I expected as much on a Saturday. I rest my purse and portfolio on the pavement, remove the concert article, fold it into thirds, and tuck it into an envelope I brought. I scribble "Dennis Roth, from JH" on the front and drop the envelope through the mail slot.

The weather is beautiful. Blooming lilacs are sweet as honey in the air, and the light-purple color against the bright-green leaves is breath-taking. I remain charmed by the fact that I can walk everywhere I need to go. I decide on the spot to make a delicious dinner for Deck this evening. I'll buy chicken, and rice, and canned carrots. I will even pick up the ingredients I need to bake a cake from scratch.

I'm running through a mental list when I spot him out of the corner of my eye.

The hook-nosed man who mugged me in Minneapolis.

CHAPTER 16

I scream, a short, involuntary sound.

He turns quickly, for only a second, but it's enough.

It's him.

It's not possible, but it's true. He's here. Here in Lilydale.

My blood pumps hot, and it's telling me to run home to safety.

My brain is louder, however, and it's trying to reason with me. It's simply not possible that my mugger is somehow here in Lilydale. This is somebody who merely *resembles* him. And if I don't face the look-alike now and verify it's not my attacker, I will be forever glancing over my shoulder.

I jog toward him.

"Hey!" I say, my voice raised.

He's walking away, but at my yell, he turns again.

He's less than a block away, his porkpie hat shading his face, but I feel certain he's the criminal who stole my wallet. Who hit me. Who knifed me. The main reason, even though I will never admit it to Deck, that I am now living in Lilydale.

My mugger—for that's who he must be—darts into the nearest alley.

As I follow him, my heart shuddering against my rib cage, it occurs to me that our roles have switched: I am hunting him. But there's no time for me to analyze what's happening. I need to catch him, to see his face clearly. I reach the alley. It's empty except for a large trash bin. There's an opening on the other end, but it's half a block away.

He can't have made it all the way through.

Is he hiding behind the garbage bin?

I'm about to dash in and see when the hand comes down on my shoulder.

I scream, nearly jumping out of my clothes. I spin to see who it is.

Dennis Roth, the willowy *Lilydale Gazette* editor, *Dennis Daddy Longlegs dispatching the news*, is standing there. He's visibly trembling. For a surreal moment, I wonder if he knows about my mugging.

"You shouldn't be running when you're pregnant."

I open my mouth. Before I can plead my case, he holds up a hand.

"No time for that. I have the story of the century," he says. He leans over, hands on knees, to catch his breath. He must have raced here. "Paulie Aandeg's been found. After twenty-four years, the boy in the sailor suit has come home."

PART II

CHAPTER 17

Dennis fills me in on the urgent walk—he refuses to let me jog—to the *Gazette* offices. I have to agree it's quite the story. A child disappears without a trace in 1944, wearing a sweet little sailor suit (Miss Colivan was correct about that), and shows up twenty-four years later. Only Amory Bauer has met with him so far, but he's convinced the new arrival might be Paulie. The man, who goes by Kris Jefferson, refused to tell Chief Bauer what happened all those years ago, but he said he'll talk to someone at the paper when he's ready.

The familiar thrumming of standing on the cusp of a big break crackles like fireworks across my skin. I don't want to outright ask for the story for fear of being turned down, so I just keep asking questions.

Dennis opens the office and leads me to the newspaper morgue—I was right that the second door led to it, wrong about how provincial it would be. He lets me pull up the stories on microfiche, reading over my shoulder as I search. His breath smells like onions.

I discover only two articles. The first:

Lad Disappears in Lilydale

September 6, 1944

The tiny desk in the Lilydale Elementary classroom still has the paper sack six-year-old Paulie Aandeg brought to the first day of classes sitting on it. He was excited to start kindergarten. He packed crayons, a tablet, a pencil and a bag of potato chips. He took the potato chips when he was excused for lunch at 11:30 and left the rest. He hasn't been seen since.

Wearing a hand-me-down sailor suit and new white shoes, Paulie attended his first day of school with considerable enthusiasm. He was walked there by his mother, Mrs. Virginia Aandeg, who sources say gave Paulie's teacher instructions to keep Paulie until she picked him up. At 11:30, the teacher excused all the kindergartners for lunch. The distraught teacher, who asked that her name not be used, remembers Paulie stepping outside with a registration card in one pocket and the chips in another, but "he was a quiet child. I don't recall him speaking all morning, and so when I didn't see him return after lunchtime, I assumed he left with his mother."

Paulie's disappearance has rocked the tiny village.

Led by Grover Tucker, Stearns County sheriff out of Saint Cloud, and with the help of local police officer Amory Bauer, an extensive, coordinated manhunt took place, but not one clue was uncovered. "We won't stop looking until we've found the child," Officer Bauer said.

Lilydale businesses have closed today to help the search. Farmers have been urged to check their barns and cisterns, and housewives have even looked inside their furnaces for the missing child. Saint Cloud-based civilian air patrols have scoured the countryside, and men have walked hand-in-hand down the shallow Crow River on the edge of town, searching for any sign of Paulie.

Two schoolgirls claim to have seen Paulie walking toward the river shortly after lunch. Mrs. Robert Cunningham, a local resident, said she saw a child walking along a ditch carrying a piece of paper around 1:00 or 1:30 p.m.

Paulie's mother, Mrs. Aandeg, says she thinks she knows what has happened to her child but cannot prove it. She refused to say any more to this reporter.

The article includes a photo of the child, smiling shyly, hair cropped short, wearing his sailor suit. It twists my heart. The second piece was published five days later and features a photo of a much-younger Stanley and Dorothy Lily posed next to Ronald and Barbara Schmidt. Stanley is standing tall, squinting at the camera, and in that youthful incarnation, he looks like someone I used to know. Dorothy and Barbara are holding their hands over their eyes to shade them. Young Ronald is such a perfect replica of Deck that it haunts me.

I read:

Home of Missing Boy Destroyed in a Fire

September 11, 1944

Tragedy has again struck Lilydale, Minnesota, hitting the same family it devastated on September 5 with the disappearance of a child. The house of Mrs. Virginia Aandeg, whose son, Paulie, left school last Tuesday and has been missing ever since, burned to the ground late last night. There were no reported injuries in the fire. In fact, locals speculate Mrs. Aandeg may be on the run in reaction to the disappearance of her child and was not at home at the time of the fire.

Paulie Aandeg was the subject of an area manhunt when he went missing on his first day of kindergarten. Stearns County Sheriff Grover Tucker was the lead on the investigation. According to Sheriff Tucker, "We've run down every tip and aren't sure where to take the case. The entire Lilydale area has been scoured, bloodhounds and Civil Air Patrol brought in and witnesses questioned. It is troubling that the boy's mother is nowhere to be found. We'll have to assume the two disappearances are connected."

The town is reeling from the double tragedies. "While this is truly terrible, we're coming together as a community," said Mr. Ronald Schmidt, owner of Schmidt Insurance. Mr. Stanley Lily, local attorney, declared that "through a local organization, my wife and I are making sure there is always a home for Mrs. Aandeg in Lilydale if she returns, and we will never stop looking for Paulie."

Lilydale truly is a gem of a community, even in tragedy.

For his part, Sheriff Tucker is not hopeful that Paulie Aandeg will be located. "While I believe we've hit a stone wall," he said, "we know there is something off in the village of Lilydale. If anyone has something to report, they're encouraged to call my office."

"Oh my god," I say, falling back like a rag doll. "That unfortunate mother."

"I'd forgotten about the fire," Dennis says quietly.

I tap the microfiche screen with my fingernail. "Only two articles. Why didn't the story get more coverage?"

"It did in the Twin Cities' papers, if I remember correctly," he says. "I was overseas when the story broke, but everyone from Lilydale remembers it. The rumor was that Virginia Aandeg killed Paulie by accident, burned down her house when the police started sniffing too close, and then fled."

I think about what Miss Colivan said about Paulie last night, that his mother had abducted him. Small-town rumors appear to provide the most vicious form of the telephone game. "If he's truly back, then that rumor is shot dead."

Dennis shrugs. "I never believed it. I didn't know her well, but she seemed like a good enough sort. Drank a little too much, that's all."

Does his gaze carry judgment? Does he know that I was out at Little John's? "I wonder what happened to the boy after all."

Dennis threads his long, elegant fingers together. "With luck, we can ask him ourselves."

I still can't believe that this plum story has landed in the *Gazette*'s lap. According to Dennis, a Father had run over from next door to say that Chief Bauer had called, saying he'd just met with a man claiming to be the original Paulie Aandeg. Dennis immediately came looking for me.

It's flattering.

"With any luck," I agree, nodding as I lean forward to reread the first article. Paulie had walked to school with his mother. She told his teacher not to let Paulie leave without her, but somehow, the teacher forgot, or Paulie wandered off, or he was kidnapped. The article isn't clear.

The only interesting nugget is the name of the local lead: Amory Bauer. Lilydale's current police chief and the man Paulie Aandeg—Kris Jefferson—first came to upon his return. And then there's Sheriff Tucker's cryptic quote: "We know there is something off in the village of Lilydale."

I shake off the chills and return to the moment at hand.

The boy in the sailor suit has returned.

"So who's going to write the article?" I ask, keeping my tone neutral.

Dennis is so pale that his emotions are broadcast in neon. My question has delighted him. "I don't suppose you want it?"

I jump out of my seat and hug him. I can hold my own wrists behind his slender back. "Thank you thank you thank you! When do I get to interview Paulie?"

Dennis waits until I release him to speak, his face scarlet. The Lilydale men must not get hugged nearly as much as the women. "Apparently, our Paulie is a hippie now. He runs on his own time clock and will 'let us know' when he's ready for an interview."

I nod, biting my bottom lip in concentration. "Don't suppose you know who the kindergarten teacher that day was."

"Yes, and I'm certain you've met her. Becky Swanson. She's the secretary at your father-in-law's insurance agency."

Blonde Becky, beautiful as a butterfly, she'd fall to the earth if she stopped smiling.

Something about that thought drops a bullet of unease into the chamber, followed by another slug, slick and scary. I glance back at the article to confirm it.

Paulie Aandeg disappeared on September 5.

September 5 is my due date.

The effort of reaching the bathroom costs me. I'm drenched in sweat, blood dripping down my thighs, my breasts vast, painful boulders. There are no identifying items in here, no names on prescriptions, no familiar shampoo. Only a bathtub, a sink, and a toilet. I use the sink to pull myself up, turn the faucet on, and gulp greedily at the cold water, drinking until my stomach threatens to revolt.

I splash icy water on my face. It brings a moment of clarity.

The faces, watching greedily as my baby came out, staring between my bloody legs as if I were a prize horse delivering their foal. I'd been drugged—a shot? two?—but the pain drew me out until the shot pulled me under, back and forth, drew me out, pulled me under, and whose faces were they? I see only grinning mouths.

But it doesn't matter.

I am Joan Harken. I am a reporter. My baby is gone.

I slide to the floor and lean against the sink pedestal. The water gurgles in my belly. The floor tile is blessedly cool. I want to lie on it, salve my feverish bones, but there isn't time. I must find my baby.

But my consciousness is being packed up and put away and I'm falling, down, down . . .

CHAPTER 18

Dennis gives me explicit instructions to sit tight on the article. It's the weekend, so Mrs. Swanson will be with her family. Better to interview her at work on her lunch break so as not to upset anyone. She hasn't done anything wrong, Dennis assures me, but it can't be a pleasant memory for her. Weekends are Chief Bauer's busy time, so a Monday would work better for him, as well. As for Paulie, we're at his whim as to when he wants to meet.

I nod and agree to it, all the while thinking that surely there's no harm in laying some groundwork. Dennis didn't want to reveal where Paulie's staying, but as far as I know there's only one motel in town, and it's the Purple Saucer. Deck and I drove past it our first day here. It's a ten-minute walk from the newspaper, and the spring day is as pretty as a peach.

When I reach the motel, I count eleven units, but the crowning glory is a large purple spaceship constructed on the roof as if it's landed there. It's straight out of *Earth vs. the Flying Saucers*, one of my mom's favorite movies. There's a thrill in seeing it resting up there, quirky and grand. The closer I get, I see the flying saucer is made out of plywood painted purple and shiny sheet metal, but I still like it.

Of the eleven units, only three have cars parked in front, and all of those have Minnesota license plates. Would Paulie have been living in his home state all these years? I make my way to the glass-enclosed room marked OFFICE, the lip of the flying saucer shading it. There's a man behind the counter, and he looks up with a smile when I enter.

"What can I do you for, ma'am?"

I planned for this on the walk over. "Hello"—I look at his nameplate—"Mr. Scholl. My name is Joan Harken."

Do his eyes grow shadowed behind his round glasses? If so, he quickly recovers. "Pleased to meet you."

"And you. I'm a new reporter at the *Gazette*, and Dennis Roth has assigned me the story of Paulie Aandeg's return. You've heard the news?"

He can't blanket his expression quickly enough this time. He knows Paulie's in town, which means he's either friends with Chief Bauer or Paulie is staying here. I sit on my exultation, which isn't easy.

"There's been word," he says cautiously.

My grin widens. "Wonderful. I'm here to interview Mr. Aandeg."

He removes his glasses and cleans them with a blue handkerchief he produces from his back pocket. When he pops his glasses back on his nose, his eyes are very focused.

"Dennis sent you, you said?"

"He assigned me the story." I keep my smile bland. Mr. Scholl can make of that what he will.

He studies me for another beat. "Well, I'm afraid Mr. Aandeg left early this morning."

Disappointment flattens my mood. I've been excited to meet him. "Checked out?"

"No. Cleaning lady says his things are still there. He could be looking for work."

Aha! "Thank you, Mr. Scholl. You've been very helpful."

"My pleasure."

"Have a nice day," I tell him, turning toward the door. I've already made up my mind to come back tomorrow, am already spinning the questions I'll ask him. *Poor Puzzling Paulie, a mystery of a man.* Mr. Scholl's comment stops me dead in my shoes.

"You want me to tell him you've dropped by, Mrs. Schmidt?"

My hand rests on the cool door handle. The patch of warm sunshine is just outside, beyond the black shade of the flying saucer, and I suddenly, desperately want to feel it on my skin. "Harken," I say.

"Excuse me?"

I start to turn, to face him, but don't think I can stand it if he's smiling.

"Nothing," I call over my shoulder. "No need to tell him a thing. I'll stop back."

CHAPTER 19

Sunday morning dawns sticky, the air slow and sullen.

"Weatherman says it's going to be a hot one," Deck murmurs in my ear, his voice drowsy. I'm surprised he's holding me, but then the pressure against my lower back tells me why. I turn and kiss him, not open-mouthed because we've just woken up, but still inviting.

Morning lovemaking is my preference. My mind isn't alert yet, so it's easy. Deck props himself up just above me, out of deference to the baby. If I glanced down, I could see the pouch, a swelling where before there was only flat, but I don't look. I grip tight to Deck and follow him into that place where there's no color or sound, just the two of us rocking each other.

He rolls off before I've climaxed. Ursula says it's like that sometimes. I've had to take her word for it because Deck's only the second man I've been with. I told him he was the first. Hearing it made him happy.

He slides out of bed and pads straight into our bathroom, so I head to the one downstairs to clean up. When I return, he's making the bed.

"That was a good way to wake up," I say shyly, staring at my bare feet.

He strides over and kisses the top of my head. "The best."

"Do you want to have a cup of Sanka with me? In the nook?"

His face twists. "I wish I could, baby, but I have to work today."

"It's Sunday!"

"I know. This first month is vital, Joanie. I'm playing catch-up with the other agents. I need to show the locals I'm worth their money. That means working harder."

Slow Henry appears and rubs against my leg, purring loudly. His glossy fur is so comforting to the touch, but I don't want to pet him, not when I'm frustrated. Deck wasn't home all yesterday. I went to bed without him, didn't even have a chance to tell him about the Paulie Aandeg story.

Deck notices my expression. "Don't be mad, Joanie. I'll be back for dinner. We can watch television just like nights back in Minneapolis. All right?"

"Fine."

"Joan, you're still pouting."

He's right, so there's no point in replying.

"You should make some friends," he says, his voice suddenly hard, the playfulness gone. "I can't be your only social life here."

But you are, I want to protest, and *you should be because it's your fault I'm here.* But then I think of my complicity in the move, and Regina, and her kindness. "I did meet a woman about our age." I don't tell him that she works at the bar or that she's from Canada in case he takes her for a hippie.

"Wonderful, baby! You should have lunch with her."

I have nothing on my calendar other than stopping back by the Purple Saucer Motel.

"I think I will."

❖

I'm timid walking into Little John's. It's foolish how I hold the wax-paper-wrapped sandwiches in front of me, all but yelling *I'm not here to drink.* Thankfully, Regina is working, and even better, she seems pleased to see me.

"Tell me those are bologna," she says when I seat myself at the bar. The dim room contains more people than I'd expected at noon on a Sunday.

"Close," I say, nudging one toward her. "Fried braunschweiger. Do you like it?"

"Is that the liver sausage stuff?"

"Pretty similar," I say. "I put pickles on it, too, but you can peel those off."

"Far out!" She unwraps the sandwich. "Can I get you something to drink?"

"A Tab?" I say, louder than required.

She smiles, holding the triangle of sandwich with one hand and turning a glass right-side up with the other. "Heard it's warm out there," she says.

It is. The middle of May, and it's already a simmering day begging for rain. "What time do you come to work?"

She's chewing. She hands me my soda, swallows her bite. "We open at ten a.m. for our shot-and-a-beer regulars. I'm here sometime before then."

I glance around the bar. Eight people, all men, none of them sitting together, all of them with a sweating drink resting in front of them. The radio is a background hum, describing a world apart from Lilydale. "Is this a typical Sunday crowd?"

She shrugs. "I suppose. Hey, you smell really good. What is that?"

"Shalimar," I say, offering my wrist. She sniffs and smiles, but then, what? A chasm lies between us. We don't know each other, but we want to. At least, I hope she wants to. "Where were you and your boyfriend headed when you came through here?"

She smiles, her overbite and dimples creating an immediate welcome. Elbows on the bar, she finishes her sandwich, filling me in. They hadn't had a destination in mind. Possibly California. Maybe New York. There'd been talk of a big folk festival in one or the other. Mostly she wanted to cut loose from her parents, who didn't approve of her lifestyle or her boyfriend.

"They were right on that last one," she says with a wink. "How about you? What brings you to Lilydale?"

I surprise myself with the truth. "A low point."

She howls with laughter, sees I'm serious, and waits for more.

"My boyfriend grew up here. He'd been asking me to move back with him for a while. Then all in one week I lost a dream job I never stood a chance of getting, Dr. King was assassinated, and I was mugged at knifepoint." I hadn't meant to tell anyone but Ursula about the mugging, but something about Regina puts me at ease. "I was desperate to run away. By the time I calmed down, I'd already promised Deck I'd move."

An old man makes his way to the bar, raises a finger. Regina pulls him a beer, glancing back at me the whole time.

"Can I tell you something?" she asks when she returns. "Something wild?"

A delicious tickle travels up my spine. "Sure."

She scans the room. The closest customer is ten feet away. She turns up the radio anyhow, and then leans across the bar. "This place is weird."

I raise my eyebrows, the thrill rippling through me. "In what way?"

"Everyone is just so . . . *nice.*"

I'm waiting for more. When it doesn't come, I burst out in laughter. She scowls, and I rush to apologize. "I'm so sorry!" I tell her. "I know what you mean. I was just expecting something a bit darker."

She wipes the bar with a dirty rag. "It's weird, is all. Everyone has a please and a thank-you, asks how you're doing. Do you know some grim-faced lady stopped by my apartment when I first moved in to ask me if I needed any clothes or food?"

"Catherine the Migrant Mother," I murmur.

"Huh?"

"Catherine Brody. She lives next door to me. Head of the welcome committee."

"Whatever. It seemed intrusive."

I take a sip of the Tab. It's crisp and sweet, perfect for a hot day. "I can see that. Like me getting in trouble for drinking here the other night. People seem to keep an exceptionally close eye on one another here." I think back to my phone call with Ursula, her scolding me like a child for thinking poorly of Lilydale. "I think it's part of the charm, though," I tell Regina, feeling only a twinge of guilt. "Every town has their own culture."

She sighs. "Yeah. I suppose you're right. Except . . ."

"What?"

"Have you noticed there's not a single bum in Lilydale? Railroad tracks run right through it, converge over by the dairy plant, and I've yet to see a single person out of place. Everyone here is so perfect and so uptight, like they were all manufactured at the same damn factory. Sometimes I feel out of place, like I might haul off and take a shit on the sidewalk."

I belly-laugh at this. "How about we promise to look out for each other. Either one of us feels the need to shit in public, we call the other. Deal?"

She holds out her hand, her dimples back. "Deal."

That evening, Deck and I are sitting on the couch, watching *Mutual of Omaha's Wild Kingdom*, a show that comforts me because I used to watch it with my mom. Deck and I are seated near one another but not touching, Slow Henry curled on my lap, purring loudly. A bowl of pretzels rests nearby on the television tray, and Deck is drinking a beer. It's cozy.

Marlin Perkins is visiting the African savanna. He's talking about springboks, a kind of antelope, smallish, with curved black devil horns. The springboks are notable because they do something called "pronking." It's as if they're drawn into the air by a helium balloon tied to their waist, hopping and then landing, hopping and then landing.

I'm delighted.

I'm turning to laugh with Deck about the silly bounce, the springboks leaping twice their height, back arched and toes pointed, when an obviously pregnant springbok appears onscreen, munching grass as her fellow springboks are popping like corn around her.

"No one knows exactly what events cause springboks to pronk," Mr. Perkins narrates, "but it's believed to be a response to a predator."

My breath catches. I cradle my stomach.

The camera pans to a leopard crouched low in the grass, tongue out, tail flicking.

My hand flies to my mouth. The gravid springbok is oblivious. She's grazing hungrily, feeding for two. She has no idea she's being hunted.

"The weakest animals make the best prey: newborns, the elderly, and in this case, the pregnant."

The large cat stalks toward the clueless springbok, her belly achingly swollen. My heart is thudding. I can't look away.

"The pregnancy makes the normally agile animal cumbersome and slow. A perfect dinner for a hungry leopard."

The large cat is nearly on her. I've stopped petting Slow Henry. My eyes feel swollen, dry. It's been too long since I blinked.

The cat leaps. It happens so fast. The predator sinks its wicked teeth deep into the pregnant springbok's leg, wrenching her to the ground. She bleats in terror, tries to run, but she hasn't a chance.

I finally rip my gaze away from the screen, tears streaming down my face.

Deck is staring at me.

Icy fingers play across my tender skin.

His expression is unfathomable, but the way he's positioned, it's clear he's been staring at me the whole time.

Watching me watch the pregnant creature get slaughtered.

CHAPTER 20

"Dr. Krause will see you, Miss Harken."

When my lower back muscles relax, I realize how rigidly I've been sitting. Despite not including Deck's name anywhere on the intake form, I've been worried that I'd be called Mrs. Schmidt, here of all places, a spot where I desperately need to be seen as my own person.

Clearly, I was silly to obsess. This is a *doctor's* office, a professional place of medicine, a neat, sanitary cube of a building that smells like rubbing alcohol and ointment. They may disapprove of me using my maiden name, but they'll talk about me behind my back rather than to my face, like proper Minnesotans.

The receptionist, an army bunker of a woman, leads me back. "Please change for the examination. There's a gown behind the curtain. When you're finished, push this button to let the doctor know you're ready."

The modern exam room is a pleasant surprise. The surfaces gleam. And I've never visited a doctor's office with a button you can push once you have yourself in order. It doesn't cure the discomfort of covering my nakedness with a flimsy piece of open-backed cloth, of spreading my legs for a strange man, but it helps.

As does Dr. Krause's appearance when he enters the room moments after I press the button. He's older, his wire-rimmed glasses two perfect circles beneath a shockingly thick swath of white hair. He's a smaller man, somewhere between Deck and me in size. He carries a clipboard.

"Miss Harken, I'm Dr. Krause. You're in a family way?"

"Hello, Dr. Krause." My tone is formal to match his. "Yes. I believe I'm five months along."

"How are you feeling?" He removes a pen from behind his right ear, poises it above the clipboard.

"Fine. Great, actually. I was worried about morning sickness, but I haven't had any." I recall the panic and nausea I felt the other morning. That doesn't count, as it started before the pregnancy.

He looks me up and down, his glance clinical. "You're in good shape. Let's get the nurse in here for your vitals."

He pushes the same button I did, and the woman who walked me to the exam room returns. Apparently, she's more than a secretary. I had thought her a large woman, but she seems to shrink around Dr. Krause.

"Cornelia, you should have weighed and measured Miss Harken before I arrived."

She doesn't meet his eyes. "Sorry, Dr. Krause."

"It's all right," I say, though I suspect it isn't, not in Dr. Krause's eyes. He's a popular doctor, exactly as the Mothers told Deck (he'd been booked up through the end of the month, but once I gave the receptionist my name, she said she could squeeze me in today), and he runs a tight ship. Coming to the clinic broke the monotony of not being able to track down Paulie—he wasn't at the motel when I stopped by yesterday or today—but that's the only good thing I can say about it. I'm no prude, but I don't know a single woman who enjoys gynecological exams.

Cornelia leads me to a wall with a measuring tape painted onto it and gently pushes me against it. "Five foot six," she tells the doctor. She then guides me to the scale. "One hundred twenty-one pounds."

I smile on the inside. I've gained only two pounds in five months.

When the nurse leads me back on the table, she takes my blood pressure and checks my pulse. All of it consumes no more than three minutes, and then she disappears.

"I apologize," Dr. Krause says. "She's new."

"It's all right," I repeat. I mean it. I also want him to hurry up and get the examination over with.

But rather than having me lie back and insert my feet into the stirrups, he walks over and feels my forehead, and then my neck. "You've been sleeping all right?"

"Yes," I say, stopping just short of adding the "sir" that wanted to line up like a good soldier at the end. "I've been sleeping like a lumberjack after a hard day's work. I've always been a good sleeper."

Dr. Krause grabs both my hands, turns them palms up, then palms down. He's so near I can smell his aftershave, soapy and spicy. He runs one warm hand up the outside of my right arm, and then my left.

He stops, studying my upper left arm. "This is an unusual erythema multiforme scar," he murmurs, almost as an afterthought.

I glance at the spot. "My smallpox vaccination?"

"Yes. Almost like a figure eight."

I rub it, brushing his hand away. "My mom said I had a bad reaction. My boy—my boyfriend, Deck, has one just like it. We sometimes joke it's what brought us together." I consider telling him the stories we made up around our matching scars—that we'd escaped an alternate world where everyone was marked and then found each other in this one, that the scar was proof of our royal lineage, or my favorite, that our ragged figure eights mean we are a fated, perfect match.

I don't think Dr. Krause would find any of them amusing.

"You two are the same age?"

"Deck's four years younger." It's an embarrassing fact I rarely think about, certainly never mention. He's so mature for his age.

"Then it's not a bad lot. That happens sometimes. A tainted batch of vaccines goes out, affecting a whole group of children. Four years is too long a span, however." He clicks his pen. "The Minnesota Department of Health is sending a medical crew through the state. Their primary aim is to collect blood samples in each community, but they're recording disease immunity, too. You may want to mention the scar you share with the father of your child."

I can't think of anything I'd rather do less, other than this exam. "Thanks for the recommendation. I do have to be at work, though, so if you don't mind."

Dr. Krause's eyes narrow behind his glasses. I shrink from his anger as the nurse did. "How many hours are you working?"

"Not many," I say truthfully. Dennis requested that I phone the *Gazette* offices before noon every weekday to find out if there's more articles for me to write or more information on Paulie. There hadn't been either. The good news is that Dennis approved of my first piece, though he'd changed the title to "Lilydale K–4 Music Program Is a Hit."

He also let me keep my byline.

"That's fine if it's not more than ten hours a week," Dr. Krause says, picking his clipboard back up. "You want to avoid exertion, particularly in the third trimester."

I ask, because Deck wants me to, "What about drinking alcohol?"

"Forbidden."

That sets me back on my heels. I hadn't wanted to drink, but now that I learn I'm not allowed, I've never desired anything more. "Not even one cocktail on special occasions?"

"No alcohol."

"In public, at least." I say this as if I'm joking, but the cottony sensation in my throat tells me there's something at stake here, the same thing that made me stand up to the bartender at Little John's. That if I walk out of this office without asserting myself, I will have walked past a piece of me that I can never return to.

Dr. Krause gets that eye-narrowing look again and scratches something at the bottom of my chart. "Nowhere. Forbidden. You're welcome to smoke, but no more than four cigarettes per day. I'll prescribe Valium if you require more to calm your nerves."

"What?" My mother had taken Valium. I'd seen it in the medicine cabinet. "Won't that hurt the baby?"

"No. It also won't hinder your milk production, which is crucial the first week of the baby's life. You intend to breastfeed?"

"I hadn't thought about it."

"Nothing to think about, at least that first week. After that, you can switch to formula."

It's a command, not a suggestion. I have never felt more insignificant in my life. *I'm not a breeder cow,* I whined to Ursula in the Dayton's Sky Room back when I lived in a world where women had choices. But did we? I'd been glossed over for the promotion at the *Star,* attacked on the streets. Maybe my sense of control has always been an illusion.

"Yes, sir," I say, hanging my head.

"I'll see you in four weeks."

"What?" My heartbeat picks up. On the one hand, that sounds like a reprieve. No examination! On the other, is it best for the baby to leave without the doctor taking so much as a cursory glance inside? "You haven't . . . looked at me."

"It's not necessary," he says, setting down the clipboard and picking up a prescription pad. "My nurse will request your records from your examining physician in Minneapolis, and that will be enough for now. If there are any changes in your condition, come back immediately. Otherwise, four weeks."

"Thank you." Now it's just relief. I don't have to let this unfamiliar man put his fingers inside me.

"Of course. Is there anything else?"

"No."

He scribbles on the pad, rips off the prescription, and hands it to me. "You can get this filled at the Ben Franklin. Good day."

Once he leaves, I dress, folding the gown and resting it neatly on the edge of the examination table. The prescription is written in a crisp cursive, five milligrams of diazepam, take as needed, three refills. I insert it into an inner purse pocket and am about to exit the room when I notice Dr. Krause has left my chart behind.

I hesitate. It isn't meant for my eyes. They're his private notes.

But they're about me.

I grab the clipboard.

It's my writing on the top half—name: Joan Elizabeth Harken. Birth date: July 4, 1940 (*you came out with a bang!* my mom would joke around Independence Day every year). Address: 325 West Mill Street, Lilydale, MN. Employer: Lilydale Gazette. Reason for visit: five months pregnant.

The bottom half is Dr. Krause's penmanship.

Patient is uncooperative. Possible risk.

CHAPTER 21

"Joan! Wait up."

Someone is repeating my name as I stumble down the street, but it sounds distant, muddy lumps ricocheting off the cold, wet walls of a deep well.

Uncooperative. Possible risk.

I suddenly crave my own mother so badly that my chest seizes. She was impossibly frail at the end, the canvas of who she had been stretched across brittle bones, hardly recognizable. The cancer took her quickly, start to finish four months. I moved home with her, worked during the day to pay both our bills, and spent every evening and weekend with her. Rubbing her arms. Brushing her hair. Reading to her.

"Remember the good when I'm gone, Joan," she'd said to me one of those final endless, too-short days.

I'd startled. I thought she'd been sleeping. This was in her last week, when she spent most of her time unaware. It was better, except when the coughs wrecked her, waking her, and it'd take longer and longer for her to remember where she was.

But this time, she'd been awake. Watching me.

Her gaze was gentle, cloudy.

"Mom." I reached for water and held it to her. "How are you?"

Her eyes traveled to the pack of cigarettes at her nightstand. She'd stopped smoking a year earlier, before the cancer was diagnosed. Now that it was consuming her bit by bit, she insisted on the cigarettes always being nearby.

I want to curse those damn things every remaining day of my life.

"Dying," she said, but there was a spark in her eyes. "You?"

The barest smile creased my cheeks. "Fine. Work was fine."

"You get your byline yet?"

"No, but I will, Momma."

"I know you will." She closed her eyes. I set the water down, thinking she was falling back asleep, but then her lids snapped open. "I want you to remember the good things."

I didn't tell her she'd already said that. "I know, Momma."

"The traveling. All the places we got to explore together. How I kept you safe. Remember that."

I stroked her thin hair, a by-product of her medication, the one vanity she'd allowed herself now more gray than red. We really had had grand times, been everything to one another. When I got offered a scholarship to the University of Minnesota, she moved to live near me.

I met Ursula and Libby there.

All that moving meant I wasn't particularly good at making friends, but I wanted to so bad. I stopped spending time with Mom, except for the occasional dinners and phone calls. I landed temp and secretarial jobs when I graduated with my journalism degree, but then I got hired at the *Minneapolis Star* when I was twenty-five—my dream job. They had me working in the women's section, but I was going to claw my way up, I knew it, and I was always looking for my big break even though I felt dirty having that much ambition. I tried to hide it, but I think I failed. A lot. I was bad at being a person, but Mom was always steady, and I'd been ignoring her, acting like she wasn't everything to me.

And now I was losing her.

"I'll remember, Momma," I murmured. "Always."

"I don't want a funeral," she said, so quietly that I could have imagined it if she hadn't continued. "I only have you, Ursula, a couple coworkers that I go out with after work. It'd be a waste of money."

The coughing took her then. She lasted another week.

When she passed, I honored her wish not to hold a funeral, but I made sure the whole world knew how much I'd loved her. I had only a handful of photos of her—her family had been from Florida, she said, either long passed or too far removed to make a difference, and they hadn't been good to her, and she'd had a Mr. Harken (my dad) for only about five minutes—so it didn't take me long to pick one for the obituary.

The obit was my finest writing to date, but I felt alone in the world. I moved back in with Ursula, but I didn't feel like she was enough. I needed someone who was just mine.

That's when Deck came into my life.

And we were going to have a child, a baby that Dr. Krause thought I might harm. I may not have planned to become pregnant, but I would never *hurt* my baby. He had no right to enter that in my notes.

"Joan!"

The grip is firm on my arm.

"Catherine," I say, turning to face Clan's wife. *Migrant Mother.*

"Didn't you hear me?" Catherine is smiling, but her eyes are pinched. "I've been chasing you down Augusta Avenue for nearly two blocks! I was visiting family at the nursing home across from Dr. Krause's office. I saw you come out."

I wish I'd brought my sunglasses. The morning is bright. "I was getting a checkup."

Catherine is suddenly standing beside me, her arm caping my shoulders, her head too close. "The whole town is so excited about your baby," she whispers. "Certainly those of us who live on Mill Street. It's been so long since we had an infant in the neighborhood. Now, you must tell me all the details."

I push her arm off and step away. I know it's rude. "There's not much to share. The baby is healthy. I'm healthy."

Her jaw hardens. "Forgive me."

A horn honks up the street. I run my hand across my face. Breathe. Realize I must appear even-tempered or people will talk. *More than they already are.* "No, it's me who should be apologizing. I've felt a little off recently, is all. The baby is truly fine. Dr. Krause seems very nice."

Catherine immediately returns her arm to my shoulders. She's herding me down the street. Is she leading me toward Schmidt Insurance? "Dr. Krause is a gem," she agrees. "We're so lucky to have him. He's not originally from around here. Did you know that? He came to us from North Dakota back in the '40s. We've since made him one of our own."

"His offices are very modern."

Catherine laughs. It's a high, tinny sound that draws some glances. "I know you think this is the boondocks, but Lilydale is not some backwater town."

How can Catherine possibly know what I think? We've spoken only the one time she dropped off a casserole. I am no open book.

Catherine leans in again, even though she's already too close. We're almost at the Ben Franklin. Her tone is conspiratorial, naughty. "I was with your husband on Friday."

I jerk back.

That thin laugh again, almost a shriek. "Got you! I'm referring to the Fathers meeting, of course. I was one of the Mothers who served them that night. Left to their own, those poor old sods would starve in a kitchen with a stocked refrigerator and a working stove." She changes tack so quickly it's difficult to keep up. "Please say you'll come to our Mothers' dinner party tonight. There will only be a few of us there, and it's at my house. Right next door! You must join us."

My skin feels as fragile as spun sugar. I realize we've stopped.

In front of Ben Franklin.

How did she know this was my destination?

"All right," I say. *Don't seem uncooperative.*

Catherine pecks my cheek. Her lips are dry, and she smells of pressed face powder. I think she must be in her late fifties or early sixties, like everyone else on Mill Street, and I don't like her at all.

"Lovely. I'll let you bring a dessert," Catherine is saying. "It is so nice to have Deck back in town. Thank you for bringing him home."

I shade my eyes so I can watch her walk two blocks before disappearing down Lake Avenue. Then, rather than enter Ben Franklin, I hurry to the phone booth on the corner. I slide open the door.

My hand is steady as I shift my handbag so I can access my coin purse. I locate a dime and drop it in the slot. I dial the number from memory.

It rings.

And rings.

And rings.

I know someone is watching me. I feel it like dead fingers up my spine. I pivot quickly in the booth, staring toward Lake Avenue.

No one is there.

I hang up and walk to Ben Franklin.

The cloisonné pineapple brooch is in my pocket.

I could return it.

But I don't.

CHAPTER 22

Deck is pleased to see me when I drop by Schmidt Insurance after filling my prescription. He's leaning over a map rolled out on a large table, his father on one side, Clan Brody—Catherine's husband, *Clan the Brody Bear*—on the other. Deck's jacket is off, his shirt rolled up to his elbows.

I still feel an electric jolt when I see him like this, engrossed, capable. When he spots me, his face lights up. It makes the whole shaky, crazy world seem solid.

For a moment.

I go to Deck. The map they're poring over is of a town—Lilydale?—with lurid red Xs carved over sections. Ronald is smiling at me, Clan is smiling at me, and Deck is leading me to the break room. I note the filing cabinets lining the walls, a mob of them, and no secretary behind the desk. Mrs. Swanson must be at a late lunch.

"How did it go?" Deck asks once he has me in the break room.

I close the door and lean against it. "Fine, I suppose."

He wraps me in his arms. "You don't seem fine."

"The doctor said I couldn't drink."

Deck steps back so he can see my face. He squeezes my shoulders. "I told you, baby. I'll quit drinking in public, too. We'll tipple at home until we're soused, if you want. When I think how much champagne we swallowed the night we made this one, I figure he must be immune to it." He addresses the next part at my belly. "Isn't that right, little buddy?"

I relax for the first time all day. "I read the doctor's notes. He put down that I'm uncooperative." I can't bring myself to say the last part. *A risk.*

Deck barks with laughter. "What'd you do? Refuse some tests?"

"Nothing. That's the truth. I cracked a joke. It didn't land well."

He kisses me on the forehead. "I'll vouch for you if it comes to that."

"Hold me again, Deck."

"Sure, darling." He pulls me back into his arms.

"I ran into Catherine on the way here," I say into his chest. "She invited me to a Mothers' dinner party tonight."

He hugs me tighter. "And?"

"I said I'd go."

"Well, look at that. Nobody would call that uncooperative, would they?"

"Will you be all right for supper on your own?"

"Dad and I talked about grilling tonight. We'll be fine. You go. Make friends. Show this town how wonderful you are."

I want to stay in his arms forever, but there's work to do. "I wanted to interview Mrs. Swanson. About the Paulie Aandeg case?" I filled Deck in about it last night. He listened with half an ear.

His chin is resting on my head. "She's taken a few days off."

I yank myself back. "What?"

He rubs the back of his neck, holding eye contact. "Yeah, but Dad might know more about the Paulie Aandeg situation."

"Can I ask him now?"

"Here?" Deck asks, a smile warming his eyes. "You want to interview my dad at his own business?"

"Why not?"

"All right," Deck says, chuckling. "I'll see if he's free."

I nod as if it's the most natural thing, biting my lip. I'm fishing my notepad out of my purse when Ronald strides in. He doesn't look nearly as pleased about this as Deck did.

"Joan, Deck says you have a few questions." The gravel of his voice is thick with friction. He leaves the door open behind him.

"Shouldn't take long," I say. "Thanks for talking to me. Have a seat?"

He scowls at the chair, walking over to lean against it, placing both hands on the chairback. "I'm afraid it's a busy day. What can I do for you?"

I sit. One of us might as well be comfortable. "You know Paulie Aandeg has come back to town?"

"That's the rumor."

I ignore his evasiveness. "Do you remember when he disappeared?"

Ronald's shoulders sag, as if he can't remain outside the memory any longer. He pulls out the chair and sits, crossing his hands on the table as if in prayer. Not only does he look like Deck, he smells just like him up close.

"A real tragedy," he says. "My heart went out to Virginia. Miss Aandeg. We tried to help her, the whole town did, but it was too much for her when her boy went missing. Then her house burned down. I believe she disappeared that night, before the fire."

"Do you know why she left?" I'm thinking of Miss Colivan's theory that Virginia had killed her son.

"I don't truck in rumor," he says, his expression sad, "but if I had to guess, I'd say she'd had enough and needed a fresh start."

"So you don't think she killed Paulie?"

"Virginia? No. What mother could possibly do that?"

His gaze is so piercing that I pretend to scribble on my pad to break eye contact. "Do you think I could interview Mrs. Swanson?" I say to my lap. "Dennis said she was Paulie's teacher the day he went missing."

Ronald leans forward and lifts my chin with the crook of his finger. It's an unsettlingly intimate gesture. "That would be up to Mrs. Swanson, but I don't see why not. She's visiting family but should return soon."

I'm leaning forward—*he looks so much like Deck*—to ask him another question, and is Ronald doing the same?

"Hey, Dad!" Deck pokes his head into the break room, and Ronald releases my chin. "We need your advice out here."

I'm still looking at my pad of paper, cheeks blazing, when Ronald leaves the room.

It occurs to me that the town might have me on a snipe hunt, leading me on, keeping the key players just out of my reach.

But to what end?

CHAPTER 23

Get called a risk by my new doctor.

Check.

Keep brooch I stole.

Check.

Have uncomfortably charged moment with my soon-to-be father-in-law.

Check.

Well, this day couldn't get better. Might as well continue the path I'm on. I blow across the street to the *Gazette* offices. I want to Xerox the two Paulie Aandeg articles, plus dig deeper in case there's any pieces I've missed.

Dennis Roth's wife is at the front desk. I do not know her first name.

"Hello, Mrs. Roth!" I say chirpily. "I'm here to look at the archives. I know the way."

She doesn't glance up from the copy she's proofing with a red pen. "They're down."

My baby hairs stand on end. *Snipe hunt.* "What? I used them just the other day."

"Everything works until it breaks," she says, glancing up. She reminds me of a torpid animal, a turtle or a sloth, with the hair of Pat Nixon.

Languid Lady Roth.

I glance toward the back of the newspaper offices. "When are they getting fixed?"

Her smile is mild. "Soon, I hope."

I match her expression. "I'll stop back."

"You do that," she says absentmindedly, returning to her work.

Languid Lady Roth, Keeper of the Letters.

Dammit. I have to make some progress today, with or without help. I step into the sunshine and consider visiting the elementary school Paulie disappeared from, stopping by the button of a town library to dig through their stacks, dropping by the police station, or returning to the Purple Saucer for the second time today. I decide instead to go outside Lilydale's circle. That will show them. I'll try Benjamin, a photographer friend at the *Star*. He was easygoing, my favorite photographer to work with. He scored as many big-ticket gigs as pink ones, but he treated them both the same. At least I assumed he did.

Fingers crossed our relationship survives outside city limits.

The phone rings twice before it's answered.

"*Minneapolis Star.*"

I'm startled. That's the number I called, but the two words are so normal, so part of a different world from the one I'm currently inhabiting. Not even three hours up the road is a city where archives don't crash for the foreseeable future, where children who've disappeared receive more than two mentions in the paper, where pregnant women aren't always being watched.

"Benjamin Ember, please. Photography."

"I'll try him."

Whirs and clicks and rings and me praying he's in.

"Benjamin speaking."

"Benny!" My relief is out of line with the circumstances, I recognize that. "It's Joan. Joan Harken."

"Joan! I heard you ended up in Podiddle, Minnesota, having babies. That true?"

"Mostly." I look around. No one's staring at me, and why would they be? I'm simply making a phone call. Except I swear I can feel eyes on me. "I'm working for a small-town paper. The *Lilydale Gazette*."

"Like I said. Podiddle. To what do I owe the pleasure? Don't tell me they need a photographer out there. Bet it pays in hay bales and farm girls. Am I right?"

"Benjamin, please." But I smile. I miss his humor. He made many a Women's News photo shoot bearable. "I need your help, but not as a photographer. I'm hoping you can visit the *Star* archives and look for anything that mentions Paulie Aandeg of Lilydale."

"Your car stop working?" he asks, but I can hear his pen scratching as he writes down the name that I spell out for him.

Benjamin the Best Man.

"Ha ha, very funny. I have a life here, is all. Five hours of driving for a one-hour search is a little drastic, not to mention I no longer have reporter access." But that's not all of it. I realize I feel panicky at the thought of leaving Lilydale, like agoraphobia but this town is my room. It's the pregnancy, I tell myself. Nesting.

"Hmmm," he says. "A favor for a favor?"

I can't imagine what I have that he'd want. "Like what?"

"You still friends with that blonde bird you brought to the Christmas party? Ursula?"

"I think I know where this is going. She has a boyfriend."

"Slow down," he says. "I got a freelance gig, a photo shoot for a downtown boutique. The model dropped out, and the owner wants me to find a Sharon Tate type. Your friend would be perfect."

"Sure." I rattle off Ursula's number. She'll be over the moon to model, though she'd never admit it. "You'll get me what I need?"

"I'll see what I can stir up," he says.

"Thanks, Benny. You're a dream."

He grumbles a goodbye, but I know he'll check for me. And if I end up with a scoop and do need a photographer, I'll return the favor.

I hang up, finally feeling good about something, something I've done on my own. I take that pleasure with me as I walk to the Purple Saucer, not really thinking of what I hope to find. There's only two cars in the parking lot this afternoon, but one of them—the blue Chevy Impala parked in front of unit 6—has Florida plates. I knock on the door, but no one answers. I scribble my name, phone number, and "Lilydale Gazette reporter" on a piece of paper I dig out of my purse, slide it under the door, and march back to the center of town.

CHAPTER 24

It's a small act of rebellion—laughable, really—but I stop by Wally's Grocery on the way home to purchase a premade Bundt cake rather than bake a dessert from scratch. I also pop into Little John's to pay a visit to Regina (not to drink, lord help me), but I'm told she's not working, and I don't want to bother her in her apartment.

When I reach home, I have time before I need to walk over to the party.

I decide to make my own work and call the Minnesota Department of Health. It sounded all kinds of boring when Dr. Krause first mentioned it, but I'm growing desperate to write. I call the operator and request the number. I scribble it down and then ask to be connected. When a woman picks up on the other end of the line, I tell her my name and that I'm with the *Lilydale Gazette*.

"Can I speak to whoever oversees the statewide blood data collection? I heard about it from my doctor and may write an article on it, if my editor agrees."

A pause on the other end of the line. Then: "You said you're calling from Lilydale?"

Her tone, a mix of incredulous and curious, unsettles me. "Why?"

"You grew up there?"

"No, I—" I stop myself. She doesn't need to know my history. "Why do you ask?"

"I've heard things. About the town."

"Like what?"

She coughs. It's a nervous sound. "Just that it's . . . tight-knit."

"I suppose it is." I wait for her to say more. When she doesn't, I prod her. "That's it?"

I can almost hear her shrug down the line. "You called about the Minnesota Blood Project?"

She's put us firmly back on topic, leaving me scrambling to figure out what I just missed. "I did."

"Well, I'm not sure if the researchers are talking to the press."

"Really?" I sit up straighter. "Why not?"

A sigh. "No reason, I don't think. It's just that no one's reached out to them, before you. We didn't think it was newsworthy. I can pass on your contact information. Will that do?"

"Yes, thank you." I give her my number. "Please call if you think of anything else you want to tell me about Lilydale, too."

The click of her phone hitting the cradle is her response.

I glance at my wristwatch.

Time for the party.

CHAPTER 25

Clan and Catherine Brody's house sits behind an alert row of shrubbery. It's stucco, a vague two-story that is more utility than style. I've waved at them leaving and entering it many times, but I've never been invited in. I find the interior as weathered as the exterior, a kitschy mix of plastic flowers, ceramic collectibles, and plastic-covered furniture. It smells faintly—and I suspect permanently—of sauerkraut and sausage.

I'm the last to arrive. When Catherine walks me to the living room, I discover Barbara, Dorothy, Rue, and Mildred seated on the couch. All four look like versions of the same person: smiling, middle-aged, bouffant hair, lips colored coral or pink tea rose, all wearing glasses.

Is this my future?

"You made it!" Dorothy stands and pecks each of my cheeks, stroking my hair for so long that I have to pull away to greet the other women.

"Thank you for having me," I say, glancing down at my feet. "I'm glad to be here." I suddenly feel shy. I'm not sure why. Their faces, with the exception of perennially sour-faced Catherine's, are welcoming.

"Our pleasure," Catherine says. She hasn't sat down. I find myself not wanting to turn my back on her. "And you brought a Bundt cake. That is *too* kind. Why don't you drop it in the kitchen, and you can join us back here. We were just discussing our charitable projects. Mildred, will you show Joan to the kitchen?"

I smile weakly at Mildred, who's clearly at the bottom of the pecking order. Maybe she can be my ally. Once we're out of earshot of the rest, we can joke about my faux pas at bringing a store-bought dessert. Or, if I'm really lucky, about Catherine's tone when she referred to it, as if I'd brought frosted dog shit rather than a packaged cake.

When Mildred leads me into the kitchen and opens her mouth, I realize it'll be neither.

"Catherine told us you visited Dr. Krause today. How is the baby?"

"Fine." It's a bark more than a word.

Mildred cowers like I've struck her, and I immediately regret my harshness. *Mildred the Mouse and her quivering whiskers.* I set the cake down. Is it too soon to go home? "I'm sorry. I'm not used to everyone . . . caring so much about me. Do you have children?"

Mildred is hammocking one hand in the other, rocking them as if she's cradling a tiny child. "Three. Three daughters."

I try to think of the neighbors I've encountered since we moved in. "Do they still live at home?"

"Heavens, no. It's just Teddy and me in the castle now." She reaches out a hand to touch me but can't quite bring herself to. Her expression is soft and moony, and it crosses my mind that I'm not the only one Dr. Krause is prescribing Valium for.

"It is lovely, isn't it, to have the whole town as your family?" she asks, her hand floating between us.

Because I don't want to be a risk, don't want to be trouble, I smile. "It *is* lovely."

Her face lights up. I've matched her tone perfectly. I let her lead me back to the living room.

❖

The food is surprisingly good, the conversation light. I find myself with more hot-dish recipes than I could prepare in a month and a backlog of stories to tell Deck. Clan Brody nearly mangling his hand trying to fix a snowblower. Scaredy-mouse Mildred traveling to Saint Cloud and getting lost in the mall parking lot. Deck's own mother trying a new beautician and emerging from the beauty parlor to discover her bouffant was the color of apricots when the sun hit it.

At some point, Saint Dorothy, who's seated next to me at the table, begins stroking my hair again. I find I don't mind. The conversation is smooth, no sharp edges, and the murmur of it makes me drowsy, these women cooing and warbling like soft-chested birds, pulling me into their nest, soothing me.

It's as if they've drugged me.

The realization makes me start. "Paulie Aandeg is back in town," I blurt.

By their exchanged glances, I can tell I've committed another faux pas, splashing lurid real life onto their smooth white canvas.

Dorothy stops stroking my hair. "We know, dear."

Now that I've blundered in, I stubbornly want to see this horse over the line. "Do any of you remember when he disappeared?"

"We all do," Catherine says icily. "It almost destroyed Lilydale."

She's staring at Dorothy as she says it. Why?

"Mrs. Lily," I ask Dorothy, using her formal name because her face is so near mine, and I want to create distance. "Did you know Paulie or his mom?"

She grabs my hand and squeezes it. "We all knew Virginia Aandeg. She was an unfortunate woman."

"But no mother deserves to lose her child," Mildred says, glancing around for approval. "We're so glad he's back."

"If it really is him," Rue says mildly. She's been quiet most of the night.

"Did Amory tell you something?" Catherine asks.

Rue's birdie shoulders lift slightly. "It's just good to be cautious."

The four of them seem to take Rue's words at face value, and Catherine changes the subject, returning to the cotton candy conversation from earlier. Church charity events they're planning, the new Simplicity MuuMuu caftan pattern 7088, a fabric trip to Saint Cloud, how Johann Lily wouldn't be fond of the too-short dress styles, a titter of laughter.

I want to be back inside the circle. "Johann Lily?" I ask.

They ignore me for a moment, burbling on to a discussion of last Sunday's church service and the choir's new song that was a hair too racy.

"Johann Lily?" I repeat. "Is he a relative of yours, Dorothy?"

It's Mildred who responds, after rolling her glance off the suddenly stone-faced women seated around the table. "Johann and Minna founded the town. They immigrated here from Germany in the mid-1800s. I can never remember the year."

"They also founded the Fathers and Mothers." Catherine is fixed on me, expression as keen as a razor, as she says this. She expects a response, but I can't for the life of me guess what it would be.

"They must have had a lot of children," I quip, "to have named the organization that."

The women at the table exchange another tight expression. And as if I've upset God, a bowling ball of thunder rumbles across the sky. I tug my cardigan closer. A storm tonight was unexpected.

"You know the Fathers and Mothers insignia?" Mildred asks. The desperation to avoid conflict rolls off her, rancid and salty smelling. She's trying to get me to back off, but I'm not sure from what. I can't find my footing with these women.

The thunder cracks again, followed by a yellow jolt of lightning.

In that electrified space, I hold up a V with one hand, like a peace sign, three middle fingers upside down with the other for the M. Mildred leans over and tucks my ring finger into the palm of my hand, so now it's two Vs, one up and one down. She moves the up

V over the top of the down V. My hands now perfectly re-create the emblem I spotted at the Washburne Avenue building.

There's something graphic about making this symbol, the pink flesh of my fingers straining apart. I pull my hands back, reclaiming them. "I understand the M for Mothers," I say. "But the V?"

Rain is thrashing the sky now, pounding on the roof and windows, drumming up the smell of earth and ozone. The lights flicker.

"*Vater*," Catherine says, the word so natural coming out of her strong, angled face. "German for father. *Mutter* is mother. The V always goes on top."

"Because Father knows best," all the women murmur in unison, like a catechism. Dorothy is caressing a necklace. I realize it's the white enameled locket she was wearing the first time I met her. It's in the shape of a lily. Surely it contains a photograph of Stanley?

I lick my lips, suddenly aware I'm gripping the edge of my chair.

The next roar of thunder is so loud, so unexpected, it startles me to my feet, a yelp escaping my mouth. The hot dish that was so comforting sloshes in my stomach. For a moment, I fear I'm going to vomit on the table, in the middle of the dirty plates, right on the plastic flowers. I gulp air, and the nausea recedes.

"I'll clean up," I say, reaching shaking hands toward plates.

"I'll help!" Mildred offers, and the other women follow suit. They bundle up silverware and cups and tureens so efficiently that suddenly it's only Catherine and me around the dining room table. I feel her hot eyes on me, but I don't meet them.

The thunder and rain argue with each other outside.

I stack some plates and am carrying them to the kitchen when I notice Catherine's ceramic collectibles for the first time, really *see* them in a blinding flash of lightning. They're scattered around the house, but here in the dining room, they have a dedicated hutch.

They're all blackface caricatures.

Mammy and Pappy saltshakers, skin the darkest black, aprons the whitest white. Ashtrays that are only pitch-black heads, mouths open to swallow the detritus. A blond-haired, black-skinned baby eating a slice of watermelon twice his size, his face so gape-mouthed that he appears more fish than human. An Amos and Andy plate.

A mix of fascination and disgust threatens to eject the hot dish yet again.

"I've been collecting them for years. Everyone knows what to get me for my birthday," Catherine says from immediately behind me. It's all I can do to swallow a squeal of fear.

She steps around so we are face-to-face. I try to arrange my expression into something neutral, but judging by her flinty eyes, I am unsuccessful.

"Are you feeling all right?" She puts her hand on my arm, her palm so hot it burns through my cardigan.

"The pregnancy," I say, hoping to distract her. "It takes its toll."

"I remember those days."

After a final glance over her shoulder, I tear my attention away from the wall that feels more like trophies than collectibles, turning my back to it, swearing never to return to this house even if it's on fire. I set the plates back on the table and pretend to gather more silverware, my back again to Catherine. "You have children?"

"One. A boy. Quill."

I pick up the plates again and turn, wondering why there are no photographs of her son displayed. "Does he live in Lilydale?"

Catherine's face is open for a moment, revealing some long-held sorrow, but then it slams closed. "I'm afraid not. He's a lifer. Never seemed to fit in anywhere else."

"I see," I say, assuming she's referring to the military.

But I don't see. Lilydale seems the perfect place for a person who doesn't fit in anywhere else.

As long as you're one of them.

CHAPTER 26

I have breakfast waiting for Deck when he tramps downstairs the next morning. I tell myself it isn't because I want to be a good wife, isn't because I must prove to him that I'm not a risk, isn't because I'm now inexplicably frightened of the Mill Street women.

I'm lying to myself, of course.

I know because I have Deck's breakfast waiting at the dinner table rather than the breakfast nook.

"Hi, honey!" I stand behind the scrambled eggs, bacon, toast, and morning paper like a prize model on a game show.

Deck's look of surprised delight washes away the stickiest of my concerns. He strides over and kisses me on the mouth. My pulse flutters. He's growing his hair out, wearing it like his father's, combed back with Brylcreem (*a little dab'll do ya!*). A red scrap of tissue marks where he's cut himself shaving. He's wearing a suit, as his father demands, and he is so striking it makes my heart clutch.

"This food looks great!"

"I woke up early to make it," I say, hoping he notices that I've also put on makeup and set my hair. "I wanted to do something special for you."

He slides into his seat at the head of the table. "Thanks, doll."

My appetite hasn't returned, so I sit in the chair next to him and reach for my coffee. I wait for him to speak, but he doesn't. He piles the eggs high on a corner of toast and tips them into his mouth, chewing loudly. Has his jaw always clicked like that?

"Quite a storm last night," I say. "You weren't home yet when I went to bed. Was it still rolling when you got back?"

He shrugs but doesn't respond.

"I had some fun at the Mothers' meeting," I say, when the silence grows too heavy.

It's a lie, but only a white lie.

His mouth is full, so he doesn't answer right away. When he takes a breath to reach for the salt, he says, "I'm glad to hear it. Does that mean you're gonna join them?"

I stare into the filmy brown surface of my mug. "I'm considering it. I learned about Johann Lily and his wife Minna last night." I take a sip of my coffee, then add more whitener. "They founded Lilydale and the Fathers and Mothers. Did you know that?"

He picks up his knife and reaches for the jelly. Grape on heavily buttered toast is his favorite. "That sounds right."

"I tried to find out more from the other women, but they didn't seem to want to talk about Johann much. Or the history of the Fathers and Mothers. I think I'm going to research it."

Deck's face goes pale. He clutches at his throat.

I stand, knocking my coffee cup, splashing some into the saucer. "Are you okay?"

He reaches for his glass of milk and tips it to his mouth. There is a strained gurgle as the wad of food fights back before flushing down his throat. He sucks in air.

"Bit off more than I could chew," he says, coughing and running his hand through his hair. I notice it's shaking. "I've been meaning to tell you, Joanie. The draft board is convening next week. We need to be on our best behavior. I don't want to end up in Vietnam."

I return to my chair, pouring coffee from the saucer back into the mug before refilling his milk. "But your dad's the head of the draft board."

He rests his hand on my wrist. "Yeah, but we need to be on the straight and narrow. I don't wanna take any chances. Do you?"

"You know I don't, Deck. It's one of the reasons I agreed to move here."

He rubs his face with a paper napkin. "Is it?"

I feel us slipping into a fight that's opened like a sinkhole in the dining room. But I don't know where it's coming from. I went to the meeting last night. I made him breakfast. "You *know* it is."

He's staring at me, so serious. So handsome. "Joan, you moved because you got mugged and you were scared. Sometimes I don't even know if you love me."

I jump to my feet and hurry to him, wrapping my arms around him from behind. "You're everything to me."

As I kiss the back of his neck, I realize that statement is truer than I'm comfortable with. Without him, I'm lost in Lilydale.

Alone.

Unprotected.

He pats my hand, pulling me around to sit in his lap. His eyes are swollen. Maybe tears are almost brimming. Maybe it's because he just choked.

"I'm sorry, darling," Deck says. "When we talk about the war, I feel my whole life slipping away. Dad says we're probably safe as long as we're in Lilydale. You like it here, don't you?"

"I'm getting used to it," I say. I stand, or at least try to, but he yanks me back into his lap. He kisses me until I go soft and melty, then he pulls away too soon.

"I'm just a little homesick for the Cities," I say, straightening my hair. It sounds like a reasonable explanation for all my moods as of late. "I need some Ursula time, maybe a visit to the paper." I mean to say coffee with Benjamin, but it doesn't come out that way. "You think that'd be okay?"

His face lights up, smile crinkles appearing at the edge of each eye. "Yeah, I think that's a grand idea. We'll figure out a day that works for you to take the car. Or better yet, maybe Ursula could visit you here."

I nod. "Sure, maybe she could."

He lets me stand this time, hugging me so my belly is pressed against his head.

That's when the baby kicks.

For the first time.

I squeal. It is simultaneously the most terrifying and thrilling sensation. I thought I'd feel claustrophobic when I first felt the baby move, but instead I am six feet tall and bulletproof. "Deck! Did you feel that?"

"Was that the baby?" His eyes are dewy and wide.

"Yes!" I put his hand on my stomach and we both wait, but our son—Deck is positive we're having a boy—isn't interested in a repeat performance. Deck and I are grinning at each other like fools.

"Honey," I say tentatively, "can you skip the meeting of the Fathers tonight? Have a date with me? I feel like we've hardly seen each other since we moved here."

His hand is still resting on my belly, but his eyes slide away. I'm certain he's going to say no. He surprises me. "How about a compromise? I'll eat dinner with you tonight rather than with the guys, maybe watch a show. I'll hit the meeting after that. Then we both get what we want. Sound good?" He's smiling his best salesman smile.

"I guess." It is better than nothing.

"How's steak sound? I saw rib eyes on sale at Wally's."

"Yum," I say, even though the thought of bloody beef sours my tender stomach.

He pulls away and tucks back into his now cold breakfast. "Why don't you pick up two steaks, then. And potatoes. You know I love your mashed potatoes."

"Now?"

"Sure." He shovels the rest of his food into his mouth, balls up the paper napkin, tosses it on his plate, and stands. "I'll clean up breakfast even."

"All right," I say. I feel rushed, but I suppose I have nothing better to do. I grab my purse. I'm out the door before I realize we don't have steak sauce, and I can't remember which brand he prefers. I dash back inside to ask him, but he's on the phone, his back to me, his shoulders so tight they're braced like wings against his neck.

It must be important. I tiptoe back outside.

CHAPTER 27

"It's so nice of you to meet with me, Mrs. Swanson," I say as Paulie Aandeg's kindergarten teacher sits across from me, smoothing her skirt for the thirtieth time. I'm thrilled to finally get a chance to speak with her. Deck told me the good news when I came back with the steak sauce. I was surprised to see him at home still, but I wasn't going to complain. He also let me know that Ronald would let us use the insurance office break room to talk, though judging by how often Mrs. Swanson glances at the door, she wouldn't be comfortable with this interview anywhere. For my part, I'm surprised Ronald's allowed me to talk to her at all. It's the first help I've gotten on the story since Dennis gave it to me.

Beautiful Becky, nervous as a nest of bees. She keeps her smile slapped on, though, her face only mildly lined, her blonde hair pulled back in a flattering upsweep.

"You must have been a young teacher," I say, trying to put her at ease.

The comment has the opposite result. Her eyes fill with tears. "It was my first and last day of teaching. I tried to go back, after . . . after . . ."

"After Paulie disappeared?"

She nods. I wish I carried a handkerchief, because her nose is starting to run. "I couldn't stay. I felt too terrible."

I grab her hand. "What happened, Mrs. Swanson?"

"That's just it," she wails. "I don't know! Paulie was there all morning. I don't remember him saying a word, probably wouldn't even recall him in my classroom if not for that sailor suit. Last I saw him, he was playing with some boys right before lunch, Quill and Aramis, I believe."

I release her hand. "Quill Brody."

"That's right. And Aramis Bauer."

I choose my next words carefully. "Aramis Bauer is Amory and Rue's son, of course."

She swipes at her tears, her face brightening like a sun appearing from behind clouds. "Yes. He was a sweet boy. A bit of a rascal at times, but it was elementary school. It was harmless. I believe he's overseas now, Aramis is."

I think of what Catherine mentioned last night. When she spoke of her son, she'd said nothing about him being the last person to see Paulie Aandeg. "And Quill?"

Her lips tighten. "I don't know. That poor boy."

"Poor?"

She pats her ears.

I squint. "He was hard of hearing?"

She shakes her head, patting her ears again but this time also tapping her chin. I have no idea what she's trying to communicate. "Even more than that? He's deaf?"

Before she can answer, the door flies open, and Dennis rushes in.

"You're not going to believe this, but Paulie Aandeg is across the street! He wants to talk to you right now."

His words echo in my chest, beneath the rumble of confusion Mrs. Swanson has engendered. "Me?"

Mrs. Swanson jumps to her feet, her closing statement coming out as one long, loud word. "It was the saddest day of my life, truly, but Lilydale has been so good to me since. They helped me to keep my home while I looked for work, and then, when I couldn't find any, Mr. Schmidt hired me here. I've never been happier."

She beams and glances out through the break room door. Ronald, Deck, and Clan are all watching us, their eyes gleaming. I'm struggling to keep up. "Thank you, Mrs. Swanson. Dennis, where is he right now?"

"Tuck's Cafe."

My smile starts slowly, but it quickly cuts across my whole face. *Finally.* The access I need for my breakthrough story. I've been paranoid, thinking the town is conspiring to keep me from digging up the truth about Paulie Aandeg. Actually, if I'm honest with myself, I was starting to wonder if Paulie Aandeg had returned to town at all. But of course he has, and I get to meet him! I am overtaken by so much bubbling champagne joy that I leap off my chair and hug Dennis. Apparently, that's what we do in Lilydale.

"You won't be sorry!"

He chuckles. "I already am. Here, I Xeroxed the two articles for you. Look for a man with dark hair in his late twenties."

I thank him and then Mrs. Swanson, give Deck a chaste kiss, and rush to the restaurant.

I'm halfway there before the question crackles up.

How did Dennis know I'd be in the break room of Schmidt Insurance?

CHAPTER 28

Panty popper. That's what Ursula would have called Paulie Aandeg. I know because she referred to plenty of men that way when she, Libby, and I were living together in Minneapolis.

Jesus, he's a panty popper.

She didn't use the term to describe just any good-looking man.

Only good-looking men who looked like Paulie Aandeg.

Kris Jefferson, I correct myself.

That's how he introduced himself.

Even if I hadn't gotten a rough description of him beforehand, I would have known immediately walking into Tuck's Cafe that he had not been raised in Lilydale. The liquid way he holds his body, his shockingly tight tan corduroys, the wavy dark hair feathered away from his face, the even darker beard and mustache with a shock of white at the chin, chocolate eyes, straight white teeth.

He's gorgeous.

A panty popper.

The intense rush of hunger I feel when I ease into the booth across from him is out of proportion, embarrassing. Animal, almost. I push Ursula's term out of my brain, honest-to-god worried that I will accidentally say it out loud.

So, how long have you been popping panties?

"Excuse me?" he says, his first words since we introduced ourselves.

My face rages with shame before I realize he's calling over the waitress.

"More coffee." He points at his cup and then at me. "You want anything?"

"Tea, please," I tell the waitress. To him: "Thanks for meeting with me. I was starting to think you were a myth. Should we dive right in?"

It's abrupt, but his attractiveness—and my response to it (*I'm practically married!*)—has me on edge. I am happy with Deck. He fills all my needs. This must be related to my pregnancy hormones, and I don't like it one bit. I yank out my notepad and a tape recorder to put some space between us. I depress the play and record buttons simultaneously and lift my eyebrows. "What can you tell me about yourself?"

Even his smirk is sexy. "Why don't *you* tell *me* about Paulie Aandeg first."

I snap the stop button. "That's not how this works. For all we know, you're an impostor." I realize I'm jumbling myself in with the town of Lilydale. *For all* we *know.* "It's on you to prove you're Paulie Aandeg."

He watches the waitress fill his cup, twirling a large gold ring on his pinkie finger. "Why would I pretend to be anybody but myself? There's no reward here. My mother hasn't been seen since the fire, if I understand correctly. What's the percentage in making all this up?"

He has a good point. I have a better one. "Why come back at all, then?"

He reaches into his denim jacket pocket and tugs out a pack of Camel straights. He taps one out. He brings it to his mouth and then reaches into his other pocket for a book of matches. The matchbook features a palm tree graphic above the name of some hotel. He strikes a match and brings it to the tip of his cigarette. The delicious smoked-chocolate scent of tobacco grinds into my senses.

"Why not?" he asks.

He has a slight southern accent. Mississippi? I hit the play and record buttons and then pull out the copies of the two articles Dennis gave me, noting to myself that the microfiche must be accessible again for him to have made copies. The type is too small for Kris to read upside down. I bank on it. "Paulie Aandeg—"

He interrupts me. "Paul."

"Excuse me?"

He shrugs. "I'm thirty years old."

"Paul Aandeg," I continue, "disappeared on September 5, 1944. What do you remember about that day?"

"Nothing, until I got hypnotized a few months ago," he says. His arm makes the smallest twitch. "After that, only chunks of my life. Snapshots, not movies. I remember the town, a little bit. I remember my mom giving me potato chips, and the sailor suit, and Mom walking me to school. The teacher wrote letters on the board. I wished I was home. Then, I left school."

"Why?" My muscles are poised like rubber bands.

"I don't remember. The brain is funny, you know? Creates a fugue state. Only tells you what you want to know. If it's too stressful, it'll rewrite the story for you."

Goose bumps blister my flesh. "I don't think that's how memory works."

"You study the brain?"

I want to write something down, to act *professionally*, but nothing comes to mind. "What's the significance of the date?"

He leans his chin in his hand. "What date?"

"September 5," I say through gritted teeth. "The day you disappeared."

He shrugs. "First day of kindergarten."

That doesn't help me, but then again, maybe that's all there is to it, just coincidence that it's also my due date. "What's the next memory you have?"

Dark clouds roll across his forehead. "A house in San Diego. My dad. Or at least the guy who told me he was my dad. He was an angry fellow. Drank a lot, listened to the radio all day."

"What kind of work did he do?"

"No kind. He was in the war. Lived off his pension." He scowls. "Got more money because he had a kid."

The pen and pad lie in front of me. I watch him speak every word. "What about a mother?"

"My father said she died in childbirth." He drags off half the cigarette in a single suck.

"So your dad lied? Banked on you not remembering you'd been abducted?"

He shrugs.

I back it up. I need to get something solid from him. "Do you remember playing with two classmates that day in kindergarten? Aramis and Quill?"

His eyes drop. "No," he says.

But he's hiding something. What would an honest-to-god journalist do with this story? It's a big one, I can feel it, but only if I get it right. "Where's your dad now?"

"In the ground."

"I'm sorry."

"I'm not." He stabs the cigarette into the ashtray. "Happened ten years ago, and he was a bastard. I took off when he kicked. Traveled all over the world. It was in Florida where I met the hypnotherapist."

The waitress sets down a cup of hot water and a tea bag for me and refills his coffee even though it's still nearly full. She's so busy smiling at him that it almost overflows. He grins back.

"What was the hypnotherapist's name?" I ask.

"You ever been to Florida?"

I'm aware he isn't answering my question. "No. Where in Florida were you living?"

"A little nowhere island called Siesta Key. It's got a couple hotels. A restaurant with the coldest beer you'll ever drink. Jobs that don't require much. They don't pay much, either, but you don't need it. Fresh fruit growing on trees. Everybody's welcome."

The way he says it, he believes it. "Sounds perfect."

He leans in. I feel the heat of him. "We could visit sometime."

My intake of breath is so loud that the man at the next table turns to look. The heat I've been feeling, he's sensing it, too? "I'm pregnant."

He chuckles, a soft, private sound. "That was quick."

"My husband. My boyfriend, I mean. We live together here in Lilydale." There was no need for me to say that. Wasn't his right to know. I don't want to lead him on, though. And I want him out of my head.

"Sexy."

I can't read his intention. "Do you mind if I take some photos? For the follow-up article?"

"Knock yourself out."

I set up the camera and begin snapping. "Hypnotherapist?" I repeat from earlier to keep him talking.

He taps out a new cigarette. He's so photogenic.

"Yeah," he says. "I was bartending in Siesta, minding my own business; then I started having these weird dreams. A friend suggested I see a hypnotherapist on the mainland. You ever been hypnotized?"

I take the last of the photos and shake my head as I put away the camera.

"It's not like you think. You don't start quacking like a duck or anything. It just relaxes you, real deep. It was when I was under that I remembered that I was Paulie Aandeg." Cigarette smoke licks his cheeks. I want to taste it so bad, that smoke, draw it in like dragon's breath.

"At first it came back in fragments," he continues. "Like Polaroids in my head. A house. A yellow room in that house with a little bed against a wall. That sailor suit. Then a name. Paulie Aandeg. When I searched for the name in the papers, I found it in the *Minneapolis Star*." He taps the upside-down articles between us. "So, I made my way up here, and now you see me."

I watch my hands reach for the tea packet, hear the crisp sound of paper opening, see the bag dunked in the water. "How can you be sure you're Paulie?"

He rolls up the sleeve of his T-shirt, revealing a tan, muscled bicep. "See this?"

On the upper outside of his left arm is a smallpox vaccine scar.

It's in the shape of a figure eight.

A scar exactly like Deck's, and like mine.

"Wake up, honey."

It's my mom, whispering to me. I don't want to wake up. My bed is so toasty. I'm safe in it. Plus, it's the weekend. The only time I'm allowed to sleep in. I'll get to my homework. I always do.

"Honey, wake up."

She's shaking me now, her voice growing urgent.

I grumble. I don't want to open my eyes, don't want to start my day. I roll over, ready to nestle back into my blanket, when my heart's gripped by a fist of ice.

My mother never calls me honey.

Joan, always, no exceptions, not even Joanie. But I don't want to end the dream, because then my mother's voice will disappear. I miss her so much. It's an ache inside the tenderest part of me. How do you go on with life after your mother dies?

I couldn't.

That's why I didn't question Deck showing up right after her funeral, adoring me, sewing me right up into his life before I had a chance to blink. I needed someone to belong to.

"Joan, wake up."

That's definitely my mother now.

Frances Harken, calling to me.

A great scraping collision happens, suddenly. I no longer know what is dream and what is reality. Am I bleeding to death after childbirth, or am I a teenager in bed, trying to steal an hour of sleep under my mother's nose?

I hope desperately for the second, and so, finally, I open my eyes. A fuzzy, candy-pink bath mat is inches from my face. Nearby, the claw feet of a tub. The subway tile is cold against my cheek. I drag my head so I can look at my body. The front of my nightgown is a deep, lush red from my blood, crusting brown at the corners. No one is with me.

I sob.

It's me, alone here, and the monsters have my baby.

I remember the pain, the breakneck ride to Dr. Krause's (*Who was driving? Why can't I see that? I must remember*), the injection.

This time I manage to pull myself onto the toilet and sit there for several seconds, shuddering, before I slide to the floor and ease back into darkness.

CHAPTER 29

The sun is shining brightly outside Tuck's Cafe. Too bright. The glare is disorienting against the murky mystery surrounding me. On my way to the phone booth, I pass an older couple. They don't look familiar, but they inspect me. Or do they? I keep walking. A woman I'm certain I've never seen before stares at me from across the street. When I catch the third person gawking at me, I whirl on her.

"What are you staring at?" I yell, my heart in my throat.

The woman recoils. Was she looking at me at all? I believe she was.

But I'm not sure I know anything anymore. Paulie's scar is in the shape of a figure eight, exactly like mine, exactly like Deck's. When he showed it to me, my mouth grew so parched that it made a clicking noise when I opened it. "None of the articles reported Paulie had that scar."

He shrugged. "Looks like you need to dig deeper."

That was the end of the interview.

As it stands, there's no story there, no career-maker, despite what I felt at the beginning of my talk with Paulie. It was at best a sad story about a boy who was likely abducted by a lonely soldier looking to make some extra bucks on his train ride home from the war, a soldier who is now dead. That doesn't feel right, though. Not now that I know about Quill Brody and Aramis Bauer being in Paulie's class, both of them the children of Mill Street royalty.

The shared date and scar probably isn't anything. A likely coincidence that Paulie disappeared on the same day and month as my due date, a fluke that Kris, Deck, and I all had a similar reaction to the smallpox vaccine. I bet thousands of people have that same scar. But when I asked Kris about those two boys, he couldn't cover his reaction fast enough. Had they been involved in his abduction somehow and the Bauers and Brodys knew about it, were worried that it would catch up with them now that Paulie/Kris had returned? That'd explain why I have been given the runaround trying to research the story.

Tired of waiting for permission—to interview Becky, to talk to Paulie, to access research on my own—I storm the phone booth and slam the accordion door closed behind me. I reach for the phone book dangling on a chain and open it to the Saint Cloud section. I run my finger down the list of names and am gratified to discover Grover Tucker, the Stearns County sheriff who originally led the Paulie Aandeg investigation. I rest the book on the thin metal shelf, remove the handset, and cradle it between my ear and shoulder. I drop in my dime and dial.

I'm aware of my heightened emotions. Imagining I saw my mugger, worried my doctor sees me as a risk to my own child, speculating that two children of the Mill Street families might know something about Paulie's initial disappearance. Tears are hot on my face. It might be paranoia, it might be due to my pregnancy, and it might be the truth. All I can do is locate the facts beneath the shifting sands.

The phone rings. And rings. I glance outside the booth. It's lunch hour, and downtown Lilydale is busy. But for one surreal moment, I think everyone is frozen, staring at me in the booth like I'm a bug under glass. My heart knocks.

I blink.

They start moving.

"Hello?"

The voice on the other end of the line is groggy and carries the bottled sound of a very old person.

"I'm sorry, did I wake you?"

"Who is this?"

"I'm sorry," I repeat, apologizing for the second time in a very short conversation. "My name is Joan Harken. I live in Lilydale, Minnesota."

When he doesn't respond, I continue. "I'm a reporter for the *Lilydale Gazette*. I have some questions for you about an old case. I'm wondering if we can meet."

"You're wondering if I have meat?"

For the first time it occurs to me that he might be senile. The articles didn't mention his age, but he was a sheriff in 1944. I didn't think you could attain that office at younger than forty-five. That would put him today anywhere from his seventies to his eighties. I speak even more slowly, louder. "No, I am wondering if I can take you out for a cup of coffee. I have some questions for you about a case you covered in 1944."

A cough. "That was a long time ago. I won't turn down company, though. I don't leave my house much, but if you bring the doughnuts, I'll make the coffee."

"This is Grover Tucker? Former Stearns County sheriff?"

"None other."

"All right, how does tomorrow morning sound to you?"

Another cough. "I like the plain doughnuts. Nothing fancy."

I'm about to confirm when the screech of a car sliding to a halt rips through the glass of the booth. It's so loud and so startling that the phone drops from my hand. Two hundred feet away, at the intersection of Highway 23 and Augusta Avenue, a car has jumped the curb. Next to it, there's a body sprawled on the road. I push against the door and step out, mouth hanging open.

I stagger forward.

The unmoving body is dressed in the same clothes as the "mugger" I thought I saw over the weekend, right down to the porkpie hat resting a few feet from the body. I'm going insane, the pregnancy eating my brain. There's no other explanation. But here he is, laid out flat on the ground. I push through quicksand, toward the contorted figure lying on the pavement. I need to see his face.

"Joan! Where are you going?"

Gray-skinned, rodent-faced Mildred appears in front of me. Behind her, the Lilydale lunch crowd closes in around the body. I try to jostle Mildred aside. She is surprisingly sturdy.

"Who is that?" I yell. "Did he just get hit by a car?"

Mildred forcibly turns me around and leads me back toward the phone booth. "Did you leave your handbag in here?"

She doesn't wait for an answer. She retrieves my purse and loops the strap over my shoulder. The far-off keen of an ambulance slams against my skin. I shuffle toward the noise. Mildred is tugging me back, I'm stretching forward.

That's the mugger on the road, I'm sure of it.

There are about twenty folks between me and him, though. How are there so many people? It's like they showed up to deliberately block my view. When the ambulance careens around the corner, the crowd steps back as one to make room. Over their heads I can see the paramedics emerge from the front of the ambulance and hurry around to open the rear. Then they disappear into the throng. They reappear in moments, the gurney heavy with a body. They slide it in the back of the station wagon, close the door, reclaim their seats, and drive off.

Away from the hospital.

I know this because Lilydale General is on my end of town, southeast. The ambulance is driving northwest.

"Mildred," I groan in a voice I don't recognize. "Where are they taking him?"

"The hospital, dear."

"But it's the other way."

"Saint Cloud hospital, then. It's bigger." Mildred is searching the crowd. I realize she's looking for help in controlling me.

I am a risk. They don't want me to become hysterical.

Was my mugger a risk? Did Lilydale take care of him? I must control myself.

"I think I need to visit Dr. Krause," I say.

Mildred's relief is so tangible that it would be hilarious if not for the circumstances. "I'll walk with you," she says.

I must be cooperative. There is too much danger, too much on the table. I smell it, and it smells thick and coppery, like great amounts of drying blood. "Thank you."

She weaves us around the edge of the crowd, distracts me with chatter, but she needn't worry. I am looking nowhere but at my own feet. I fear there is no one in Lilydale but Regina who would believe me, no one, not even Deck, who wouldn't commit me and take my baby away if I tell them that I'm certain I'm always being watched, that I have the same scar as my boyfriend and a stranger who claims to be a boy who disappeared twenty-four years ago, that somehow the man who mugged me in Minneapolis showed up in Lilydale, and now he's been hit by a car.

Hell, I'd commit whoever told *me* that story.

I've heard of that before, of women who lose their mind because of the disequilibrium of pregnancy. They never get it back.

I don't want to be crazy.

I hug myself tighter, letting Mildred lead me inside the doctor's office. She murmurs something to Cornelia at the front desk. I am immediately guided to a back room.

Dr. Krause appears moments later. I'm not surprised.

"I'm not feeling well, Dr. Krause. Not like myself." I won't offer details. I will not tell him that either this entire town is insane, or I am. "I feel like I'm overstimulated. Growing upset over minor things."

"I'm glad you came," he says, nodding, his expression concerned. He has brought a chart with him. He opens it. "September 5 due date. That's right."

He peers at me through his round, rimless glasses. He has yet to examine me beyond the cursory check last visit.

"You're being a thoughtful mother, very obliging, following medical orders," he continues, his gaze serious.

Silence shrouds the room, a quiet so forceful that I can feel its heat.

The doctor's threat is clear. *Follow my rules, or else.*

I nod to show I understand.

"Very good," he says. "I'll increase your Valium, and you'll promise to come back if you feel unsettled again, won't you?"

"Yes, sir."

CHAPTER 30

"I think it may have been the heat," I say. I'm standing next to Deck, holding the relish dish I forgot to put out with the rest of the food. Ronald and Barbara have joined us for dinner, which I've cooked. It's too late for relish, the main course is almost finished, but I need to show them I'm trying. Deck is carrying brandy to refill his glass as well as Barbara's and Ronald's.

I've prepared a new recipe from one of the women at Catherine's gathering. It's a hamburger hot dish that calls for corn mixed in with the cream of mushroom soup. I'm grateful everyone appears to have enjoyed it.

"We're just glad you're okay," Ronald says. He scoops out his third serving of the hot dish. He seems to especially enjoy the cornflake crust. "That's what's most important. You're carrying our grandbaby in there."

I smile and let Deck slide his arm around my thickening waist. "I agree. That's the most important," I say. Then, almost as if it's an afterthought: "I was also upset by the accident I witnessed."

Barbara and Ronald exchange glances. I notice because I'm watching for it.

Deck is oblivious. He selects a sour gherkin from the dish and pops it into his mouth. "What accident?"

"A man was hit by a car." I gamble on keeping my focus on Barbara because I can watch only one of them. I'm rewarded as she blanches.

"He's fine," Ronald says. "Dennis is going to run a bit about it in the paper."

I swivel my gaze to him. He's been studying me like I've been watching Barbara, just like he was reading me the first day we drove up. Tendrils of warning brush my flesh. I force a smile. "I'm so glad to hear it. When the ambulance drove in the opposite direction of Lilydale General, I worried it was really serious."

"An abundance of caution," Ronald says. "Now, what did you learn about Paulie Aandeg?"

Deck drops into his seat, and I rest the relish tray on the table and take my place kitty-corner to him.

"He's a good-looking fellow," I say. "But it's impossible to know if he's really the boy in the sailor suit."

"I wasn't even born when Paulie disappeared," Deck says, "but I'd like to meet this fellow. I think I'd know if he was telling the truth."

"He has a scar," I say. I hadn't planned to bring it up, but I find I want to see their reaction. "The man who claims to be Paul. Deck, it looks just like ours."

Barbara's fork clatters to the floor. "Deck doesn't have any scars."

I pull up my sleeve, smiling. I've unsettled them, but they won't know that's why I'm smiling. They'll take it for innocence. "It's a small-pox scar."

"Everyone has one of those," Ronald says quickly. "*I* have one of those."

I notice for the first time that he and Deck hold their forks the same, like they're stabbing their food.

"Not like ours," Deck says. He's stopped eating. His brow is furrowed. "Joan and I have figure-eight scars."

For the first time since we've moved to Lilydale, I think the Deck I fell in love with might still be here. I fuss with my napkin so he can't see my grateful tears.

"Did you actually see this scar on the man who claims to be Paulie?" Barbara asks.

I nod. "He showed it to me. Problem is, I have no idea if the real Paulie Aandeg had it. It's not mentioned in the articles, the local ones, at least. Would either of you know about vaccinations both Paulie and Deck would have received?"

"It's so long ago," Barbara says brightly. "Impossible to remember. Did you make this cake from scratch, dear? It's so much better than the one you brought to Catherine's."

CHAPTER 31

I shouldn't have to manipulate Deck to leave for work an hour before he planned—*early bird catches the worm, honey!*—or lie about why I'm driving to Saint Cloud (*shopping!*). I especially shouldn't have to slouch in my seat as I motor out of town, worried that someone will see me and stop me.

But I do, aware that I've gone from being afraid to leave Lilydale to desperate to escape.

Hunched in the driver's seat, I drive past the lonely ramblers at the outskirts of town, feeling their sleepy, sticky pull: a life of work, family, growing more familiar every day as responsibility and inevitability pour like gravedirt onto my shoulders. But that's dramatic. The situation doesn't call for it. I agreed to move to Lilydale. We have a nice house, Deck's job is solid, and I've just been granted the biggest story at the newspaper. The pregnancy is making me unreasonable.

Hysterical.

Barbara's and Ronald's behavior last night could be explained away as completely normal. Of course Barbara went pale when we talked about a car accident. Obviously they would be concerned about my health. And a porkpie hat does not a man make. Still, it's not until I pass through the dark sentinel trees surrounding Lilydale, pass through the thick skin of the town with a pop—just like the day I arrived, except out rather than in—that my neck relaxes, that I can loosen my grip on the steering wheel, that blood returns to my fingers.

Saint Cloud is charming, a river city that's so open it feels familiar. On the drive, I unclasp my purse, locate the bottle of Valium, and swallow one dry. Then, I close my eyes and anchor myself in the memory of my mom. She understood how important my stories were. She didn't think it was foolish how I saw the world. She loved my imagination, and she loved me.

I park in front of Grover Tucker's house.

"What do you think, sweetheart?" I ask my stomach, stroking the firm bump. "You ready to go inside?"

The house is a cozy Cape Cod with a well-kept lawn. I park and walk up the granite walkway. A soft breeze murmurs through the neighborhood trees, making the honey-scented pink rosebushes on each side of Mr. Tucker's front porch wave. I knock on his door.

He answers immediately.

My jaw drops.

He laughs, a wheezy sound. "Not what you expected?"

CHAPTER 32

"Thank you for the coffee."

He'd brought me to the sunroom on the back of his house, where I'd tried to hide my surprise as he poured me a cup. It wasn't that I hadn't seen Negroes before, of course. *Of course.* Mom and I had lived in the South. It's just that in my wildest imagination, I never pictured a black sheriff in Stearns County in 1944.

"There weren't a lot of us," he says.

My embarrassment doubles. "You're reading my mind."

He laughs. It's a friendly sound. "Your face, anyhow. You haven't recovered from the shock."

"I'm so sorry. It's just that . . . I haven't lived in Lilydale long, but in the short time I've been there, I haven't seen a single Negro."

"And you probably won't. It was the same when I was elected—thanks to a mix of blacks in Saint Cloud back from the war and the fact that I ran unopposed—and it'll likely be the same for a while. Didn't make my job any easier, but then again, the only people who ever like a sheriff are the innocent. I didn't run across much of those in the execution of my duty. Are those doughnuts for me?"

I had set the box down but had failed to open it. I lift the lid. "Yes. I bought some plain ones, but also frosted. For me."

He smiles. "All right, then. I might as well try those, too. Now, you didn't drive all this way to watch an old man eat, did you?"

He moves slowly, as if his bones are made of glass.

"Do you mind me asking how old you are?"

He throws back his head and guffaws. "That's right. You mentioned you were a reporter. Not afraid to ask the hard questions, are you? Well, I'm glad to have lived as long as I have, and I don't mind telling you about it. I'm seventy-seven."

"I hope I'm half as sharp as you at that age." His face is leathered, a newsboy cap pulled over his white hair, but his mind is quick. "I'm here about the Paulie Aandeg case. Do you remember it?"

He stops halfway in the middle of pouring himself a cup of coffee. "The boy disappeared on September 5, 1944. Can't ever forget that. His mother's face will follow me to my grave. Broke my heart we couldn't find her boy for her."

"What if I told you he's shown up?"

Mr. Tucker tugs his hat off and fans himself. "You don't say."

"I do. I met with him yesterday." I open my portfolio and remove the photos I've taken of Kris. "This is what he looks like now. Do you think it's Paulie?"

Mr. Tucker handles the pictures, examining each. He sips his coffee. He takes a bite of his doughnut, and then another. Finally, he says, "Could be. Age is about right. Coloring. Paulie had brown hair and eyes. It's hard to know for certain."

"Did Paulie's mother mention anything about him having a scar?" I pull up my cap sleeve. I chose the dress for this reason. "Like this one?"

Mr. Tucker grabs his reading glasses off the table. Beyond the sunroom are more plants than I've seen outside of a park.

"Smallpox?" he asks.

"Yes, but shaped like mine. A figure eight."

He sits back. "Can't say that I remember. I can get my hands on the old file, though. Maybe."

My eyebrows shoot up. "Would I be able to see it?"

"Not if there's any sensitive information. But if I can call in a favor—and that's a big *if*—and if I come across anything that might make up your mind about this man claiming to be Paulie—a littler *if*—I'll call you."

"Thank you, Mr. Tucker."

"Grover."

"Thank you, Grover. Do you mind if I ask you a few more questions?"

"As long as there's doughnuts, you may ask questions."

I yank the article copies from my portfolio. "My research says Virginia Aandeg's—Paulie's mother's—house burned down five days after he went missing, and she was never seen again. Do you have any theories about who started the fire?"

Grover squints into the past. "That's right. There was a kerfuffle around that. An insurance fraud investigation, if I remember correctly."

My pulse picks up. "They think it was arson?"

"Something like that. All I remember is that the town of Lilydale received the insurance payment for Mrs. Aandeg's house burning, and that was enough to draw some attention."

I turn the fire article to face him. "This fire?"

He skims it. "Yes, that's right." He taps his finger over Ronald's name. "That man. Ronald Schmidt. He still around?"

"He is," I say cautiously.

"Always thought that one knew more than he let on."

"He's my boyfriend's father."

Grover sets his doughnut down. "Forgive an old man."

"Nothing to forgive." My smile is tight. I'm walking a thin rope, trusting this man I've just met. "I think there is something off in the village of Lilydale."

If Grover recognizes his old quote, he doesn't let on. "That's true of many places." He brushes sugar off his hands. "You know, I find myself mighty tired all of a sudden."

A chill envelops me. Is he going to tell on me? Is he one of their agents, like Dr. Krause? "I'm so sorry, Mr. Tucker. Have I said something to offend you?"

"Grover, and no. I'm getting up in years, and that's the beginning and the end of that story. Leave me your phone number, and I'll reach out if I hear anything. In the meanwhile, you're always welcome to drop by."

I jot down my number and let him lead me to the door, feeling like I've lost an opportunity. I can't think of any more questions to ask, until: "I saw an accident last week in Lilydale. A man got hit by a car. An ambulance took him away. Looked like it was coming this direction. Did you happen to hear anything about it?"

Grover leans against his door, shaking his head sadly. "I didn't see anything in the papers, but I'm so sorry you witnessed that. Once you hear the thump of a car hitting a body, that's a noise you won't likely soon forget."

He closes the door, but I can't move.

My heartbeat is pounding too loudly, realization crashing through me.

There hadn't been a thump.

Just the screech of the car, and then the body lying there.

CHAPTER 33

I won't call Ursula again.

And anyone else would lock me up.

That's how I explain what I'm doing outside the alley entrance to Regina's upstairs apartment. I almost turn around rather than knock. She isn't expecting me. I don't want to intrude. She was welcoming in the bar, but she might not want me in her home. Seriously, what the hell am I doing here?

I spin on my heel and start down the rickety wooden stairs, hitting the ground behind Little John's. I'm halfway to my car when I meet Regina coming toward me, carrying a Wally's grocery bag.

"Joan! You stopped by."

Her pleasure seems so genuine that I don't question it and instead follow her inside. Her apartment is small, a studio with her living room, kitchen, and bedroom combined, and the only doors lead to a bathroom and closet. It's cluttered, and I feel safer here than I have anywhere else in Lilydale, including my own home.

"It's a nice place," I say, watching her toss her purse onto a pile of clothes on the floor before setting her grocery bag on the counter.

"It's a shithole," she says. She pulls out eggs, milk, bread, and butter. "Can I get you anything to drink?"

"Do you have cola?"

She tugs her fridge open, biting her bottom lip in concentration, her hair braided in a single plait down her back. She's wearing a peasant blouse and a miniskirt so short that I get a peek of her red underpants when she bends over. Her outfit is cute, and young, and makes me realize I'm dressing like an old maid, that I've been sliding down that path since moving to Lilydale, growing big and slow and domestic.

"Questionable orange juice, water, or whiskey. That's what I can offer you."

"Water will be fine."

"Suit yourself," she says, closing the fridge and pointing to the cabinet to the right of it. "Cups in there, water in the tap."

I open the cupboard. It houses four jelly jars and a chipped mug. I grab a jar, run the tap until it's cool, and fill it. "How long have you lived here?"

"What's the date?"

"May 27."

"Six months, then. Can you believe I showed up here in winter and still decided to stay? How long are you planning on being a Lilydale resident?"

"I'm working here now. At the newspaper."

"I know. I read your article on the music pageant. It was good." Once the groceries are away, she yanks open the cupboard, pulls out another jelly jar, and splashes a shot of whiskey into it. She shoves clothes off a chair and indicates I should do the same.

She laughs when I move them to the bed.

"They're dirty," she says. "Might as well be on the floor."

"Is there a laundromat in town?"

"Yes. Since I'm down to one clean pair of panties, I'll have to visit it soon." She drinks her whiskey. "You drove here. I saw you pull in. Don't you live over on Mill Street?"

"I do." I force myself to relax. "I was in Saint Cloud working on the Paulie Aandeg article. You met him yet?"

Now I have her interest. "He's been to the bar every night this week." She drapes the back of her hand across her forehead, miming a woman fainting. "I do declare, he is one dreamy hunk of love."

My cheeks pink against my will.

She crows with laughter. "It's no crime to have eyes, lady."

I reach for her whiskey and take a sip. "It's not just eyes. My loins saw him, too."

She's still chuckling as she pours me my own glass of whiskey. "Had an aunt that got pregnant when she was forty-eight. Can you believe that shitty luck? Anyhow, she swore the pregnancy made her hornier than a sailor on shore leave. The baby's daddy wasn't around to help her out in that regard, either. It got harder and harder for her to pick up men as her belly grew."

I grimace.

"I'm not saying that's you," she says, furrowing her brow. "You've got a man at home. I'm only telling you that it's normal to have extra-strong urges when you're pregnant."

"I went to see the sheriff who handled Paulie's case back in 1944," I say, changing the subject.

"How old's he?"

"Seventies." I refrain from saying he's a black man. I get the idea Regina wouldn't care. Or maybe I don't want to seem like I do. "He said Kris could be Paulie. He's going to look into it."

Regina polishes off her whiskey and reaches for more. "It must be exciting, being a reporter. You said you did that when you lived in Minneapolis. Did you cover your own mugging?"

She's smiling, has no idea she echoed the same crazy thought I had while the man in a porkpie hat held a knife to my throat, and just like that, the whole story tumbles out. Not only the mugging, or the fact that I'd won Slow Henry out of it, but that I'd imagined I'd seen the mugger here, two different times, and the second time he'd looked dead as a doornail on the road.

"It's silly, isn't it?" I ask when I finish, positive that Regina is going to judge me as harshly as Ursula did, desperate for her not to. I need someone else to believe my stories, crave it.

Regina shakes her head. "It's not silly; it's this town. It was either a guy who looks like him, or it *was* him. Stranger things have happened." She reaches across the Formica table and pokes my stomach right where it's bulging. "You have to trust your gut."

I want to weep with relief. "I haven't told anyone about thinking I saw the mugger here. Not even Deck, or my best friend in Minneapolis."

She paints an X over her heart. "Your secret dies with me."

"You think I should go to the police?"

"You positive he was the one who got hit by the car?"

"That's just it. I don't know that *anyone* got hit by a car. I know a vehicle went off the road downtown and that a man who looked like the mugger was on the ground immediately after. Did you hear any buzz about it at the bar?"

She glances toward the ceiling, like she's sorting through memories. "Not that I recall. But I tell you what. If it was me, I wouldn't go to the police. First of all, I avoid them on principle. Had some run-ins. Second, it sounds like the situation sorted itself out one way or another. I think the real problem is that you don't feel comfortable talking to your old man about it."

I notice for the first time that she's wearing a necklace, a tiny tooth-colored pearl on a gold chain, very much like the one I stole for my mom. I smile and take another tiny sip of the amber whiskey, its warmth rolling down my throat and unhitching my bones. "It's not Deck I don't trust," I finally say. "It's Lilydale, like you said. It makes me jumpy. I've never lived in a small town before. I always feel like I'm being watched."

"Ain't that the truth," Regina says. "Welcome to the fishbowl."

It could be the whiskey, or the fact that she isn't treating me like I'm mad, but I suddenly want to tell her everything about the Fathers and Mothers. I haven't been sworn to secrecy, but I sense they wouldn't want me to share.

To hell with them.

"You know that Johann Lily who founded the town? Well, he started a group, too. They're called the Fathers and Mothers. Can you believe that? And they want me to join!"

I hoot, and Regina laughs along, exactly like I wanted Ursula to do. I'm beaming.

"Would you like more whiskey, Mother?" she asks.

Impossibly, my laughter doubles. "Yes, please, Mother. But we mustn't tell Father."

She can't breathe, she's laughing so hard.

"I think I am going to ball Kris," she says.

I hold up my glass in a toast. "Go with God."

She clinks her jelly jar to mine. "Not like there are a lot of men to choose from, with them all off at war. Why isn't Deck?"

"War's for uneducated men," I say, before I realize I'm mirroring Deck's own words, something he said to me back in Minneapolis.

Regina stiffens.

"I'm sorry," I say.

Her face seals like an envelope. "And waitressing is for uneducated women, I suppose?"

I grab her hand. "Please, Regina. My mom was a waitress, and she's the best woman I've ever known. It was a stupid thing to say. I'm a jackass. Forgive me?"

A slow smile blows across her mouth. "Your Mother forgives you, child."

And we start belly-laughing again. I'm desperate to stay connected to her, to remain in this easy, amber-colored girlfriend space.

"You have a scissors?" I ask.

She glances around the kitchen. "Somewhere. You wanna sew?"

"I want you to cut my hair."

Her eyes go wide. "What?"

"Yep. Cut it all off. I'm turning into an old lady, Regina, fast-track dying right in front of your eyes." I tug out my headband and bobby pins, shaking out my shoulder-length hair. I've used so much hairspray that it barely moves, even without anything holding it in place. "Save a gal, would ya?"

She grins and stands, rustling through the drawers. "You're lucky I used to cut my boyfriend's mop all the time. I hope you're okay with a flip."

"I was thinking more of a pixie." When I close my eyes, I see Mia Farrow on the cover of *Vogue*. "Could you do that?"

She spins, holding a pair of scissors in hand. "I can try."

CHAPTER 34

She does a marvelous job.

I help her clean up bundles of my hair.

She doesn't blink when I ask if I can use some mouthwash to rinse away the perfume of whiskey. I touch myself up in her mirror—I look so different, so young, my eyes wide and innocent when framed by the pixie cut—and walk back to my car. My plan is to drive it home so it's there if Deck needs it and then walk to the newspaper offices.

Now that I've talked to Grover, I want back in those archives. Meeting with the retired sheriff made me realize how lax I've been in researching the article, how complacent Lilydale has made me, either deliberately or because it's the nature of a small town.

When I reach home, Slow Henry is the first to greet me.

Deck is the second.

He goes white when he sees me.

I feel the hot itch of guilt, and I don't like it. "You're home early!" I say with false cheer.

"Look at your hair," he says, still pale. He swallows, seems to collect himself. "I love it."

I touch it self-consciously, all the buoyancy I felt with Regina draining away. Should I have consulted him? "Thanks. It was a spur of the moment decision."

He nods. "How was Saint Cloud?"

"Good." I scramble to remember what I told him I was doing today. "You liked the shopping?" he asks.

I try to hold the mask on my face. That's right, I said I was going to the mall. "It was wonderful! I didn't stumble across anything I needed to have, though. Maybe that's why I got the haircut. So I didn't drive all that way for nothing."

I go to him. I want to be in his arms if for no other reason than that he can't see my face.

He doesn't return my embrace, but I nuzzle in.

He finally wraps his arms around me.

"I adore you," he says.

The emotion in his voice catches me off guard. He squeezes me tighter. "And this baby," he says. "I'm going to love it more than I've ever loved anything."

My eyes grow warm with tears.

"Hey, you know what we should do?" he says. "We should buy a crib. There's a store over in Cold Spring that's supposed to have quite a collection. I can sneak out of work over lunch tomorrow and take you shopping. Would you like that?"

"I'd love it, Deck." In the safety of his arms, I speak the closest truth that I have, hoping to bridge the distance that's grown between us since we've moved. "I haven't been feeling like myself, you know that, right? I'm so jumpy, worried all the time."

"You've been through a lot this year, Joanie."

"I know, but—"

"We're having people over for dinner tomorrow," he says, talking right over me. "It'll be a big party. Everyone on Mill Street plus some others, so all the important Mothers and Fathers."

I stiffen and extract myself from his arms. "And I suppose I'll be cooking?"

He reaches out to touch my cheek, but I pull back.

"Honey, don't be like this," he says. "The other women will lend a hand if you want. You just have to reach out. It wouldn't kill you to ask for help every now and again."

They're not going to like my hair. "Do I get a say in who's coming to my house?"

"If you'll only listen, you'll understand this is really for *you*. The Fathers and Mothers want you to invite Kris so they all can meet him, and you can spend some more time with him. Won't that help your article?"

"I don't need help."

"See? That is exactly what I'm saying. You won't accept assistance from anybody."

I feel trapped. "I want to invite Regina."

Deck reaches down to pet Slow Henry, who's braiding himself between his legs. "Who?"

"She works at Little John's."

Deck straightens. "She won't fit in."

"Neither do I."

❖

Deck doesn't leave my side all night, even following me to bed when I finally tell him I'm tired. Old me might say he's a doting boyfriend. New me wonders if I'm being babysat. Anyone but Regina would call that foolish, tell me that the pregnancy has tipped me off-kilter. But it hasn't. I'm feeling fuzzy headed, more tired than usual, but that's a natural part of carrying a child. Having a whole town watch me? My husband keeping me on a short leash, even though he calls it our "romantic night in"?

That's crazy.

For all my exhaustion, though, once I crawl into bed, sleep eludes me. My nightgown twists around my stretched belly. The room is hot.

A mosquito buzzes near my head. Deck snores with a rhythm that is so consistent I want to smother him with a pillow.

When I can't take it anymore, I trundle out of bed as smoothly as my ever more cumbersome body will allow. I recognize my belly is hitting more things. That I can't stand as quickly. As much as I'm excited for this baby, the vulnerability scares me. I pad downstairs and into the kitchen. Underneath the sink, tucked in a bucket hidden beneath clean rags, I locate the pack of cigarettes.

Dr. Krause said I can have four a day.

I step into the backyard, moonlight settling like silk across my shoulders. The temperature is ten degrees cooler out here. I shove sweaty hair off my face and go to one of the Adirondack chairs.

It must be two in the morning.

Nighttime's cloak is the closest thing I have to privacy in Lilydale.

I sink into the chair, feeling drowsier already. Maybe I could sleep outdoors tonight? I bring a cigarette to my mouth and light it. The smell instantly drops Ursula into my consciousness.

Joanie, she's saying softly, *you have to stop making up your stories. You spin everything better or worse than it is. You know what happened to Libby that night. After the party.*

The orange ember at the end of my cigarette starts fluttering like a trapped insect. I bring it to my face but can't find my mouth for the shaking.

You know what happened to Libby that night.

I begin to sweat with the effort of holding the snapshot image from Halloween: Libby, Ursula, and me, laughing, in our costumes at the end of the night.

That's what happened! Laughter. Friendship.

But the cigarette smoke isn't letting me hide, not when it smells like Ursula, not when it drifts like poison fog across the anxiety I've been swimming in, not when I can no longer keep all my stories straight.

Libby was a vivacious redhead with a laugh that lit up a room, and she reminded me of my mom the second I met her, though I don't suppose it mattered as much then, when Mom was alive. The three of us—Ursula, Libby, and me—had been assigned to the same dorm floor, and we'd immediately grown as tight as a book, with Ursula the ink, me the paper, and Libby the glue.

That had been something for me.

My first real friends.

So many good memories. Ursula setting off the fire alarms in the dorms while teaching me and Libby to blow smoke rings in the bathroom. The three of us catching the Beatles at Metropolitan Stadium. Eating my first Chinese food with Ursula and Libby, gobbling down chow mein that was all salt and sweet and tender strips of pork. Smoking grass with them, stumbling home after parties with them, sharing my dreams and fears.

Laughing in that Halloween photo.

You know what happened to Libby that night.

I do, know even more than Ursula.

Ursula went home with her boyfriend after the Halloween party, which is probably why Libby sought me out, crying, resembling my mom more than ever. I'd tried my best to listen. She wanted to meet with the abortionist Ursula recommended, but she was Catholic, and terrified she'd go to hell, and what did I think?

I thought it would all look better in the morning.

That's what I told her.

She killed herself that night. I found her body the next morning.

Joanie, you have to stop making up your stories. You spin everything better or worse than it is. You know what happened to Libby that night. After the party.

Suddenly, I can't sit in this Adirondack chair another moment. I'm busting out of my own skin, too awful, too fragile to go on. *It's my fault Libby died. I didn't say the right thing, wasn't a good friend.* I jump up and stab out my cigarette and walk the butt to the trash can. I slip the lighter into the pocket of my dressing gown. I tread across the wet grass, toward Dorothy and Stan's home, the night's dew gluing grass clippings to my feet.

If I don't do something to calm myself, something I know I shouldn't, I'm going to lose my mind.

I slink to the rear of the house, where I guess the kitchen to be.

I approach the door.

Unlocked.

I slip into Stan and Dorothy's kitchen, my pulse thudding, the sharp yellow light of the moon revealing a floor plan identical to my own house. Which means—if the upstairs truly is no longer in use because of Stan and his wheelchair—there is only one main-floor room that can be used as the bedroom.

The slashes of moonlight I walk through brush against my skin like cobwebs, warning me back. It's dangerous, what I'm doing, insane, and I can't stop myself. I need Dorothy's white enamel locket.

I need it.

I pad through the dining room, put my hand on the cool doorknob of what I believe is their bedroom. Every hair on my body has become a nerve, a feeler, a shivering caution.

I turn the knob. The door opens with a click. Soft snoring, the stale smell of sleeping bodies. I step into it.

The moonlight is weak, secondhand, on this side of the house, but I make out two forms in the bed, a wheelchair next to the larger. My heart sits in my throat, thick and wide, throbbing, and I'm not thinking about Libby at all, or Ursula or my mom or Lilydale. I'm seeing only the jewelry box on the dresser.

In the second before I open it, it occurs to me that it might be a music box.

But it's too late.

I open it. Silence, except that one of the bodies in the bed turns and sighs, dropping me into a full-body ice bath. I dare not turn, do not have the muscles or eyes for anything except that white enamel lily locket, the shape and color of the Fathers and Mothers pin, surely holding a photo of Stanley.

It burns in my hand, burns deliciously, when I clasp it, and I taste something like relief. I can't control anything in Lilydale, not who comes to my house for dinner, not whether I can drink in public, not anything except this. I have Dorothy Lily's necklace, and when she comes over for dinner with the rest of the Fathers and Mothers, I will know something none of them do. I will have some power.

The snoring has taken on a different tenor—is it one, rather than both people snoring?—but I don't look. I keep my face to myself, clutch the locket to my chest, and slip out of the room like a ghost, an exultant ghost.

I am calm when I step outdoors, the air cool, the moonlight shining golden across my skin.

My walk is confident across the driveway. I do not waver as I stride to my own house, not even when I spot the man in the alley, watching me from the shadows, unaware that I can see him, too.

CHAPTER 35

I tape the necklace to the back of the main-floor toilet tank, rinse my feet in the tub, put the man in the alley (*Clan, sneaking home late?*) out of my head, and sleep like a baby. I don't even hear Deck leave the next morning.

True to his word, he returns at eleven thirty to take me crib shopping. I lay my head on his shoulder as he drives. It's a short trip, only one town over, but I soak up this time with him, hanging on his every word. He's clearly so happy to be back living in Lilydale. He's pleasantly boyish, gushing about his new clients and the memories that keep rushing back. Football games. An awkward first kiss. His freshman-year job stocking shelves at Wally's.

I smile and listen. I don't tell him about Grover or visiting the Lily house last night. I just enjoy him. Deck's been so busy at the insurance agency that I've missed him. We've grown apart, but I can feel our hearts knitting back together.

When he pulls up in front of Oleson Furniture and rushes around to open my door for me, I grin and burst out, surprising him with a big, passionate kiss.

"Well now, what was that for?"

"For being the best boyfriend a girl could ask for."

He smiles. "You're angling for the largest crib, aren't you?"

I giggle. I'm smiling up at him, about to make a weak joke (*we only need a small one, silly, it's for a baby*), when the color drains out of his face like someone's pulled the plug in his stomach. I whirl to see what he's seen.

When I spot her, I gasp, my hand flying protectively to my stomach.

A rapidly breathing woman is hunched beneath a tree just on the edge of the parking lot. She isn't here to shop, I don't think. In fact, it looks as if she's run here, barefoot, her hair tangled with twigs and leaves. She's glowering at Deck, whether intentionally or because that's her natural expression, I can't be sure.

When she steps out of the shadows, I moan.

Her face isn't right.

Her head is impossibly narrow at the top, eyes melting into cheeks, her nose an unformed lump of clay floating between. Her chin juts out enough to balance a coffee cup on, pulling her bottom jaw so far that I can see every one of her bottom teeth. She looks feral, her chest rising and falling with the breath of effort or a deformity of her heart, I can't be sure. Her body appears normal beneath her shapeless dress.

I avert my eyes. It's cruel to stare, would be even crueler to run, but that's what I want to do, to get my baby far away from here, to protect him from whatever caused that.

"Do you know her?" I whisper to Deck.

"We're leaving." Deck pulls me back toward the car.

"But we haven't even looked at cribs!"

I steal a peep over my shoulder. The heaving woman hasn't moved, but now she's grinning, a horrible jack-o-lantern smile that eats the bottom half of her face. And then she darts behind the store, her movements as quick and unsettling as a silverfish.

I shudder, letting Deck guide me to the car. Once inside, I lock the doors, but I hope the woman doesn't see. I don't want her to feel bad. I can't help wondering if it's contagious, though, whatever did that to her, and if my baby is safe.

I weep on the drive home, but softly, so Deck won't be alarmed.

CHAPTER 36

The dinner party is that night. Dorothy and Barbara are in my kitchen, as proper as ever, helping me prepare. I am only able to hold myself together by thinking of that enamel locket taped to the back of the toilet tank.

Dorothy is wearing a button-down shirt over drainpipe slacks. This is her work outfit. She'll be in a smart suit for tonight's party, I'd bank on it. Her hand keeps going to her bare neck so often that Barbara, who's also there to help, finally asks her about it.

"Minna's necklace," Dorothy says. "I seem to have misplaced it."

I cough to cover the unexpected burst of pleasure. *I stole more power than I thought.* "The necklace belonged to Minna Lily?" I ask. "Wife of Johann Lily?"

Dorothy tries to smile, but her lips are too pinched. "That's right, dear. She brought it over from Germany. It's a locket, actually, containing dirt from our ancestral homestead."

I fall against the countertop. It isn't personal that I've taken her necklace. She's never been anything but nice to me. I realize I've gone too far.

Dorothy takes it for sympathy. "You're too kind, darling, but don't worry. It'll turn up."

She's mixing a Cool Whip and mandarin orange salad with maraschino cherries. Both she and Barbara were visibly shocked by my hair when they showed up, but they've bitten their tongues.

"Barbara, I think you can put the ham in to warm now," Dorothy says, dismissing talk of the locket with such alacrity that I wonder whether I've met my equal in focusing on only the positive.

The thought leaves me strangely cold.

But Dorothy and Barbara are buzzing around my kitchen, so confident, so at home, both of them cooing over my pregnancy and the town happenings and their excitement for the party, that I decide to go with the flow. It's so cozy, almost like being mothered.

Between them, they've brought serving platters and a large ham, already cooked. It only needs to be warmed. Same with the scalloped potatoes. Dorothy even brought a nut-covered cheeseball, Ritz crackers, and sliced olives for appetizers. That leaves me to boil vegetables, set Jell-O salads, and warm bread. It's pleasant, mindless kitchen work. Our conversation stays on the surface, avoiding all but the easy things.

When the first people begin showing up, the house smells wonderful. The china and sterling flatware Barbara and Ronald left in the built-ins are laid out, a feast served family-style. My own mother would be proud. I feel a sharp ache as I realize I've missed the one-year anniversary of her death.

"Joan, come over here," Ronald calls to me from the front door, where he's standing next to Amory Bauer. Ronald has been manning the door as if this were still his house. (And unlike his wife, he didn't keep his opinions of my hair to himself. When he first saw it, his face went tomato red, and he sputtered, "And isn't long hair a woman's pride and joy? For it has been given to her as a covering," before Deck led him away.) "You haven't spoken to Amory about Paulie Aandeg yet."

It no longer bothers me that Ronald knows that, that he probably knows everyone I've spoken with since I moved to Lilydale. I separate myself from the pack of women I've been chatting with. Mousy

Mildred, stern-faced Catherine, beneficent Barbara, Birdie Rue, Saint Dorothy.

"I'm so glad Ronald told me it was you," Amory says, his eyes glittering dangerously as I approach. "With that hair, I'd have taken you for a new boy in town. What is it you want to know about the Paulie Aandeg case?"

I try to force the smile to reach my eyes, but it gets hung up at my mouth. *Whether your son had anything to do with his disappearance,* I want to say. "Thank you for coming. I guess I want to know if there is anything that didn't make it into the newspapers."

"You know newspapers," he says. "They get half the story and make up the rest." Though he's grinning, it's not kind. He wants me to feel bad.

I mirror his smile. "If you give me the whole story, I won't have to make up a thing."

His eyes narrow. "Not much to tell. The boy disappeared, and then his mother went missing the same night her house burned down. What do you make of that?"

He wants me to say that it sounds like Mrs. Aandeg had something to hide. "Your son, Aramis, was in Paulie's class."

Amory's smile slides toward ugly. "Who told you that?"

Ronald puts his hand on Amory's shoulder. "I told you she spoke to Becky Swanson. The boys' teacher the day Paulie disappeared."

It's interesting to see the effect Ronald's touch has on Amory. It deflates him. I had assumed the police chief rather than the mayor had the power in the relationship, but that's clearly not the case.

"Aramis is overseas," Amory tells me, his eyes burning into me. "We're lucky to get a phone call every few months. You won't be able to get ahold of him, but if you did, he wouldn't have anything to tell you. He was a child."

"Same with Quill Brody?" I ask.

"Same with Quill Brody," Amory says, copying my words exactly.

I don't want to give up, not without at least a single piece of new information. "You met Kris Jefferson, the man who claims to be Paulie Aandeg?"

"Interviewed him when he first came to town. Not much to learn there."

I won't let this go. "Do you think he's Paulie?"

Amory claps me on the back. "We'll find out tonight!"

He pushes past me. For a moment I wonder if he's too big for my house, like a giant who's wandered into the land of humans. But that's silly. He fits in just fine. These are his people, and he's only a man, not even as large as Clan.

I'm about to close the screen door when I spot the couple strolling up my walk. Everyone who Deck invited is here except Dennis from the newspaper, who couldn't make it because he had to cover the baseball game.

That leaves the two people I invited: Regina and Kris.

Kris is empty-handed. Regina is carrying a jug of Mountain Red. She hands it to me. "Hope your group will like it!"

She's going for funny, but she's clearly nervous. She's wearing a miniskirt that this crowd will think is too short and a blouse that is scandalously low cut. Kris, earthy and gorgeous as ever, is wearing patched jeans and an India print shirt. He'll also stand out like a sore thumb, but his languid body posture informs the world that he couldn't care less if he tried.

I kiss Regina on the cheek. "If they don't like Mountain Red, they're assholes," I whisper.

"I dig your hair, and something smells delicious," Kris says perfunctorily, stepping past me to strut into the house. "Let's get this done and over with."

I wonder what he knows that I don't. There isn't much time for speculation, though. The food is growing cold. Deck and Ronald set up three card tables next to the dining room table so we can all eat in

186

the same room. It makes four separate conversations, but I catch bits. Amory joking that the whole city council is in my dining room, plus the draft board. The Jacksons, who own Little John's, speaking to Regina about a belligerent customer they had to kick out the night before. Clan, Deck, and Ronald talking insurance and, when Clan mentions how it's time for a crow hunt to let off some steam, the men laughing. Mildred Schramel is trying to keep my attention, telling me she is sure she'll get used to my hair and that she hopes I have a boy, because it's so much work having girls.

It's surprisingly all right. I begin to relax.

There is a lull in Mildred's questioning. That's when, without forethought, I let the words tumble out of my mouth. "I thought I saw someone in the alley last night," I say to her, "between our house and the Lilys'."

The head table, where I'm seated, goes church quiet. It takes the smaller tables a few seconds to catch up, but soon the entire room sits in the spotlight of silence.

"Impossible," Amory says. "There's no safer town."

"It must have been a trick of the light, then," I say, wishing I could swallow my words. I know better than to speak out in this crowd.

"When was this?" Deck asks.

I knead the napkin in my lap. "I couldn't sleep last night. I went out for fresh air."

"You said you saw somebody in the alley?" Regina asks from across the room.

"Like I said, impossible," Amory barks.

"It isn't impossible for someone to walk in an alley at night," Regina argues.

"Really?" Amory asks. "Would you like to tell me more?"

The ugly in his voice is unmistakable.

"I don't know about Lilydale," Kris says from the other end of the main table. "But where I come from, people walk by houses that aren't theirs all the time."

"Tell us where you hail from," Ronald says.

"Besides Lilydale," Mildred says, tittering nervously.

"The last place I called home was Siesta Key, Florida," he says, staring at me.

I look away. He shouldn't flirt in front of these people. Not with me.

"That's where I discovered that I was Paulie."

"How *did* you find out?" Ronald asks. "I think we're all curious about that."

I understand this is why we're all here, in my house. It's not for my article. It's so the Fathers and Mothers can put on a show of force, get their questions answered, find out exactly what Kris has revealed to me so far.

Kris seems fine with it. He repeats the story he told me in the café, about the hypnotherapist stirring up old memories of the town, and his mom, the sailor suit.

"You say the man who raised you was military?"

Kris nods. "He probably took the train through Lilydale on his way back from the war. Saw a kid, knew he could get a bigger pension with a tyke, and brought me back with him to San Diego. It's the only explanation that lines up."

"That's horrible," Regina says.

"People do terrible things," Ronald says. He's looking at me.

Deck covers my hand with his. "Dessert time!" he says. "We'll get out of the way so the ladies can clean up. Gentlemen, who wants to enjoy cigars in the backyard?"

I excuse myself to use the bathroom upstairs. I rinse off my face and wash my hands, taking deep breaths. I fumble the Valium bottle out of the medicine cabinet and swallow one. I can't hide here for much longer or I'll be missed. A soft knock on the door gets my attention. I open it, hoping Regina is on the other side.

It's Kris.

I jump back so quickly that I bash my elbow on the sink. "What are you doing here?"

Kris is smiling, but it's a lopsided grin. He's ingested more than wine tonight. He reaches behind him and pulls a postcard out of his back jeans pocket. It features a palm tree against the most glorious sunset I've ever seen, tangerines and lemons fading to lavender, a larger version of the matchbook he used at Tuck's Cafe. "Siesta Key, Florida," is written across the top.

"Leave with me," he's saying. "Tonight. Before it's too late."

I throw up my hands. *Stop.* "What's wrong with you?"

"Yes, what's wrong with you, son?"

The growl of a voice nearly loosens my bowels. I hadn't noticed Amory in the hallway. He has Kris in a headlock before I can register what's happening, yanking so hard that he drags Kris off his feet, the rug bunching beneath him as he hauls Kris out the door.

I fall against the wall. A commotion erupts downstairs, and then the front door slams. Regina appears in the bathroom doorway, her face flushed.

"You okay?"

She helps me toward the closed toilet, but I push her off. "I have to get downstairs. We must pretend like everything is normal, or it'll get worse."

"All right," she says, glancing over her shoulder. "But what just happened?"

Rather than respond, I lead the way downstairs. I understand that how I play this has very real consequences, even if I don't yet know what they are. I step onto the main floor. Everyone is still, quiet, the whole room of guests watching me. Then, like robots who've been plugged in, they start moving again, laughing and drinking and acting like this is normal.

My bones turn to jelly.

I pivot so I'm facing Regina, who's behind me on the stairs. I smile and nod as if I'm telling her a joke but pitch my voice so only she can hear it. "I shouldn't ever have asked you to come. I'm so sorry."

Regina is pale. "What are you talking about?"

"You need to go," I say, the lightness in my voice and the way I'm holding myself belying my words, I hope. "I've invited you into the lion's den. Please, just act like everything is normal."

She steps ahead of me. She threads her way through the crowd. I follow. At the door, I hug her. In the reflection of the front window, I catch Amory staring at me with such naked hate it feels like a punch, but when I turn, he's wiped the expression off so completely that I wonder if I imagined it.

But I know I didn't.

I am in way over my head.

CHAPTER 37

"You'll want to join us on June 1," Catherine says. It's a foregone conclusion.

"What?" I ask.

Regina left forty-five minutes ago. The table is cleared, the dishes are done, and the kitchen is clean. One of the women—I'm not sure which—has even thought to make little tinfoil packages of leftovers for everyone to take home, a delicious pocket of ham and potatoes. The guests are filing toward the door. The evening is almost over.

Soon, I can lie down and close my eyes.

But then the women turned on me. Almost as if they had it planned.

"Join you for what?"

"Mothers' initiation," Dorothy says, hand going to her bare neck before she catches herself. "I mentioned it while we were preparing dinner."

I am positive she did not. And I want to destroy that damn necklace now.

"We hold it the first of every month," Mildred says. "It's been a while since we had anybody to initiate, though." She looks to the other women for confirmation. They ignore her. I am struck by how very much like a high school clique these Mothers are. Mildred is the hanger-on, Dorothy the leader, Barbara the heart, sharp-faced Catherine the enforcer, and Rue the brain.

"That's a very kind offer," I say. I don't feel strong enough to turn them down.

Clan Brody nearly crashes into our ladies' circle. I put out Regina's wine with dinner. He drank that like water and then pulled out a bottle of his own whiskey. The sour smell rolls off him in waves. It mixes with his sweat and creates something oversweet. I swallow a surge of bile.

Clan holds his arms out toward me. The green grip of nausea tightens.

"Thank you for having us," he says, his words slurring.

I think he meant to whisper in my ear, but he's too loud.

I step back. "You're welcome."

The women are shifting, fluttering, birds again, not sure how to handle this interloper in their nest.

Clan glances at my stomach, the gesture exaggerated, like his head is perched on ball bearings. "The town can't wait for that little one."

Catherine grips his arm, her fingers sinking deep into his flesh. "Yes." Her bright-chip eyes lock on mine. "We're all so excited."

She starts pulling Clan toward the door. It seems she'll get him home without a further scene, but at the last minute, he swivels and lurches back to plant himself in front of me. Where are the other men?

"You look like your mother, you know," he says, his voice blurry.

I hold myself as still as stone. "My mother's not from around here."

"*A* Mother," Catherine says, her words like a punch, but whether directed at Clan or me, I cannot tell. "He said you look like a Mother, and we couldn't agree more. That's why we want you to join us on June 1. Make it official."

Clan is swaying, and all the women are smiling and nodding at me. I have the sudden sensation of falling. Light reflects off the glass of Mountain Red Mildred is clutching. The smell of the wine, though, the red liquid shimmering thick and salty like blood, pushes me over the edge. I do not even have time to excuse myself. I barely cross the threshold of the main-floor bathroom before I drop to my knees and vomit into the toilet.

I throw up with such force that I worry I'll eject the baby. I flush and vomit some more. When I'm completely empty, shuddering, I push myself to my feet and wipe down the toilet. I check for the necklace, which is taped safely behind the tank. Knowing it's there grounds me. I won't destroy it. I'll use it like a talisman.

I don't have a toothbrush in this bathroom, so I can only rinse my mouth with water. I catch my expression in the mirror. I look like a haunted-house version of myself, too-short hair tufted around my ears.

When I step out, everyone has left except for Ronald and Barbara. Barbara pats me on the shoulder. "Are you all right, honey?"

I nod.

"Don't worry about Clan," Ronald says. "He has a drinking problem. We'll talk to him."

I nod again. Did they stay around to tell me that?

When they leave, Deck brings me a Valium and a glass of water.

I swallow them both and let him lead me to bed.

I slip into sleep, no longer worried about getting my story.

Now, I wonder if I'll get out of this town alive.

CHAPTER 38

Deck lies heavily on his side of the mattress. There's an ocean between us. I want to reach over and touch him. I want to return to the days when we would tease each other, and make love, and explore Minneapolis. I don't know when precisely the world shifted so it's him against me, but we're no longer on the same team.

The Valium, or maybe the pregnancy, or possibly the pressure of everything makes me cry. I think I am so quiet that Deck doesn't hear me. But then, he bundles me into his arms.

"You don't like it here."

It's not a question, and so I don't give an answer.

His voice is so low that I almost don't hear it. "If I have to choose between your health and getting drafted, I'll choose you every time," he whispers. "We're moving back to Minneapolis."

"Deck!" I can't believe it. I sob even harder but for a different reason. I get to leave this town where they know my secrets. Where they don't accept me. Where everyone is watching me.

He starts kissing me, gently. The tenderness turns to passion, which morphs to naked, reckless need. Soon, I can't get enough. I'm ripping off his pajamas, climbing on top of him. He's never seen me like this. I've never seen *myself* like this. I ride him, pounding, until I climax. I fall onto his chest. He rolls me over and kisses me on the forehead. Then he turns away, his back to me.

I'm embarrassed by my sexual aggressiveness. I've never finished before him. My hunger to feel him against me isn't sated, either, so I roll onto my side, curving my body against his. In this position, I run my finger over his vaccination scar.

I think of mine, just like it. How no matter what, we're connected, me and Deck.

In this relaxed state, a new thought inserts itself into my brain.

"Maybe *you're* Paulie," I say drowsily.

He laughs. He sounds very much awake. Has he been pretending to fall asleep? "It'll take me a few weeks to close up business here before we can move back. I need to see which accounts I can transfer. I'll have to land us an apartment, too."

It feels so good to be taken care of. I murmur something vague.

"It'll be best if we go to church this Sunday. Are you okay with that? Put on a good face before we ride off into the sunset?"

I'm exhausted from weeks of paranoia all twisted up with moments of calm. I nod. He must feel the movement against his back, because he relaxes, then drifts off to sleep for real. I'm not far behind, floating in that warm forever between sleep and waking. So tranquilized am I that at first, I think the lullaby is coming from my dreams. I strain to hear it, trying to place it in my childhood.

But the song is insistent, not soothing like I thought at first.

In fact, it's jarring, a hurdy-gurdy melody that finally yanks me awake. I sit up in bed. I look around. The moon is muffled behind clouds, too weak to pierce the deep ink of a small-town night. The bedroom window is open, the softest breeze tickling the curtain. I walk toward the shadowy opening.

The jumpy melody is coming from outside.

I see nothing out of place, but then a shadow moves in the alley.

The same place I saw the man last night.

The hurdy-gurdy lullaby is coming from him.

My body goes numb and heavy, my limbs great sacks of sand, as if I'm trapped in a nightmare. I will not go outside at night on my own ever again. There's no need. We're moving soon.

I return to bed and burrow again into Deck's strong back.

The jangly, terrifying music continues. I jam a pillow over my head.

It takes a long time, but I fall asleep. When dreams come again, they're horror-laced visions of my baby cut from my belly by leering, deformed carnival clowns.

CHAPTER 39

Deck and I do not talk about moving the next morning. We both simply return to living our Lilydale lives. I trust he'll take care of what he promised. Very soon, once he's gotten all the loose ends tied up, we'll be back in Minneapolis. If Ronald and Barbara want to see their grandchild, *they* can visit *us*.

That we'll be escaping soon gives me all that much more reason to nail down the Kris/Paulie story. Having a feature piece in my portfolio might help me get my reporting job back. With that in mind, after Deck leaves for work, I decide to stop by the Purple Saucer to check in on Kris.

The phone rings on my way out.

"Joan? It's Benjamin."

I'm so fully immersed in Lilydale that it takes a moment to place him. The *Star* photographer. "Benjamin! How are you doing?"

He groans. "Don't tell me I did all this work for nothing. You remember calling me earlier this week?"

I'm glad he can't see my face. "Yeah, of course. What'd you find out about Lilydale?"

"That it should be called Eden. The town's perfect. Better than perfect. They have an outreach system, historically and currently, that makes sure every townie is taken care of. There's fluff pieces about it, short and sweet bits here and there since the Great Depression. Speaking of, Lilydale is one of the only towns whose economy thrived during the '20s. Some community fund that invested back into the town. The place is heaven on earth."

"Except for Paulie Aandeg," I say, trying to hold back the dread his words give me. Because if Lilydale is as perfect as it seems, then the problem is me.

"Except for Paulie Aandeg," he agrees, "but that could've happened anywhere. And frankly, I'm relieved that the town isn't flawless. I'd think it was a front for a cult."

"Thanks, Benjamin," I say.

"You okay, Joan? You don't sound happy to discover you're living in paradise."

"No, I know. I'm sorry. I had a late night last night. Of course I'm thrilled Lilydale is as perfect as it seems." *On the surface.*

He chuckles. "Yeah, you really sound like it. Do yourself a favor and don't borrow trouble."

His words echo my mom's. "Got it. Stay cool, Benny."

"See you on the flip side."

I think about his research on the walk to the Purple Saucer. I decide both things can be true: Lilydale can be a haven for many and still be threatening to me.

Except hasn't it treated me well, mostly?

I think of Ursula, telling me I must stop telling stories.

The tales need to go out, not in.

I reach the motel. The car with Florida plates is gone. I knock on the door of unit 6. No answer. When I go to the front desk, I'm relieved to see Mr. Scholl isn't working. The young clerk tells me to check down by the Crow River. He points me in the general direction, suggests a route.

Reluctantly, I head out. I wanted to get this over with quickly.

But the day is pretty, the town buzzing (for Lilydale) with people doing their business—disappearing into the barbershop or grocery store, buying fabric, visiting the library. For a moment, I worry that I'll miss this quaintness when Deck and I move, but then I walk down another street and find the sidewalks deserted. The sudden emptiness is unsettling. In a few more blocks, the town has dwindled, the only visible structure a large, squat building that resembles an abandoned factory. According to what the clerk told me, the Crow River is another two hundred feet behind that.

That's where I find Kris sitting on a fallen tree.

The river flows silver and placid in front of him, the land around so forested that it feels like we're in an unspoiled wilderness rather than six blocks from the edge of town.

"Hey," I call. I don't want to startle him.

He doesn't respond, so I say it louder. "Kris!"

"Yeah," he says. "I heard you."

I step closer, wading through the tall vegetation. "Mind if I join you?"

"It's a free log."

I drop down beside him. He's wearing the same jeans and India print shirt as the night before, his face more lined in the bright sunlight than I'd noticed.

"Don't suppose you have that Siesta Key postcard on you?" I ask.

He yanks it from his back pocket. I take it, running my fingers along the weathered edges. "Are you okay? Were you hurt last night?"

"You mean when I was kicked out of your house? I've been treated worse."

I hand the postcard back to him. "Why were you flirting with me?"

"Would you believe it's because you're cute?" He runs his fingers through his hair. I can see the start of a smile in the lines around his eyes.

"No," I say. But I like the warmth between us. I like *everything* now that I know Deck and I are leaving Lilydale. I was fine in Minneapolis, just fine. It's small towns that are the problem, just like my mom said.

He chuckles. "Maybe it's that I like to live dangerously, then."

I want to ask him what that means, but I spot a flash of metal across the water. A wristwatch catching the sun?

I stand, putting distance between Kris and me. Am I being watched again? My pulse is jittering unpleasantly. "I want to talk more about your time here. When you were Paulie."

He's staring across the river at the same spot. "I've told you everything I remember."

"All the same," I say, "I have a few more questions for you. For later." *When we're in public, with witnesses. When I won't get in trouble.*

"Then I guess I'll catch you on the flip side," he says.

Same way Benjamin signed off only an hour ago.

I back away. The flash has not repeated.

I make my way to the library. I'm jittery, as if my behavior will decide whether Deck and I get to leave. Nobody seems to be openly staring at me today, though. I want to keep it that way. The inside of the library is approximately the size of a postage stamp. The only person inside is the librarian, who informs me that if I want to research the Aandeg case, the newspaper office houses the only records.

I'm not surprised.

I make my way to the *Gazette*. Dennis is out. When I ask his wife to see the archives, she tells me they're still not accessible.

"But you said they'd be fixed."

She shrugs. *Guess I was wrong.* "What'd you want to look up?"

I don't feel like tipping my hand (my hand that consists of one dinky card: the Paulie Aandeg story), so I keep it neutral, even though I'm growing frustrated at how impossible it is to get any new information about this case. "When I saw Dr. Krause, he mentioned that there was a Minnesota Health Department survey coming through. I thought maybe I would see if there was any history of them visiting here before."

She claps her hands. "That sounds like a wonderful article!"

Is she a little too excited that I appear to be laying off the Paulie story?

It doesn't matter. I'm getting out of Lilydale either way.

I come to this time with a yell.

It's fury (*the Furies*) fighting on my side, finally, and it raises me up, off the bathroom floor, my legs trembling only slightly this time. I hardly even need to lean on the sink. Once upright, I slowly, delicately make my way from the bathroom into the lemon-walled bedroom. Oh yes, I recognize this room.

Finally, I remember where I am.

The Furies redouble.

I cock my ear. It's early evening now. I hear them outside, know what they're doing. I smell the meat they're roasting, hear the brittle bubbles of their laughter popping in the humid night air and releasing blurts of joy.

They're demons.

But I know exactly what to do.

Have been planning for this.

I gingerly, haltingly return to the bathroom, remove my bloody, crusty clothes, and step into the shower. The water runs red, and then pink, and then clear. I express milk from both breasts, the relief exquisite. I towel off, and below the sink, I locate thick belted pads for my underpants and thinner ones for my brassiere.

In the top drawer of the oak dresser, I discover loose, clean clothes. The basic comfort of standing, of cleaning and clothing my body, of having fresh pads to soak up my blood, is so overwhelming it nearly brings me to tears.

But there isn't time.

Clarity is returning by the second. I remember the bottle of Geritol and the strawberry Pop-Tarts I hid in the rear of the closet, inside a musty box of children's clothes. I rip the tinfoil and eat two so fast I hardly taste them. Screwing off the Geritol cap, I take two deep swallows. The salty, slimy metallic taste almost brings the Pop-Tarts back up, but I force my gut to accept it. I need the iron to make it through what I must do.

The next package of Pop-Tarts I take to the bathroom, where I chew slowly, drinking water from the faucet between bites, reveling in the returning focus.

Because it's not just the Geritol and Pop-Tarts I've hidden.

A smile (*maybe a grimace, maybe the mask of war*) stretches across my face.

I have prepared for this.

They are going to pay.

I am Joan Harken. I will take back my baby.

CHAPTER 40

Knowing that I'll be moving back to Minneapolis soon has me antsy. I can't talk to Kris at the moment, not if someone is spying on us. It might jeopardize my escape. Regina doesn't know anything about what happened in Lilydale in 1944. The microfiche machine is down. No one on Mill Street will tell me the truth. The two classmates who might have seen something, Quill Brody and Aramis Bauer, are out of my range of contact.

I walk, mulling things over. No way can I wander into businesses and start asking the workers if they remember Paulie or Virginia Aandeg. When I think about my goodwill mission here just a week ago, I'm embarrassed at my naivete. I thought I was making friends. More likely, I was creating informants.

I'm glad I stole the pineapple brooch. And the locket full of Lily dirt that thank god I never opened.

I can't go door to door, either, knocking, asking people what they know.

What does that leave?

I find myself in front of Dr. Krause's. He isn't originally from around here and so wouldn't be a help even if he were the obliging sort, but I spot my answer across the street: the Lilydale Nursing Home. Surely someone inside remembers Virginia and Paulie Aandeg.

I walk in like I know what I'm here for. I ignore the unsettling, overpowering smell of antiseptic and stride to the front desk. I assume my mildest expression.

"Hello, how are you?" I ask.

The older woman behind the desk glances up, her eyes narrowing. She's nondescript. Brown hair under a nurse's bonnet, brown eyes, crisp white uniform. "I'm good, Mrs. Schmidt. What can I do for you?"

The familiar chill settles in my bones. Everyone in Lilydale knows me. Small-town insanity. Well, I will use it to my advantage. "I'm good, thank you. You know I'm writing the article on Paulie?"

The woman leans forward conspiratorially. "We all do. How exciting! The boy has come home."

"So it would appear," I say. "There aren't any residents here who would have known him before he was abducted, are there? Maybe a neighbor or friend? He doesn't remember much of anything from back then, and I'm trying to flesh out my story."

The woman taps her chin with a pen. "I think I can do you better than that. We have Rosamund Grant here with us. She used to watch the neighborhood children back in the day. The poor kids, anyhow. They didn't call them babysitters back then, but I suppose that's what she was. Maybe she watched Paulie, too?"

I try to keep the excitement off my face. This might be the first uncensored, unbiased lead I've had. "I'd love to speak with her. I promise not to say anything upsetting."

The woman snorts. "You don't need to worry your pretty head about that. Mrs. Grant is an old battle-ax. She was mean back then, and she's even crabbier now. I'd be more concerned about you."

❖

"Yes, Paulie had one just like that. Remember it as plain as the back of my hand. So unusual."

I let my short sleeve drop. "Did any other kids you took care of have a similar scar?"

"Well, I suppose your beau, Deck," she says.

I blink rapidly. "Did you used to watch him, too?"

She cackles. She's the oldest woman I've ever spoken to, her back a hump that rises higher than her head as she sits bent nearly double in her wheelchair. Her eyes are bright, though. "That family would sooner die than let me within an inch of their child. Same with all of those Mill Street snoots. But I assisted Dr. Krause when the vaccinations were given. Not a nurse, exactly. Just a helper. I also cleaned the wounds when they got infected."

"Wait," I say, my heart pounding. Something is drifting into place, something important, but I'm too close to see it. "Dr. Krause from across the street administered the vaccinations to Paulie and the other kids?"

"None other."

Skittering apprehension tickles my skin. "So he'd know that Deck had the scar like me and Paulie?"

"Decades ago, I suppose he knew it. No telling if he'd remember. Not everyone has a brain built like mine." She taps her scalp, visible beneath thin wisps of white hair.

I didn't bring a notebook. "Is it correct that none of Paulie's family is still around?"

She squints. "It was just Virginia and Paulie, which means no Aandegs in town since 1944. I don't blame that poor Virginia for leaving. It wasn't her choice to get pregnant, and then her boy is snatched from her."

My mouth drops open. "Virginia Aandeg was raped?"

Her eyes dart up, drilling into mine. "That's not what we called it back then."

I'm reeling. "Who raped her?"

Her face grows cagey. "I only know rumors."

"What do the rumors say?"

"They say Stanley Lily visited many women back in the '40s, whether they wanted him to or not." She twists a gold ring on her knotted finger.

Sad Stanley. My brain sparks and spits. *Sadistic, Sinister Stanley.*

"Not just poor ladies, like Virginia. Rich ladies. Rich like Barbara Schmidt."

I gasp and jump to my feet.

She cackles. "Maybe your Deck and Paulie Aandeg are half brothers?"

My jaw opens and closes before I find the words. "It can't be. Deck looks exactly like his father."

"Does he?" she asks, her grin evil.

Yes, of course he does. "Deck is Ronald's son."

She shrugs again. "I may have mixed up names. It was so long ago, and all those Mill Street men liked to plant their seeds far and wide back then. Plant a seed, harvest it, plant a seed, harvest it."

She's singing, her eyes growing rheumy. I grab her arm desperately, unwilling to get off topic. "Do you know who took Paulie?"

Her smile creases her face. "If you see pretty trinkets, don't you take them?"

This woman is old, I remind myself. Her memories are all jumbled. She doesn't know what she's saying. I must stick to facts. "Mrs. Grant, do you remember where the Aandeg house was? Before it burned down?"

"South side," she says, quick and sharp as a paring knife. "A little Baptist church stands where it used to be. The church has been empty for a few years. Guess religion couldn't find root in that cursed soil." She cackles again.

"Cursed how?" I ask through tight lips.

"Why don't you ask the ghost next door?"

My breath freezes. "Excuse me?"

"You're living next door to Johann and Minna Lily's original home, didn't you know? Oh, the house has been rebuilt for Stanley and Mrs. Lily, but the underground is the same. The well out back, too, though you may have to dig a bit to find that."

Suddenly, I am no longer tethered to my own body. My eyes are sticky, but I can't seem to blink, my chest tight but I can't draw a breath. We're sitting at a card table in the communal room. A nurse appears and tells Mrs. Grant it's time for her medication. The nearby residents are watching us.

"You've been very helpful," I tell Mrs. Grant, forcing my mouth to shape the words. "I won't keep you any longer."

Her eyes grow crafty. "You shouldn't be working, you know."

I feel an increasing pressure at my throat. "Excuse me?"

"Not when you're pregnant like that. Your father-in-law won't like it. And here's one final piece of advice, and this one's free: whatever you do, don't wander into the basement."

The spit in my mouth turns to paste. Does she mean the nursing home basement, the one below the Lily house, or my own dirt base-ment, the one I've refused to enter?

Before I can ask, she leans forward, a shadow falling across her ax of a nose. "I'll give you one hundred dollars for that baby."

Her cackling hooks my skin as I stumble out of the nursing home.

CHAPTER 41

Have I underestimated the power of this town, been overconfident in my ability to bust free? If Stanley is a serial rapist—and Paulie Aandeg's father—and the Mill Street families are covering for him, how far would they go? Would they have murdered Virginia Aandeg after they'd shuttled Paulie—the only evidence of Stanley's crime—out of town, destroying any chance of her turning in her rapist? And if so, if he's really Paulie, how much danger is Kris Jefferson—walking proof of the bloodline—in?

Or is Rosamund Grant simply a crazy old lady, stirring up a kettle of trouble?

I'm hurrying toward my house, walking as fast as I can without exploding into a run, struggling not to shatter as I go. I don't look around. I certainly do not want to talk to anyone. So when the shape separates from the tree and glides toward me, I turn my face away.

"Joan."

I recognize the voice. I don't want to slow, but I must. "Ronald."

He ambles up to me. If someone is watching, they'll witness a charming scene: a middle-aged man and the mother of his grandchild taking a stroll. I confirm that Ronald and Deck are nearly identical, twins separated by age but not appearance. I should never have let Mrs. Grant worm her doubt into my mind.

"Visiting someone at the nursing home?" he asks.

"Yes." I'm brittle. "How about you?"

"I was on my way to speak with you. I just received very disturbing news."

My hand instinctively tracks to my belly, to the curve that is visible no matter how shapeless my clothes. *Be still, Beautiful Baby. I am here. I will protect you.* Has Deck told his father we're moving? He wouldn't.

"I'm sorry to hear that," I say. I want that to end the conversation. I turn to walk home alone, but Ronald doesn't let me. He stays at my side.

"It's about your mugger."

This stops me in my tracks. Ronald might know about the day I got Slow Henry, if Deck told him against my wishes. That's all Ronald could mean, because the only person who knows that I thought I spotted my mugger in Lilydale is Regina, who promised she'd carry my secret to the grave.

I hold myself still. "What about him?"

"I heard you think you saw him. Here in town."

I blink rapidly, too shocked to respond. *Regina.* But she wouldn't have told, at least not told Ronald. There must be another explanation.

Ronald continues. "He followed you here, Joan. We don't know why. We want to help you, though."

I speak through clenched teeth. "Who is 'we,' and who told you I saw him?"

Ronald holds up his hands. "You mentioned at dinner last week that you saw a man get hit by a car. Amory told me the gentleman was fine, but when Dennis followed up by calling the Saint Cloud hospital, he was told the fellow had taken a turn for the worse."

"You said he didn't die. When you were at my house for dinner. You said he was alive."

Ronald shrugs. "Internal injuries."

I swallow past the horror of learning the man is dead. "What does any of that have to do with the mugger?"

Ronald sighs deeply. "You seemed upset by the accident, far more upset than would be expected. Deck was worried about you. Thought maybe you knew the man. So, he and I drove to the hospital, looked at the body. Joan, the man who you saw get hit by a car perfectly matches the description of your mugger."

"You're wrong."

Ronald scowls but keeps walking. "How's that?"

"I didn't see anybody get *hit* by a car. I saw a car run up the curb, then I saw a man on the road. *Deck* never saw my mugger. Yet he identified a corpse in the morgue as the man who mugged me?"

Ronald cuts to the side, stepping away while keeping pace. When he turns back to me, he's a different person. His kind, grandfatherly presence has been replaced by a dreadful storm of a man, his words dripping with condescension, his lip curled in a snarl.

"You know," he says, "the Fathers and Mothers kept this town out of poverty even during the Great Depression. What we do is provide leadership. That takes balance. It's about doing what's the best for the majority. Most people want to live life on the surface." His gravelly voice drops even lower. "Very few want to go to the deep dark below. The Fathers and Mothers roll up our sleeves and dive down there, managing the townsfolk's nasty business. Protect them like the children they are. 'Honor thy father and thy mother, that long lived upon the land which the Lord thy God will give thee.' I hope you can learn to respect our authority."

He glances at my stomach. "And I hope you're well enough to care for your child. Deck has mentioned some troubling things. I'd hate to see your firstborn taken away because you're unfit."

I'm stunned. Immobile. A pregnant springbok with nowhere to hide.

He leans toward my ear, his breath hot on my neck. "But if that's the case, you can trust that the Mill Street families will raise him as if he's our own."

He strolls away, hands in his pockets, whistling a merry tune.

I watch Ronald go, panic crawling across my flesh because after our conversation, I now know two things for sure: I really did see my mugger in Lilydale, and now he's dead.

And only one screw can possibly hold those two pieces together.

My mugger was from Lilydale all along, and he's been murdered for the mistake of letting me spot him here, in his hometown.

CHAPTER 42

I let Saturday, June 1, come and go.

I know it's the monthly initiation ceremony for the Fathers and Mothers. I garden. I clean. When the phone rings and Deck answers, and I hear him tell somebody that I'm not home, I don't ask any questions.

When later that day, Deck drops to his knee and proposes with his grandmother's sapphire ring, I say yes. I will say yes to everything and no to nothing. I know now, after walking with Ronald, that it's no longer about staying to finish the investigative story so I can land a reporting job in Minneapolis.

It's about survival.

Paulie probably is Stanley's child. A child of rape, a Lily, and despite their best efforts to get rid of him, he's back in town. The Mill Street families are dark and dangerous, and they want my baby, too. Or, more accurately, they want Deck's baby. To escape with my child, I must be smarter than smart.

The leopard, not the springbok.

When Sunday rolls around and Deck asks if I still want to attend church, I behave as if he's offered me the moon. I even make chocolate-marshmallow bars for the fellowship meal after the service.

The Catholic sermon is rule bound and oddly violent with threats of harsh punishments and notions of an unforgiving God. I act as if

Jesus is speaking directly to me the entire time. I let the engagement ring glitter on my finger and catch the light to distract myself.

It's beautiful.

I will keep it, once I escape. I want Deck to go with me, but if he takes much longer, I will leave without him. Protecting my baby is all that matters.

We're seated in the front pews with the other Mill Street families. All of them Fathers and Mothers. The Schramels and the Bauers, the Lilys and the Schmidts. Do the women look happy?

I study them as they watch the priest.

They appear purposeful. Like they have a place in this world. It's different from how the people in the rear of the church look. It's not just because those people have darker skin, are migrant workers judging by their dress and rough hands. It's that the people in the back seem like they cannot quite relax. Not like the Mill Street families can.

When I twist my head, I spot Angel Gomez, the beautiful child I first noticed at the school musical, with his family. He's still impossibly lovely, with his dark curls and deep-brown eyes. His mother and sister are doting on him, bribing him with a cherry-colored lollipop to keep him quiet.

I catch the mother's eye and smile. She smiles back.

My sight is pulled to the right by the vision of Clan Brody arriving late to church, Catherine at his side. It takes all my will to not gasp out loud. His face is covered in green and yellow bruises, his eyes swollen nearly shut. Deck must feel me go rigid.

He glances in the direction I'm staring, then leans over to whisper in my ear. "Heard he was so drunk when he left our place the other night that he fell down his own stairs."

Deck laughs.

I stroke my neck, wondering what Clan has done to displease the others. The net is closing in.

CHAPTER 43

Deck wants to meet with the Fathers after the fellowship gathering.

"Are you going to tell them about our move?" I don't want to bother him, am afraid it will cost me, but I can't stop the question from spilling out. I need to know what he's planning, at least as much as he'll tell me.

He kisses my forehead. "Everything I do from this day forward is about making the move smooth."

I lean into him. "Do you need me to stay?"

"It's probably better if you don't."

I pull back, studying him. "Why not?"

"You look tired," he says, brushing my cheek. "That's all."

That's how I find myself walking home alone and noticing for the first time that I'm moving like a woman who's expecting. I am five and a half months pregnant.

There is no longer any outfit that can hide my condition.

I'm tempted to jog. To see if it's still possible. To see how fast I can move.

A car pulls up, driving slow enough to roll alongside me. I look over. Kris is behind the wheel of the blue Chevy Impala with Florida plates, the same one I spotted outside unit 6 of the Purple Saucer. It's a nice car, or at least it was. A rear panel has been replaced with a sheet of black metal, and rust rims the wheel wells.

"Need a ride?" he asks. He's wearing a soft-looking tie-dyed shirt, its blues and greens and purples faded by age and sun. His curling hair and impish smile are as attractive as ever, but the lust I felt for him is no longer there.

I lean in, looking for evidence of Stanley Lily in his features and build. It's impossible to say, as eroded as Stanley is. I glance around to see who's watching us before opening the passenger door and sliding in. "Thanks. Remember where I live?"

"You want to go straight home?"

"It's closer than Siesta Key." I shouldn't be in this car. Eyes are always watching me.

He laughs. "True enough."

He drops a relaxed hand on my shoulder. "You won't believe Siesta Key once you get there. It's beautiful. If it was a different life, I'd drive there right this second, just take off."

"With me?"

Smile lines bloom beyond the edges of his sunglasses. "If you like."

He starts driving. I don't have a plan. I don't even really have interview questions. It just feels good to be with him. The attention. The freedom.

"Take a right here," I find myself saying. Mrs. Grant didn't exactly pinpoint where Paulie's home had been. Lilydale isn't that large, though, and there can't be an abundance of abandoned Baptist churches around.

The Sunday traffic is slow on this warm, bright day. We cruise through the sleepy neighborhoods I'm familiar with, then toward the edges of town, where the houses are mismatched and in need of paint, kids and dogs playing in the yards. The south side of town looks like a whole different realm from Mill Street.

We locate the church in under fifteen minutes. "Pull in here," I say.

Kris does. "This place should be condemned."

He's right. The single-story square of a church was charming in the not-too-distant past, judging by the prim, smug-looking white paint protecting its exterior. But now, "Nixon for President" posters are choking the entrance (Ursula would feel vindicated), and red paint has been poured across the front stairs. The glass is busted out of the windows, and the bushes are overgrown, the grass a wrestling tangle of weeds.

"Seems like it could be a nice area," I say. "If it was kept up better."

Kris throws a cursory glance around the landscape. Most every house here looks abandoned; black licks at the windows of many, suggesting they've had a fire; and the block is oddly quiet. It's a ghost town on the edge of Lilydale.

"If you say so."

I'm watching him. "Any of this look familiar?"

He glances around again. "Nah."

"This church used to be where Paulie's house was."

His expression doesn't change, but his hands grip the steering wheel tighter. "I don't remember it."

I feel sad. It's not that I expected him to recognize his childhood neighborhood, but . . . he doesn't seem to know anything about Lilydale or the life that Paulie lived here, hasn't since I've met him. Regina told me to trust my gut, and it's telling me that Kris is not Paulie.

Because Deck is.

CHAPTER 44

I immediately dismiss the ridiculous idea. Ronald and Barbara couldn't possibly have suddenly introduced a new child, not with the attention Paulie's disappearance got. The whole town would have had to be in on something like that. Of course, Deck being Paulie would explain why they wanted my baby in Lilydale so bad. If Virginia Aandeg was raped, Deck's irrefutable resemblance to his father means she was raped by Ronald Schmidt, not Sad Stanley.

And my baby—Deck's baby—would be blood evidence of this crime.

I start laughing.

"What is it?" Kris asked.

I become very aware that I'm in a car with a stranger, on the edge of town, and I haven't told anybody where I've gone. Maybe I *should* be watched at all times. The laughter doubles until I can't breathe and tears are streaming out of my eyes. Kris watches my hysteria grow, but he lets it happen, driving steadily until I'm wrung dry.

"I'm sorry," I say, wiping my face. The emptiness feels good.

"No problemo," he says.

I don't think Deck is Paulie, not really, but I no longer think Kris is the real Paulie Aandeg, either. He knows nothing about Paulie's life, nothing that you couldn't find in the paper other than the smallpox scar, and for all I know, that detail was included in an article in a different newspaper. I want to ask him why he's impersonating the abducted child, but instead I say, "That's okay that you don't remember that house." I paraphrase what he told me when we first met at Tuck's Cafe. "I heard that a big shock can wipe out memory."

I rub my hands across my face and through my hair, still not used to the short length. I'm exhausted. "Please, just take me home."

He turns the car around. We say little on the drive, exchange cursory goodbyes after he pulls up to my house. Once inside, I swallow a Valium and lie down with Slow Henry. I might have slept the afternoon away if Deck hadn't appeared, shaking me gently.

"Joan! Wake up."

It takes a while to dig my way out of the dream. It had featured a boy in a sailor suit, leading me to a river. I'm disoriented, unsure where I am at first.

I focus on Deck. "What is it?"

His expression is twisted, an ugly mix of scared and something I can't identify. "Another boy's been taken."

My hand flies to my mouth. "Who?"

"A boy from church."

I repeat the question, even though, with gruesome certainty, I know the answer. "Who?"

"You wouldn't know him. Angel Gomez. He's not even in kindergarten yet. He was playing outside his house with his brother. His brother went inside for a glass of water, and when he came out, Angel was gone. The whole town is joining together to look for him."

I leap to my feet as well as I can, my expanding belly throwing off my balance.

That's Angel, Miss Colivan is saying. *A boy shouldn't be that pretty. He'll get snatched right up.*

"You shouldn't go," Deck says, his hands on my shoulders to hold me back.

"I'm going," I say, quivering. "I want to help."

As I grab my cardigan, I realize what the second emotion on Deck's face was: naked anticipation.

CHAPTER 45

Hundreds turn out to search the woods behind the Gomez house. I'm grouped with the Mill Street regulars. They have guns. I don't know why.

I can't shake the sensation that I'm part of an elaborate stage production.

The Fathers are leading the search. Ronald is barking orders. We're all given a section to scour, holding hands so there's no possibility a child could slip through. The foliage is thick, the jungle undergrowth making it difficult to forge through some areas. I struggle to keep my balance, my lower center of gravity throwing me off.

There is a thrum of excitement flowing through the Mill Street Fathers and Mothers—I don't know how else to explain it. They're out looking for this missing boy, which is the right thing to do.

But their mood feels oddly celebratory.

Me, I can't shake the feeling that Angel could be my own child. Lost. Alone and crying for his mother. Mildred is holding my hand on one side, Dorothy on the other, as we've been instructed to do. Their embrace feels sticky. I don't want them touching me but can't think of how to say that, how to live with releasing their hands and possibly walking past Angel without knowing it.

"I am sure he's back here somewhere," Mildred says, smiling encouragingly at me. She seems the most animated of them all, almost competitive in her desire to locate the boy. "Or maybe he's already home."

"That's such a kind thing to say," Dorothy says. "If we don't find the unfortunate child, it won't be for lack of trying."

A root grabs my foot and brings me to my knees.

Dorothy kneels to help me up. "However this goes, at least we'll have your baby," she says quietly, too quiet for the nearby searchers to hear.

Over my dead body, I think, brushing myself off as I stand without her help.

CHAPTER 46

Come Monday, Angel still hasn't been found.

I cannot be the only person in town who didn't sleep last night. Out there somewhere, a child is alone and missing his mother. He could be hurt. He could be imprisoned by the worst sort of evil.

Before Deck left for work, he tried to calm me down. Said the police were the only hope.

The same police—at least one of them, Amory Bauer—who let Paulie Aandeg disappear.

That isn't good enough for me.

Because of yesterday's search, I know exactly where Angel's home is, on the south edge of town, the poor part. Deck has the car. The walk takes me an hour.

The house appears empty when I approach, but Angel's mother pulls the door open before I knock. I learned from Barbara that her name is Mariela, and she's unmarried. She's aged a decade since I last saw her, her skin faded gray, her eyes muggy. She is heartbreak come to life.

"Any news?" she demands.

I don't know if she recognizes me from church, or the search, or will simply ask this of anyone who shows up at her door for the rest of her life.

"I'm sorry. No. Can I come in?"

She hesitates but steps aside.

The interior of her house is small and tidy. She's burning a Virgin Mary candle below a picture of Jesus on the cross. The table beneath the candle is strewn with plastic beads and dried roses. She leads me to the dining room table and indicates I should take a chair.

I pull out my notepad. "Do you mind if I take notes?"

"What for?" She hasn't sat down.

"I'm a reporter for the *Lilydale Gazette*. I'm hoping I can write a story on Angel's disappearance, bring some attention to it."

"You're one of them."

"Excuse me?"

She shifts to stare out the back window, toward the woods I searched with a hundred other people yesterday afternoon. "You're one of the Mothers."

I can hear her capitalization of the word. "I am *a* mother." I point to my protruding belly. "I have not joined the Mothers."

"Still." She's still looking away from me. "You're one of them."

"What do you mean?"

"I didn't ask for this. I paid the price, the Lilydale price. That should have been enough."

My blood turns to sand. "The Lilydale price?"

She's still facing outside. "I think you should go."

"I can help."

"They will take your child, too," she says, turning finally. Her face is shadowed. "If they want."

Her words lash me. "Who?"

She steps toward the door and opens it. "I'm sorry. I should not have let you in."

I stand. I notice two wide-eyed children watching us from the kitchen. They are still. Scared. I don't want to make this worse.

I pause at the doorway. "Can you tell me if Angel has a scar like this?" I lift my sleeve. She studies the figure eight but doesn't so much as blink.

"No. He doesn't."

She closes the door gently in my face.

❖

"Benjamin?"

"Who is this?"

My stomach twists with anxiety. I'm wagering so much on this call. I called the *Star* and was patched through to the photography department, just like before. "It's me again. Joan Harken."

"Joan! We must have a bad connection. I can hardly hear you. Can you switch to another line?"

I can't tell him that I'm at a phone booth because I'm too scared to call from my own house. "I'll just talk louder. I need another favor. Some more research."

He pauses. For a horrible second, I think he's going to turn me down. Finally: "What is it?"

"Do you have pen and paper?"

I hear a rustling on the other end.

"Got it."

"A second child has gone missing from Lilydale. A boy named Angel Gomez."

A whoosh of breath. "Oh, damn. Those are the worst stories. I'm sorry, Joan."

"Yeah, me too. Lilydale isn't such a paradise now, is it?" I can't tell him I think they're connected, that I think I know what the "Lilydale price" is, the cost of staying in this protected bubble where no one goes hungry, all have medical care, there are no homeless: it's not speaking up when the men of Mill Street come for you, or later, when they decide to dispose of the evidence of their attack.

It all makes sense, the morbid glee in the Mill Street families when they "searched" for Angel, Angel's mother's strange comments, Rosamund Grant's cackling words. *Plant a seed, harvest it, plant a seed, harvest it.*

I think not only is Kris not Paulie Aandeg but that Paulie Aandeg has been dead since 1944, and his mom, too. The same is probably true of Angel Gomez, though I can't bear to think it.

I can't say any of this, not until I can prove it. If the Mill Street families got word of my suspicions, they'd have me institutionalized in a heartbeat and take my child. Ronald very nearly promised it.

I make up a lie that will get me the same information I'm after. "I think the danger's not over," I say. "I think there might be a copycat kidnapper here."

Benjamin's whistle pierces the line. "No shit."

"None." I beg him to dig deeper, find out if there were any less-publicized child disappearances from this area, any other fires that got only a passing mention. "While you're in the archives, can you look up any investigations into a Ronald Schmidt or Stanley Lily of Lilydale? Something you might have missed in a general Lilydale search?"

I hold my breath. He could hang up, and then I'll have nothing.

"Joan?"

"Yeah?"

"What the hell have you gotten yourself into?"

"Will you help me, Benjamin?"

"Yeah. But you owe me a beer next time you're in town. Make that a whole case of beer. And you have to drink it with me. I don't care how pregnant you are."

I wipe my nose with the back of my hand. I hadn't noticed the tears rolling down my cheeks. "Wild horses couldn't keep me from paying that debt."

CHAPTER 47

Benjamin will get me the information when he gets me the information.

If he gets me the information.

All that I can do now is wait. Deck insists he needs the car, so the next day, I repeat the one-hour walk to the Gomez house. This time no one answers, even though I see a curtain fall inside the house when I knock. Unable to sit at home, helpless, I travel house to house asking the questions I was trained to ask.

Who. What. When. Where.

No one has seen anything unusual. The Gomez family is large, but they keep to themselves and don't cause trouble. Mrs. Gomez cleans houses. She receives food stamps, that's what her neighbor tells me with disdain, but I suspect it's because he believes I'd look poorly on such a practice.

You're one of them, Mrs. Gomez had said.

The only hint of something troubling I get is three blocks down. The house is the same size as the rest in this part of town, but it's neater, the trim a crisp black, the paint white. The lawn is mowed. The crew-cut man who answers the door stares down at me, and something about him chills me to my core.

"Hello," I say.

He doesn't reply.

"I'm Joan Harken, reporter for the *Lilydale Gazette*. I'm doing an article about the missing boy. Angel Gomez? I was hoping I could ask you a few questions."

The man steps aside. I gulp. There's a young man teetering immediately behind him, a lantern-jawed teenager. His eyes are vacant. He's just been standing there, like a piece of furniture.

"Come in," the man says.

"That's all right," I stammer, my heartbeat clattering in my chest. "I have a lot of houses to stop by. Can I ask you if you saw or heard anything that would be helpful?"

"No, but you can ask my stepson." The man turns to the dead-eyed teen. "Gary? Have you seen anything?"

"Un-unh," the stepson says.

"Thank you," I say, stumbling backward off the steps. He should be in Vietnam, the young man, but he doesn't look like he's right in the head. Maybe that's why he hasn't been drafted? I note the name on the mailbox.

Godlin.

There's something terribly wrong with that family. Is it enough to report to the police? I finish canvassing the neighborhood. Nobody else has offered anything of use. One moment Angel was there, and the next he was gone.

The Lilydale Police Department adds a half an hour to my walk, but I need to be thorough. I'm surprised to find Amory Bauer inside. I don't know why. I assumed he would be in the field, somehow. He's not pleased to see me.

"Hello, Mr. Bauer," I say, unsure of his title at work. His uniform impossibly adds size to his already large body.

His silver-streaked hair is immaculate, his blue eyes shocks of color beneath the sagging fat of his face. "What are you doing here?"

I hold up my notepad. "I'm writing an article on the missing boy. Angel Gomez. Have you uncovered any leads?"

"Have you?" he asks.

He means to belittle me. I play submissive. "I interviewed everyone in a five-block radius, everyone who was home. No one knows anything, but I did meet a strange man and his stepson. The Godlins?"

Amory is suddenly standing in front of me, hands gripping my upper arms too tightly. I'm caught off guard that a man his size can move that fast, but I shouldn't be. He demonstrated his agility the night he kicked Kris out of my house. "You want to avoid the Godlins. The stepdad doesn't do right by that boy. They're trouble."

I struggle to keep my voice even. "You think they had something to do with Angel disappearing?"

"Not that kind of trouble."

I twist out of his grip. "So no news on Angel, none at all?"

The phone rings behind Amory, and he turns away.

"None," he says, hand on the ringing phone. "I'll let your husband know if I hear anything. Makes sense you'd be worried about a little boy with your own baby on the way. We'll find him. I promise."

Amory picks up the call.

I leave, taking my time, not ready to return home. I walk past the newspaper office. When I step inside, Mrs. Roth, who looks more like Pat Nixon than ever in her red suit and pearls, tells me that Dennis has traveled to Saint Cloud and that the archives are still down. I peek inside the Fathers and Mothers hall next door. It still looks like it's halfway unpacked. That doesn't leave much to do in Lilydale. I don't need anything from Ben Franklin or the grocery store, and I'm not hungry.

That leaves only Little John's. I suddenly realize how hot and thirsty I am, how much my back and feet hurt. Yet I've been avoiding the bar ever since Ronald cornered me outside the nursing home. While I'm now certain—*almost positive*—that my mugger was from Lilydale, there's always the distant chance that Regina ratted me out. Next time I see her, I'll have to ask about it, and then I risk losing my only friend in town.

But my feet are steering me toward the bar. Maybe it was a mix-up. What if Regina innocently let it spill? Or what if it happened exactly like Ronald said, with Deck worrying about me and going on to identify the man based on the description the night of the mugging? That's a lot to swallow, but believing it is easier than confronting Regina.

Little John's is ahead on the corner. It's late afternoon, another hour before everyone gets off work.

Anyone inside the bar is either unemployed or trouble.

The door swings open, and Kris stumbles out.

Or both.

A woman follows him. I don't recognize her, but they're so comfortable with one another that I wonder if they came to town together. She tumbles into him, laughing before kissing him passionately.

I duck into the nearest alleyway until Kris and the woman pass, weaving in the general direction of the Purple Saucer. Once they're out of sight, I have a choice. I can go home, or I can simply walk into Little John's and ask Regina straight up what, if anything, she's told Ronald.

It would be the responsible thing to do.

But I can't bring myself to step through the door. I don't think I could bear discovering I'm alone in Lilydale, as alone as I feel. Instead, I hurry toward the phone booth and dial the number to the *Star*. I'm told Benjamin is on assignment and that it's not known when he will return.

I ask to leave a message.

When that's done, there's nothing for me to do but go home and prepare Deck's supper.

CHAPTER 48

When I wake up the next morning, I see Deck's already left for work. I
don't even know what time he got in last night.

Late.

It occurs to me that I can pack a bag and hitchhike to
Minneapolis, beg Ursula to take me in, convince her of the danger
in Lilydale, that we must get the police involved. But I'm safe here as
long as I'm pregnant. This fact buys me time to help Angel, if such a
thing is still possible, to plan, to think of a way to escape this town
that guarantees they can never hurt me or my baby or force us to
move back here.

Deck hasn't remarked on my anxiety. He has been working late
nights. He's been distant. I think I saw him flirting with Miss Colivan,
the fourth-grade teacher, at church. He may not have initiated it, but
he didn't seem to mind when she laughed at something he said—he's
never been funny—and snaked her arm around his waist. It saddens
me, but it also makes planning my escape that much easier.

I jump when the phone rings.

"Hello?"

"Joan Harken, please."

"This is she." The person on the other end of the line sounds so
civilized and normal. I want to scream at them, *Save me! Get me out of
this crazy village.* "To whom am I speaking?"

"Samantha Beven. From the Minnesota Health Department. I'm returning your call."

About what? I almost say.

But then I remember. I called them a lifetime ago when I thought the world had rules and that I could write an article about blood collection and censuses.

"Thank you for calling me back," I say, thinking quickly. "I'm a reporter for the *Lilydale Gazette*. I wanted to find out more about the blood survey you're bringing to our town. What you're hoping to find."

"What we *were* hoping to find was one of the purest Germanic bloodlines in all of Minnesota. Unfortunately, Lilydale refused us access."

"They can do that?" But of course they can. They can do anything they want. And boy, would they want to avoid a blood collection, if my theory is right, if Ronald and Stanley—and probably Clan the Brody Bear, Amory Mountain, and Browline Schramel, too—have a decades-long history of raping local women, exacting the price of staying "safe" in Lilydale.

"A city council does have the right to turn away our blood research, yes."

"I understand." The phone clicks. Has she hung up on me? "Hello?"

"I'm still here."

"It sounded like you ended the call."

"I heard it, too."

I feel a dozen eyes on me, or should I say ears? But curiosity—no, terror—is pushing me to get answers. I need a logical reason why Deck, Kris, and I all have the same scar on our arms. "I have another question, and it's an odd one. You might not even be the person to ask."

"Try me."

"I have a scar on my upper left arm."

"Vaccination scar?"

"Yep, smallpox. But here's the thing. It's in the shape of a figure eight almost."

"That happens sometimes." She sounds polite but bored. "Sometimes certain bloodlines will have a similar adverse reaction to a vaccination. It's uncommon but not unheard of. Most of the time, though, it's a bad batch creating a specific reaction."

Exactly what Dr. Krause mentioned during my first visit with him.

"Could one batch be shipped to different states?"

"It's possible."

I'm about to ask my last question when something clicks into place. It wouldn't *have* to be possible. Kris said his first memory after Lilydale was in San Diego, the city I was living in when I stole the pearl necklace for my mom. Both he and I could have easily gotten vaccinated there from the same bad lot. Deck having a similar reaction to another lot four years later was just one of those things. But was it coincidence that Kris and I were living in the same city at the same time when we were kids, and now we're both in Lilydale?

"Is that it?" Her voice has gone from bored to annoyed.

"One more thing." I'm thinking about the locket taped to the back of my toilet, the one containing ancestral dirt. "You mentioned the German bloodline here in Lilydale. Do you know anything about Johann and Minna Lily?"

I hear her exhale through her nose. "Nothing other than that they're Lilydale's founders and that Lilydale is the state's epicenter of German immigration. They really kept the marriages insular there. One of the shallowest gene pools in the country. The Stearns County Historical Society could tell you more. Are you familiar with them? They meet in Saint Cloud. I'm an honorary member but have never attended a meeting."

I reach for the paper and pen next to the phone. "Do you have their number?"

❖

I'm tempted to leave the house and walk to the phone booth to call the historical society. If I do that, though, I'm admitting that I think my phone is tapped, and that seems like a straight train to Crazy Town.

Browline Schramel and Mildred the Mouse live inside a telephone, one that Browline Schramel is always tinkering with.

I shake my head to loosen the story. I dial. When a woman answers, I give her the spiel about being with the *Lilydale Gazette* and writing an article about the town.

"Oh!" she says. "Lilydale is such a lovely village. I've driven through it many times. It has the perfect small-town feel. You're so lucky that you get to live there!"

"Thank you," I say through clenched teeth. "What can you tell me about the town?"

"It was founded in 1857, but I'm sure you already knew that."

"By Michael Lily?" I'm testing her.

"No, dear, it was founded by Johann and Minna Lily. There's quite an interesting story with those two. I'm going to run to the archives right now to make sure I have it right. Do you have a moment?"

"Yes."

I hear the click again. I tell myself it's only her setting down the phone, but my skin is crawling with tiny insects. I wait two minutes. Then three. At four, I am sure she's never coming back. I'm about to hang up when I hear another click.

"Hello?" The voice is unfamiliar.

"Hello," I say. "Where's the woman I was speaking with earlier?"

"She had to take another call. Personal business. She told me you wanted to learn about the Lily family. Is there something I can answer for you?" The chilliness in her voice is unmistakable.

"The woman I was speaking with said there's an interesting story about them. Do you know what that was?"

"Other than the fact that they came to a land they didn't know and founded one of the most stable, kindest communities in Minnesota? I think that's incredibly interesting."

"Yes," I say, the earth opening beneath me, swallowing me whole. They've gotten to the other woman, the first one I was speaking with. Their reach is wide. How wide? "I agree. It's a wonderful town. Thank you for your time."

"Will that be all?"

"Yes. Thank you again." I hang up. I sit at my typewriter and begin slamming the keys. I don't even pretend it will be an article anymore. I just want to see the black words on white paper.

> Lilydale, Minnesota, a town of 1,476 people, is ruled by a small cadre of men and women who call them-selves the Fathers and Mothers. They look so nor-mal and act so kind, these Fathers and Mothers, but they're not. They rape women and kill the children, and they want my baby. I think they brought me here to—

The phone bleats, making me shriek. I yank the paper out of the typewriter and cram it into my pocket before I answer, my heart still beating so fast it's dizzying.

"Hello?" My voice quavers. Have they seen me typing? Do they know I know?

"Joan?"

My relief is so strong that I whimper. "Benjamin. Can I call you back in five minutes?"

"Is everything all right?"

"Yeah, I just need to . . . I need to call you back."

I hang up and race out of the house, but not before I burn what I typed, letting the charred flakes of paper drift into the sink.

CHAPTER 49

Catherine meets me at the end of my walkway. It must be her shift to chaperone me.

"Joan! What a beautiful day. Are you off to see Deck? I'm bringing Clan his lunch. We can walk together."

I rub the back of my neck. It's so sensitive that it feels covered in blisters. Or eyes.

"How wonderful," I say, smiling as if my life depends on it, because it might. "I'm sure they'll be happy about us dropping by."

I pretend I can't see her watching me from the corner of her eyes.

Risk. Uncooperative.

That's what she thinks of me, what they all think of me.

But as long as I follow the rules, I—the host of a precious Mill Street baby that they wouldn't have to hide for once—will be allowed some freedom of movement. Not much, but some. Once the child is born, though, unless they believe I'm one of them, I have no doubt I'll suffer the same fate as Virginia Aandeg and the mugger who was so careless as to let me see him.

I have no intention of staying around long enough to test my theory.

I know that hatchet-faced Catherine is about to ask me about my health and then the weather—it's part of their script, to stay at the surface—so I answer before she can speak.

"I have been sleeping so well lately, despite the unrelenting heat. I've never felt better. This summer weather sure agrees with my pregnancy."

Does her smile slip?

"How lovely," she says.

We're both pretending we're normal. I'm going to pretend better, even though my chance to speak with Benjamin is slipping away. I ask her about church, fertilizing roses, and baking casseroles, anything to keep her from asking me questions. And when we're only a block from Schmidt Insurance, I act as if I've just realized something.

"Oh my gosh! I didn't take out meat to thaw for supper before we left. I'm sorry, but I better run to the grocery store or Deck won't have a thing to eat tonight."

"I'll go with you," Catherine says, too quickly.

"No reason both husbands should be lonely this lunch," I say, smiling. I touch her arm. "Maybe you and Clan can join us for dinner? I can shop with the two of you in mind."

There is no misreading the anger on her tight face. "We're dining with the Schramels. Maybe another evening?"

"Maybe." We face off at the corner, neither of us wanting to be the first to walk away. I win, my brittle smile stronger than hers. I burn my eyes into her straight back until she steps into Schmidt Insurance. Then I walk quickly in the other direction and close myself in the phone booth. I retrieve Benjamin's phone number and a coin out of my purse. I drop the coin into the slot and dial.

"Joan! What took you so long? I have to go out on a job."

"Benjamin," I say, breathless. "Thank god you're still there. Tell me what you found."

"Okay, but I only have a minute. Joan, I'm worried about you. Do you have a doctor there you can talk to?"

Not Benjamin, too. The tears are instant, but I keep my voice level. "Did you find anything else?"

"I didn't uncover anything connecting Paulie and Angel, if that's what you're wondering. Could Angel just be part of a migrant family? They move their children in and out of schools."

I remember Angel's mother sobbing. "No, that's not it. You didn't find any other children missing from Lilydale over the years?"

"None. Joan—"

I cut in before he can finish. "I have one more favor. Can you find out anything suspicious about Johann and Minna Lily? They founded the town in 1857."

Benjamin's tone—slow, enunciating each word—suggests he's at the end of his rope. "Why don't you come to Minneapolis and look it up yourself?"

I've been peering across the street our entire phone conversation. Two men are staring back at me from the front window of the Fathers and Mothers building, not even bothering to hide their surveillance. "It's complicated. Please. I wouldn't ask if it wasn't important."

"Fine," he says, sighing. "I'll see what I can do. But I'm busy, so it might not be right away."

"Thanks, Benjamin. I owe you one."

"You owe me twenty. You're lucky I'm a sucker for beautiful women."

The men step back from the window, as if they know our conversation is over. I hang up. I feel a trembling, a cry coming. I think it's rising in me, but I soon realize it's fire trucks. They scream through town, racing south.

Toward Angel Gomez's house.

CHAPTER 50

I race into the *Gazette* offices, startling Dennis.

"I need your keys!" Deck won't give me ours. I know this without being told. If I allow Dennis too long to think about it or, even worse, time to seek permission from the Fathers, I won't get his, either.

I lunge at him, grasping for the key chain that he's pulling out of his front right pocket, his social conditioning moving faster than his brain. His jaw drops when I rip them away.

"I'm sorry!" I yell.

I dash out to the back door and slide into Dennis's Coronet. I start it up, slam it in reverse, and peel out of the alleyway. The fire trucks are out of sight, but I can still hear them. I speed to catch up.

Of course. Once they kill the boy, they murder the mother and burn any evidence. I must save Mariela. And her children.

The ones who are left.

Except the trucks don't stop south of town. They veer east and keep driving straight past the dark trees, pop through the skin of Lilydale and into the real world. Soon, I can smell rich black ash burning and see soot rising in the air miles ahead. I drive toward the fire, all the way to Cold Spring. A barn is blazing on the edge of town. Fire trucks from the nearest municipalities are there fighting the roaring flames.

It has nothing to do with Lilydale.

I keep driving.

I could drive forever, I think. I could motor all the way to Siesta Key and never look back. I can raise this baby on my own. I'll change my name. They'll never be able to find me.

Except women like me don't do that. We don't start new lives. And I can't leave, not if there's a chance Angel is still alive.

Saint Cloud is ten miles ahead, Lilydale twenty miles behind. I keep driving all the way to Grover Tucker's house, telling myself I'm buying time until I can figure out a plan. I find him in his lush backyard sitting in the shade, sipping lemonade.

"You got my message," he says without getting up. "I wasn't sure if your friend would pass it on."

I step closer. I want to see his face. The shade is too dark, though. "What message?"

"I called Saturday morning. Said I had news for you."

I glanced down at the sapphire on my ring finger. Saturday was the morning Deck proposed, just after the phone rang. *That bastard is their puppet.* "You heard about Angel Gomez disappearing?"

"I did, but that wasn't what I called about." He stands slowly. "Let's step into the house."

I follow him into his spotless kitchen, the light blue of the cabinets picking up the checkered pattern of the linoleum. He has lace curtains. I wonder if he was ever married.

There's a pile of papers on the counter. I recognize the picture of Kris I left with him on top. Below that is a manila folder. He hands the stack of papers to me, his face lined and sorrowful, his eyes cloudy.

"He was telling you the truth about his name. It really is Kris Jefferson. Maybe where he'd been, too. The rest is a lie. His military papers and rap sheet are in the envelope. He's two years too old to be Paulie."

My throat is sticky. "Rap sheet?"

"Nothing too dark. Lifted some cars. Wrote a few bad checks. He's a grifter and a drifter, but I don't think dangerous."

I know the answer to the question, more or less, but I ask anyway. "How'd he end up in Lilydale?"

Grover turns his hands palms up. "Who knows? He might of told you the truth of that, at least part of it. He heard about the missing boy. Had nothing better to do, so came north to see what he could make of it."

That's one possibility. There's another one, though. If the Mill Street families hired a man to mug me so I'd be scared enough to move here, is it too much of a stretch to imagine they'd also hired a drifter to distract me until I gave birth, to flirt and give me a chance to play a reporter? I lean against the counter. I hate to think of myself as so vain, so easily diverted. "Don't suppose you know who Paulie Aandeg's father was?"

Grover shakes his head. "I'm trying to track down his birth certificate, but that's turning out to be a lot more work than it should be. I have one last favor to call in, but the outcome doesn't look good."

My shoulders slump. "I'm scared."

Grover's face has been drooping, but it tightens up. I see the sheriff he must have been: commanding, smart. "It's that damn town," he says. "Is there anyone there you can trust?"

I think of Regina, and how she may have told Ronald that I'd spotted my mugger. I don't tell him about her because I can't even trust him. Lilydale has separated me from the herd and is coming in for the kill.

He reads my face. His own grows grim.

"Get out of that town," he says. "Get out of there now."

CHAPTER 51

I am going mad.

Really and truly, I am leaping out of my mind. I sense it as I drive home, grow certain of it as I return the Coronet keys to a furious Dennis, sink into it as I walk up my driveway and enter my house.

There is nowhere else to go.

Slow Henry bounces off the sofa, twines around my leg, purring.

His touch pulls me back to myself, just like it did after I was mugged.

I cradle the phone in my neck and dial Ursula's number. Her Ansafone picks up. I glance at my watch. She must be at work. When the machine prompts me to leave a message, I let it all out. To hell with her thinking I'm insane. I have to tell her.

"Ursula, it's Joan. I know you think I'm mad, but you need to listen. This is real. I must get out of Lilydale. Deck's one of them. That's not even the worst. I think they killed Paulie Aandeg. I think the men who run the town take advantage of the women and expect them to keep quiet, even when the women get pregnant. And now, they've stolen another child. Do you hear that Ursula? They steal kids!"

I am yelling so loud I almost don't hear the click.

But I do. My flesh melts into my bones, and I groan.

"Ursula," I croak, not caring that I sound insane, "I'm going to wait for you to call me and tell me what to do. But I need to know it's you.

When you call, tell me you know who Amelia Earhart is. Tell me you know who she is on Halloween."

I take a Valium and I crawl into bed.

❖

Someone is hammering a nail into the door.

Pound.

Pound.

Pound.

It's a very long nail. Or many nails. I don't care. I just want it to stop so I can sleep. I feel a stirring next to me. *Deck.* He's in bed. It's another night that I didn't know when he came home.

And it's not a hammer pounding.

It's somebody knocking at our front door.

I shoot out of bed so fast that I get dizzy. Ursula! She's come to save me. Maybe she's brought the police! I'm halfway down the stairs before I realize how unlikely this is. But I keep going.

I yank open the door.

Clan is standing on the other side. He has pulled on trousers but is still wearing his pajama top. His hair is disheveled. He's barefoot. It must be near dawn because I can see his face clearly in the outdoor murk.

"Get Deck. It's an emergency meeting of the Fathers and Mothers."

My blood slices at my veins. "What is it?"

"There's been a shooting," Clan says. "Don't worry. We'll keep everyone safe."

❖

Hands shaking, I call Ursula again, after Deck and Clan have left. Clan refused to tell me who shot whom, but whatever has happened tonight has gathered all the Fathers in one place. I will never be safer in Lilydale than I am right now.

She picks up on the second ring, voice groggy. "Joan?"

Relief floods my body. She's been waiting for my call. "You got my message?"

"I . . . yes. Where are you right now, Joanie?"

"At home. I mean, in Lilydale. Can I stay with you? I might be bringing danger with me. It's bad, Ursula, really—"

"Goddamn it, Joanie, stop that right now." She's angrier than I've ever heard her. "There's no conspiracy! No one is trying to steal your baby. Nobody is watching you. You need help, Joanie. Deck and I are very worried about you."

"You called Deck?" I slide to the floor, my voice etching the air.

"Don't be mad," she says firmly. "You're going bananas, Joanie. I was worried after that first call, but then Deck called me last night. After you left that cuckoo message. He told me all the insane ideas you've been having. He's worried about you, Joan. He's a good husband."

I swallow the sharp rock in my mouth. "A good *husband*."

"Yes." Her chuckle is dry. "I can't believe you didn't even tell me the two of you eloped. If nothing else proved you were going crazy, that would have done it."

And that's when I realize, finally, how powerful they are.

They have made sure I have no one to turn to.

"You're right, Ursula. Thank you for your concern."

I drop the phone and flee into the night.

CHAPTER 52

I don't get far, obviously. They would never allow that.

It's Catherine who finds me sobbing, running barefoot in my nightgown, and brings me to Dr. Krause. He administers a shot. When Deck shows up, Dr. Krause tells him that Senator Robert F. Kennedy's shooting—that's what got the Fathers out of bed—has made me hysterical. The radio playing in the doctor's office says the senator's condition is critical, and I understand he will die, and most of Lilydale will not care because we live separate from the real world here, and *boy do we.*

Dr. Krause tells Deck I cannot drive, or work, or experience any distress or I will lose the baby. He prescribes sleeping pills in addition to the Valium, enough of both to sedate an elephant.

After, Deck leads me to the car.

"Darling," he says, "what's wrong with you?"

You brought me to this town, you sorry bastard. You dropped me in this crazy stew.

"I'm sorry, Deck," I say. It sounds as if I'm speaking in another woman's voice, a soft, acquiescent woman. "Can you drive me home?"

It's a short ride from Dr. Krause's to the craftsman, white with blue shutters, home to avocado appliances and charming built-ins and my jail. Catherine, Dorothy, and Barbara are waiting. They help me into the house. Dorothy wants to tuck me into bed, but Deck says he can do it. I hear him shooing out the Mothers.

The baby kicks.

I'm so sorry, Beautiful Baby. So, so sorry.

I start weeping.

❖

Church next Sunday is lovely. That's what I make my face say if anybody looks at me, and my mouth repeat if anybody asks. The priest speaks of the promise of eternal life, offering hopes and prayers for the Kennedy clan, and then, as an afterthought almost, for the Gomez family. I bow my head and murmur the right words. I'm even wearing white gloves. I've chosen a dress that displays my belly in all its pregnant glory.

I am pure, and I know my role.

I let no one see what's inside: my escape plan, fully hatched.

When I approach Dennis after mass, he appears nervous. It's only recently that I tricked him out of his car keys, which has certainly gotten him into all kinds of hot water. He glances around the church. There are Mothers and Fathers nearby, but it doesn't matter if they're sitting on my shoulders. Every word I say is going to pass muster.

"Hello, Dennis. Such a wonderful service."

He tugs at his collar. "Yes. I'm so glad to see you well. I heard about . . . I'm so glad to see you well."

"I shouldn't have let myself get so excited. You understand. The assassination."

Senator Kennedy succumbed to his wounds twenty-six hours after he'd been shot. Deck keeps me away from the television and the radio, but when he isn't watching me, I have begun listening to the world again. It has me keening with grief. Boys dying in war. Riots. Children starving. I've neglected my responsibility as a reporter and a woman, entering the morbid snow globe that is Lilydale, cutting myself off from the tides of the world, from my duty.

"Yes, terrible news, that." Dennis is glancing around, desperate for a reason to excuse himself. I don't have much time.

"Mr. Roth, I'm worried about my health. I'm so sorry, but I think I shouldn't write articles for the paper until after I have the baby. Maybe not even until he's school-age and my days free up."

Dennis is so relieved that he encases my gloved hands in his long insectile fingers. "That's probably for the best. Don't you worry. We'll hold your job for you until you're ready."

I squeeze his hands back. "I would like to write one final article," I say, keeping my smile firm.

His face falls.

"I've so admired the gardens belonging to the Mill Street women. It would make me joyous to write an article honoring their talent." I chuckle heartily, leaning forward as if I'm about to share a delicious secret. "Who knows? With any luck, I might pick up a miracle that would help my own gardening."

His eyes tear up. I scared him, and then I offered him a gift. "I promise I'll make room for it."

"You're too kind." I perch on my tippy-toes to kiss his cheek, and he leans forward so I can reach. Afterward, when I'm about to walk away, almost as an afterthought, I say, "Do you suppose I could borrow your camera for a few days? The article would be so much better with pictures of the lovely flowers."

He's smiling so wide I fear the top of his head is going to tip off. "Stop by later. I have some work back at the shop and will be in this afternoon."

I nod and make my way to the church basement. I walk straight to the five core Mothers: Catherine the Migrant Mother, Mildred the Mouse, Birdie Rue, Saint Dorothy, and Bland Barbara. I stand next to them meekly. I can tell they're mad at me. I *have* been a lot of trouble.

I won't be anymore. Eventually, when I don't ask questions, they relax. When Mildred mentions the next crow hunt and I keep a placid smile stapled to my face, Catherine asks if I would like to help cook for it. I say yes. They're no longer asking if I want to be initiated, but being asked to help in the kitchen is the next best thing. I just need them to let down their guard.

I stay late to clean up. When Deck is waiting impatiently by the door, I tell him I'll walk home without him. He hesitates. He doesn't particularly want to stay home with boring old me. Yet he doesn't want to get in trouble, either. Letting me walk unchaperoned might be a bad decision for him.

I grip his arm softly. "Deck, I don't want anything to happen to this baby. I'll walk slow. The fresh air will do me good."

He relents.

I'm the last person besides the priest to leave. I make my way leisurely, smelling flowers along the way. When I'm halfway home, I pause as if a thought has come to me. I step into an alley, a shortcut to Wally's that passes alongside Regina's back entrance. I come out the other side whistling. Inside the grocery store, I buy eggs and milk. Enough food to show the necessity of the trip, but not enough to make anybody worry about me carrying something too heavy.

Slipping the note under Regina's door was the one risk in my whole plan.

I wrote it in a way that I'm covered, though.

If she tells on me.

She probably will. Everyone is against me.

CHAPTER 53

"Sister, I thought you were avoiding me," Regina says.

I smile stiffly. "This pregnancy. Makes it impossible to get out of the house some days."

My note asked her to meet outside the Lilydale Public Library first thing the next morning. While it doesn't offer much, it carries encyclopedias and a handful of dusty volumes on pregnancy. When we step inside and check out the shelves, I'm relieved to also discover a comprehensive collection of cookbooks.

The librarian watches me from across the room. She can observe which sections I take books from, but I retrieve so many that it's impossible to make sure what exactly I'm pulling.

I discover validating information in a leather-bound encyclopedia, but it's the cookbooks I'm really here for. When I find what I'm after, I return all the books to the shelves, smiling at the librarian the whole time. Then I wait for Regina to finish reading the magazines.

She plays an important part in my escape plan, though she doesn't know it.

We stroll to Tuck's Cafe at my suggestion.

"How's work going?" I ask her.

She shrugs. "Same old, same old."

She seems so kind, so normal. I wish there were any other way.

But I can't trust anyone, not anyone but myself.

I catch the door handle on my stomach entering the restaurant. She laughs. "You're getting pretty big."

I pat my belly. "You don't know the half of it. All my clothes are dirty right across the tummy because I rub it into everything."

"How's it feel? I mean, what's it like to carry another person around?"

"Amazing."

She smiles. It's wistful. I almost lose my courage. But I have no other option. There's a good chance she's on their side, has already told on me. If they got Ursula to turn, surely they got Regina. Believing that makes what I'm about to do possible.

She slides into the booth. She's waiting for me to do the same. Instead I raise my voice. "I will not!"

She stares around the restaurant. She has no idea what I'm talking about.

"I'm a mother-to-be. The last thing I need to do is smoke marijuana!"

Regina's jaw goes tight. Her overbite is barely visible. "You don't have to do this."

"*You're* the one doing this," I say, my voice shrill and loud. Everyone in the restaurant is looking at us. Exactly as I planned. "I don't ever want to see you again."

Her face crumples. I hate them so much in that moment, the people of Lilydale. They've made me into a monster, but what choice do I have? I must make them trust me, or they will take my baby and they will kill me.

I storm out. My work is done. Within minutes, the Mothers and Fathers will know that I've severed ties with Regina. They'll recognize that I am compliant. That will buy me the twelve hours I need to get the hell out of here.

❖

I have Deck's favorite supper and a bottle of ice-cold beer on the table when he arrives home from work. I massage his shoulders before I join him. If his conscience bothers him at all, he doesn't let on. When he finishes his beer, I get him another one.

The first one had the sleeping pills ground up in it.

The second one is just for show.

The doctor prescribed me one a night, and so I ground up four into Deck's beer. I need him to fall asleep early and stay there.

I'm escaping Lilydale tonight.

Before I do, though, I need a guarantee that they won't follow me and the baby, and I finally figured out the only thing that would suffice.

Deck doesn't even make it all the way through dessert before he crashes face-first into his plate. I consider gluing his balls to his thigh. I have some time to kill until it gets dark, after all. I decide I don't have the luxury of petty revenge, though.

Survival is my only priority.

I clean up supper, even though I will not be back. It's something to do, busywork to distract me until it gets late enough to leave. If a Father or a Mother stops by, my plan is shot. I believe they won't. I hope they won't. I hope my stunt in the café with Regina assuaged them.

When the phone rings, I jump. I smooth the front of my shirt. I need to calm myself. Whoever it is, I will tell them that Deck is out.

When I have my emotions under control, I pick up the phone. "Hello?"

"You're not going to believe what I uncovered," Grover says, his voice strangled. "It's worse than I imagined."

I nearly swallow my tongue. In my plan, I never considered that Grover would call. "I think you have the wrong number," I say.

I hang up. A drop of sweat rolls down my neck. I intended to hold off on phase two until later, but now it's too much of a risk. They've been alerted.

I check on Deck. He's still out cold.

After I finish tonight, I'll never see the shitheel again.

CHAPTER 54

It's dark outside, but I still sneak out through my back door. I'm wearing a pair of Deck's dress pants belted above my bulging belly. Over that, I've donned an old shirt of Deck's that I used for painting, and then a jacket. His matching fedora is crammed low on my head. I wouldn't pass any close inspection, but from a distance, I look more like a man in a hurry than a pregnant woman fighting for her life.

I toss a nervous glance at the Lily house next door. There are no lights on, but it still takes all my willpower not to dash to the car. It's like their *house* is watching me. I start the Chevelle. I steer it toward Schmidt Insurance.

Once I have *my* insurance, I'll be out of town immediately and forever.

Lilydale is a ghost town at 10:00 p.m. on a weeknight. I pass a single lonely patrol officer, offering a wave and a tip of my hat brim as I drive past. I pull into the lot behind the insurance company, park, and take out the business keys I stole from Deck. I let myself in the back door.

I have the camera, a flashlight, and an idea of what I'm looking for.

I start with the filing cabinets. Becky Swanson is meticulous in her filing. I locate the Aandeg file in the *A*s and confirm that Schmidt Insurance took over insurance payments as an act of goodwill two months before the fire, naming the town of Lilydale as the beneficiary until such a time as Virginia Aandeg could resume payments.

If a person didn't know how evil Lilydale was, this would look generous.

I locate the same setup in the Gomez family file.

I learned from a library encyclopedia that it's possible to burn down buildings and leave no evidence. Naming the city as beneficiary is a further way to throw off fraud investigators. Of course, the city and the Mill Street families are one and the same, but an outsider wouldn't know that.

There's a roll of maps beneath the desk in the center of the office. I want to know what the Xs were on the one Deck, Clan, and Ronald were studying that day I stormed in after my first meeting with Dr. Krause, when he'd called me a risk, back when I still thought I knew Deck.

When I locate the map, I'm horrified to discover that not only are there red Xs over where Paulie's house was, the Gomez house is, and four other spots, but there're also percentages written on each of the poor neighborhoods. The biggest concentration is around the Baptist church Kris and I visited, the one surrounded by houses that had been licked by fire.

Is Ronald controlling the makeup of the town?

Very few want to go to the deep dark below.

I bet if I matched up the X'd houses with property insured by Schmidt Insurance that listed Lilydale as beneficiary, I'd find a perfect match. I'm confident I am looking at one source of Lilydale's benevolence: controlled burnings of people's homes—poor people, migrant workers—after they've been coerced into handing over their insurance premiums. And then what? They probably move on.

A house or two burning every few years wouldn't draw too much suspicion. But what else have the Mill Street families done to create the balance they are after? How else have they terrorized families, made them move on to keep the percentages where they want them?

It's the price of living in Lilydale, where "everyone" is protected.

Ronald's hubris in keeping this information in plain-enough sight is breathtaking. It's better than I could have hoped. It will be his downfall and my baby's guarantee of safety. I lay out the evidence I've gathered. It's crucial that Ronald *not* know exactly what I have—he must live in as much fear as me—and so I cannot simply take the files and the map. Instead, I will snap photos and then return everything as I found it. To get clear pictures, I must turn on the light.

I have the *Gazette*'s Kodak with the flashcube.

It's not nearly powerful enough to capture a legible photograph in the dark.

I go to the window and peer out. The street is empty. If it stays that way for the next sixty seconds, I might pull this off. My pulse shredding my veins, I hold the camera in one hand, flick the light switch with the other. I snap photo after photo, my hands moving so fast they're a blur, making sure to take close-ups as well as wide shots that show the incriminating evidence in the identifiable office.

Click flash.

Click flash.

Click flash.

I'm sick with fear that I'll be caught, but I have to do this. Without incriminating evidence to hold over them, they'll always come after me. *Always.* I snap more photos. Finally, the camera's shutter won't click. I've used up the film. With a shaking hand, I flick off the light.

Within seconds, brightness sears the front of the window.

I drop to the floor, landing hard on my butt, but not before I spot the patrol car flashing its searchlight into buildings. I hold my breath. The car stops outside the store. The light returns, now a glare of yellow in the office. Can he see the files I've left out? I slowly pull my knees toward me, making myself as small as I can around my swollen belly.

Waves of nausea overtake me.

It can't end like this.

I squeeze my eyes shut, counting down my last moments of freedom. I think of my mother, beautiful Frances, a survivor, always looking out for me, always keeping me safe, me and her against the world.

You can do this, Joan. You've got this.

My eyes snap open at the sound of the car pulling away.

Finally, a stroke of luck.

Nauseous with adrenaline, I roll up the map, return it to its storage location, and then do the same with the files.

I'll drive until I'm out of Lilydale, and then I will mail the film to Benjamin with instructions to develop it and bring the prints to the publisher at the *Star* should anything happen to me. I have the padded envelope stamped and ready to go. The city paper may not care much for small-town affairs, but when it's arson and possible murder, they'll have to stand up and pay attention.

Then I'll send Ronald a letter telling him I have enough evidence to put him away for murder. He doesn't need to know it's only theories. He has too much to lose to take chances. I'll tell him that if no one follows me, the evidence will never see the light of day. If I suspect I'm in danger, I will destroy him and the Lilydale demons who have benefited from his evildoing.

Plan in place, I go.

Or I should have.

CHAPTER 55

The curiosity is too much. It yanks me back like a lasso before I reach the back door.

I must know if they have a file on me.

I return to the cabinet. I slide it open. I search under "Schmidt." I discover a regular life insurance policy for Deck. It's dated December 14, 1967. The day he took me to the Gobbler and got me pregnant. His beneficiary is his child. Such arrogance.

There's no mention of me in that file.

I locate my policy under "Harken."

Skim it.

My tongue goes sour.

The policy is brief and to the point: if anything happens to me, Deck receives $1 million.

It's almost enough to make me go back and glue his balls to his leg.

❖

I intend to drive to Interstate 94, take it east until I hit a southbound highway, drive until I'm far enough away, and then drive some more. No one will even know to look for me until tomorrow morning, when Deck doesn't show up for work.

That gives me at least ten hours.

I flip on the radio. Van Morrison is singing "Brown Eyed Girl."

I stab the button, remembering Deck and me dancing to the song in the tiny apartment before we moved. Why did he have to fall in love with me, and me with him? Couldn't he simply have married some woman who *wanted* to be in Lilydale, someone like Miss Colivan?

It hits me again with a fresh wave of grief: Ursula believed Deck, not me. I'm alone, alone except for my baby, and I will not let anything happen to him. I roll down the window and let the night breeze glitter across my skin. I am so close to free.

When I reach 94, though, I remember Grover's phone call, the one I hung up on hours earlier. He'd discovered something important. Would it confirm who Paulie's father was?

I realize I need to know if my child's grandfather is a rapist.

It will take less than an hour. I have the time. It's late, but I won't ever be in this state again, so it's now or never. I drive through Saint Cloud, reveling in the feeling of invisibility. When I pass a blue mailbox, I pull over to scribble a note to Benjamin, toss it in the prepared envelope containing the film, and sink the works into the box.

One step closer to safety.

I don't know what I'll find at Grover's, but I think it's likely that he's discovered that Ronald was Paulie's father, Ronald or Stanley.

I grow more certain of this as I steer toward Grover's house on the north side.

I'm so focused on untangling the pieces that, at first, I don't register the ambulance's wail. Grover lives close to the hospital, the hospital where I would've been forced to give birth had there been any complications. I rub my belly absently, for comfort. But as I near Grover's house, I realize with dawning horror that the ambulance is pulling up outside his home, screeching to a stop alongside the police car already there, its lights flashing.

My heart galloping, I park the car. I leap out, watching, unbelieving, as the medics jerk out the gurney and race into Grover's house.

Moments later, when they hurry out with an unmoving body on the stretcher, I fall to my knees. I can see Grover's impassive face and a corner of his hand, both still under the glow of the streetlamps.

I retch into the grass.

They killed Grover.

And it's my fault.

I never warned him how dangerous they were. How deadly. I wipe my mouth with the back of my hand. I use the car door to pull myself to my feet. I need to see him one last time, to beg forgiveness even if he can't hear me. I step forward.

The sheet moves, and the man coughs.

"Grover!" I scream, running toward him. The ambulance driver tries to block me, but I'm a wild creature. I growl and push through. Grover's wrist is warm where I clutch it. "What happened?"

The ambulance driver speaks, not unkindly. "He was attacked, ma'am. A burglar, they think. We have to get him to the hospital."

"Gave 'em more than they bargained for," Grover says, his voice weak. "I think they heard I got my hands on this." There is trembling under the sheet, but he doesn't appear to have the strength to move his arm.

I reach under and come out with an envelope, bent into an impossible shape.

Grover's gurney is guided into the back of the vehicle.

"Is he going to be okay?"

They don't answer.

"Is he going to be okay?" I scream. They close the rear door, leap into the front seat, and slam their doors before driving away, their lights flashing. A police officer steps out of Grover's house, his face questioning. I stumble into my own car and start it up, clutching the envelope the whole time. I don't know who's watching here. I drive downtown and park the car beneath a streetlight.

I open the crumpled envelope with shaking hands.

I discover Paulie Aandeg's birth certificate inside.

Grover's favor had come through. It had nearly cost him his life.

It may yet.

My eyes glide over the words without understanding. I reread them, disbelieving, and flip to the image clipped to the back of the birth certificate. A picture of Virginia Aandeg. My lungs shrink as my body goes leaden. I suddenly realize what about Stanley in that 1944 photo looked familiar.

Dear God save me.

It finally all makes sense.

PART III

CHAPTER 56

I fumble for the key in the ignition, my fingers numb. I'm positive I've forgotten how to drive, but within moments I find myself in front of the Saint Cloud Police Department. I leave the car running as I bolt in. I realize from a great distance that I'm hysterical. That I'm screaming and yelling. That I am saying that my life is in danger. Swearing that I have proof of things. I'm waving the birth certificate and photo in one hand and the empty camera in the other.

I am led to a room and seated across from two men out of uniform.

They hand me water.

I tell them everything.

Everything.

They keep exchanging incredulous glances. Against all odds, I see they believe me. Finally. *Finally* someone trusts my story.

When I'm finished, the dark-haired of the two detectives reaches for the phone. He turns to his blond partner. They nod at each other, and then the dark-haired man turns to me.

"We'll handle this. You rest. Let us do our job."

I nod. My blood feels sluggish. I am so tired. But finally, I'm not the only one who knows about Lilydale. I'm led to a room with a couch. I lie down. The detective pulls a scratchy blanket over me.

Somebody else is in charge now.

Somebody else will take care of everything.

❖

I wake to a commotion outside. It takes me a moment to remember where I am. The smell of stale coffee. The industrial furniture. I'm inside the Saint Cloud police station. They have Paulie's birth certificate. Irrefutable evidence. I run my hands through my short hair and stand.

This is the story that will make my career.

I grimace at the thought. It's a dying gasp from the old version of me, the girl who believed in ambition and love and happy endings. Still, Grover and Angel deserve their stories to be told.

I reach for the doorknob. The people in charge may want me to stay around for questions, but I'm hopeful I can simply check in at a nearby hotel and get to work writing this up. It's no longer about the byline. It's about the truth.

The doorknob turns under my hand. I jerk back.

Amory Bauer strolls in, as big as a mountain, pistol straining at his side. He's pleased, as glossy as a snake who's swallowed the whole rabbit.

I choke on my own tongue.

His smile is vicious.

"She's awake!" he calls over his shoulder.

He steps aside so Ronald and Deck can stride in. Deck appears as shamefaced as a child and still groggy. *Son of a bitch.* I lunge at him and start pummeling him with my fists. Amory pins my arms at my side with no effort at all.

"Better take it easy. You won't like it any other way," he says.

He pushes me out the door, marching me past the two plainclothes officers. They won't meet my eyes. "See you at the next meeting," Amory says.

He doesn't speak again until we are in the car, him behind the wheel and Ronald and Deck on each side of me in the back. Amory adjusts the rearview mirror, our eyes meeting in the glass.

"I can't believe Grover tracked down your birth certificate. I was sure we'd destroyed all your papers, Paulie."

CHAPTER 57

I remember little of the drive back to Lilydale. When we reach town, we drive straight to Dr. Krause. They've woken him up, and he looks disheveled and annoyed. Oddly, I don't think he's in on any of this. I think he's just a plain old-fashioned sexist. He tells them I'm to be under constant supervision, not alone until the baby is born. Krause administers another injection. It must be stronger than the one he gave me after Kennedy was shot, because I remember nothing after the needle pierces my flesh.

I wake up in the lemon-colored room. I stand, teetering, and stumble to the window. It's open a few inches. I can look across the way and see the bedroom I've shared with Deck for over two months, the flowered wallpaper splattering the walls like blood.

A roar deafens me, the sound of my reality splitting.

My childhood memories are coming back, coursing like boiling water over my brain.

They took me to this room, only for a night, before they moved me to the basement. I was wearing a sailor suit.

The jolt is so strong that for a second, I feel as though I'm standing next to my own body. Bile races toward my mouth. I hold it down, just. I see Slow Henry standing below, on the driveway. He meows up at me. I can't get to him. My tears start pouring out.

Ronald's voice comes from the doorway. "Can you believe Paulie Anna was your real name? I wouldn't have let Stanley and Dorothy keep it, even if we didn't need to hide your identity. It was too on the nose. You've always been such a goody-goody girl, at least until recently. So placid, when you were young. So docile."

I don't turn immediately. I can see his reflection in the glass. The birth certificate that Grover finally tracked down had been clear. Paulie Anna Aandeg had been a girl.

She was me.

Virginia Aandeg was my mother, though I knew her as Frances Harken. The man I'd been told was my father must have given my mom the new surname and me the birth certificate with a new name and birth date to hide us from these monsters. I shudder at what it must have cost her.

"The newspaper articles," I say. "They referred to Paulie as a boy."

Ronald steps closer. "Virginia cut your hair herself. It was identical to the atrocious mop on your head right now, by the way. You looked like a boy then, you look like a boy now. Between that, the sailor suit, and it being the first day of kindergarten, poor Becky Swanson didn't know who was what. When the newspapers descended on Lilydale for a day or two, I made sure they thought you were a boy. Made it easier for us if they were looking for a male. The town got on board."

I lean my cheek against the cool glass. It's going to be a scorcher out there, yet I'm shivering.

"You've always known," he says, now standing immediately behind me. "You wanted to pretend you didn't, *but you knew*. You were six when Dorothy took you. You couldn't possibly have forgotten."

A rage explodes inside me. I want to punch through the wall, through the glass, through his face. I whirl. "I was a child."

"A slow one, by all accounts. But we still took you. You were *chosen*. The Mill Street families only had you for five days, Joan, but we loved you like our own."

He walks over to the oak dresser. Opens the top drawer. Takes out a folded sailor suit.

I suck in my breath.

"We didn't want you to find out this way. Lord knows it almost broke Dorothy's heart that it's fallen to this. We were hoping you would come around. Deck offered to bring you home, you know. No one better for the job."

I think of the night I first met him at the 620, how he pursued me. I grow ill all over again. I was so naive, thinking he was infatuated. He'd been acting. My eyes fill with acid tears. "Did you set him on me, back at the bar?"

Ronald shrugs. "Think of it as an arranged marriage." His tone is strangely syrupy. "You and Deck have so much in common. You just didn't know it. Children of Lilydale, reunited."

"Did Stanley rape my mother?"

"Stanley and Virginia had an affair. When Dorothy found out, she snatched the product, as was her right, though we would have preferred she waited for us to get your mother to agree beforehand. It would have kept the out-of-town newspapers out of Lilydale. Still, everything would have gone smoothly if your mother hadn't sobered up and come after you."

I imagine my hands around Ronald's neck. It's all I can think about. Squeezing his bones until his lips turn blue. He will thrash and scratch, and I'll revel in the blood I draw. He must see the murderous hatred in my face, because he scowls.

"You stole me from my family," I growl, not recognizing my own voice.

He moves surprisingly fast, rushing forward to pin me against the window. "*We're* your family," he spits. "Virginia was only a vessel. You're half Lily, which means you're ours."

I want to weep with frustration. "Please. I'm an adult now. You can't keep me."

His face shifts like a kaleidoscope. "Whatever do you mean? This is the only way."

"What happens if I leave and tell the whole story of what you two did?"

His eyes narrow, and his tone is mocking. "Like you tried at the Saint Cloud police station?"

My bravado drains out. "Kris will help me," I whisper. It's ridiculous, a child's nonsense, but who else do I have?

"The man who pretended to be Paulie? We let him stay in town because he was harmless. A small-time con artist. We made sure he didn't hurt you. Don't you see how much we've done for you?"

"Regina, then," I say desperately, but I ruined that.

"If she's smart—and I think she is—she'll be one of us soon."

My mind's racing. Ursula believes them, and Grover, if still alive, is hospitalized. Deck was always an invention, a lie I fell for like a dazzled schoolgirl.

"You want to be very careful," Ronald says, his smile brittle, his resemblance to Deck the cruelest of quirks. He's using the singsong voice of a kind teacher speaking to a naughty child. "The police in Saint Cloud think you're crazy. The doctor's records show that you're unstable and have subsequently been prescribed heavy doses of Valium and sleeping pills. You've said some very odd things to several people, including your best friend in Minneapolis. She saved your message. The rantings of a paranoiac."

The sticky, awful truth paints itself across my mouth and nose, suffocating me. I either follow their rules or I'm put away.

"If you stay and keep the peace," he says, "we can all finally have everything. If you don't, you know how it ends."

"The obituary," I rasp. *The one my mother hadn't wanted me to write.*

Ronald raises an eyebrow and then smiles. "That's right. All this time, Dorothy has been watching for news of the daughter she'd lost. The name was different, but she'd recognize Virginia Aandeg's face—survived by one daughter, praise be—anywhere. By that time, Stan was lost to us, couldn't be of assistance in retrieving his child, but she convinced Barbara and me to send Deck to bring you back. It would take only a few months of living in beautiful Lilydale to fall in love with it, and you and Deck would replenish the next generation of Lilys."

As he tells me all of it, every detail of what happened leading up to my birth, I begin weeping.

Johann and Minna Lily were brother and sister as well as husband and wife. They left Germany to found Lilydale in 1857. They had twelve children, only two of whom lived to adulthood, a son and a daughter. The rest were born horribly deformed; those who survived childbirth were kept hidden until their deaths days or weeks later. To guarantee the Lily bloodline (which they thought was pure, and the reason for their intelligence and success) and keep their wealth intact and in the family, Johann got other women pregnant.

Minna raised the children as her own. In exchange for their half-Lily children, these women and their families got to live in Lilydale and be protected by the Lilys. By 1938, though, there were only ten Fathers and Mothers left, the lowest number since it had been founded, all of whom lived on Mill Street and ran Lilydale.

Stan Lily believed it was his obligation and right to sleep with any of the women of Lilydale, including Virginia Aandeg, my mother. The Fathers and Mothers were fine with it because it made more Lily offspring, but when Virginia would drink, she'd tell townspeople about the night visits. The Fathers and Mothers paid Virginia a small stipend to keep her quiet, and it was working.

Then, Dorothy spotted me in my sailor suit on the way to my first day of kindergarten and decided she wanted the beautiful child for her own; since I was half Lily, and since the Fathers and Mothers had done so much for Virginia and for the town, Dorothy felt entitled. She lured me to her house with candy. By the time Stan returned home that afternoon, Virginia had called the Lilydale police to report me missing.

Stan was furious when he found me in his house, said Dorothy should not have been so impulsive, but Dorothy stood up to him for the first time in her life. She wouldn't give me up, so Stan created a plan. They would wait until everything blew over and then present me as their own daughter. The town would look the other way, as it always had, and if the state police or papers ever came back to Lilydale, they'd be looking for a lost boy, not a lost girl.

Stan gave Virginia a generous donation that very day. He said it was from the Fathers and Mothers to cover her heartbreak at the loss of her child and to give her enough for a clean start in a different town, where she wouldn't always be reminded of her lost child. It was clear it was a bribe, though Stan never said as much. Virginia, drunk, took Stan's money, and she stayed drunk for the next five days while Lilydale was overrun with papers and police.

On the sixth day, a Sunday, Virginia sobered up, broke into Stan and Dorothy's house while they and all the Mothers and Fathers were at church, found me catatonic in the basement just as she'd suspected she would, and fled Lilydale with me. The Mothers and Fathers wanted me back because I was half Lily, but they didn't want the police to find me, because Virginia could reveal that Dorothy had been the one who'd kidnapped me. So no one reported Virginia missing, they burned down her house to destroy any evidence she might have left, and they encouraged rumors that Virginia had killed me and then fled town to escape justice. Dorothy, for her part, kept reading the city papers for any word of Virginia and Paulie, because she believed I was hers.

I am still crying when Ronald finishes his story, because I know what he doesn't. Virginia moved to Florida, taught me to paper over the bad memories and remember only the good until those years in Lilydale were a nightmare, changed her name to Frances and mine to Joan, and we would have made it . . . if I hadn't written the obituary against her wishes.

Ronald makes an exasperated noise. "Stop all that blubbering. Deck is a good man. He doesn't deserve all this worry. You really should be a better wife."

The baby kicks my kidney.

He sees me flinch. He guesses what it is and rests his hand on my belly. I want to shove it off, but I'm too afraid.

"It won't be so bad," he says, flashing his teeth. "We're going to have the biggest party when this baby is born! We'll welcome him into the Mill Street family. We'll all be there. Everyone who matters. We'll restore order."

That's when I understand that not one part of me is my own.

Never has been.

Ronald turns away. He picks up the sailor suit and drops it into the trash. His back is to me as he speaks. "We're all Lilys here, you know."

I'm crying by now, but he won't stop.

"All of us on Mill Street. Direct descendants of the only two of Johann and Minna's children to survive. You have the purest bloodline in the nation."

CHAPTER 58

July turns the air into liquid. I find myself constantly drenched in sweat. We have fans set up in every room of the house, but it doesn't matter. My body is cooking in the world's oven.

I'm living at Dorothy and Stan's now.

They let Slow Henry move in with us.

Dorothy is thrilled to finally have her "daughter" home.

The Mill Street Mothers will not let me out of their sight, not even to use the toilet, certainly not long enough for me to escape. They take shifts watching me.

If I'm good, I can live, and I can hold my baby.

I must make them believe I'm good.

I laugh at my previous Nancy Drew plan, the idea that I could snap photos of Ronald's questionable business practices and drive away. No, these people will not let me go so easily.

I finally know what I'm up against. I also have one chance of escape, a sliver of light in a raging sea of dark. Ronald unwittingly gave me the idea when he mentioned the party they'd have when my baby was born. The elegant, impossible timing, so much balanced on a razor's edge. I can't think about it. I just plod toward it, knowing there are only two ways it will end: I will be dead, or I will be free.

I seldom leave the sauna of the house. I grow more ponderous in my pregnancy, and as I do, I write articles, but they are about the joys of being pregnant and cooking and gardening. I've not been asked again to join the Mothers.

They allow me to attend get-togethers at Catherine's house. There, I let them teach me how to crochet. We make blankets for the less fortunate. There is talk of Shirley Chisholm, and we all make faces of disgust. I learn the value of saving flower seeds from one season to the next.

Sometimes I spot Regina around town, but I'm never without one of the Mothers. I hope they leave her alone, but I'm too deep in the soup to warn her. The heat and my growing body conspire against me, making me slow and clumsy. Mildred reminds me it's a precious life I'm carrying and that I should be grateful.

She doesn't need to tell me. I *know* it.

I'm leaving Dr. Krause's with her when she realizes she left her purse in the examination room.

I'm momentarily alone when the car pulls up.

A woman steps out.

I cover my mouth to stifle my scream.

She looks at me, then past me. I'm used to this invisibility as a pregnant woman. Lilydale tells me I am serving my purpose and don't deserve a second glance. But she gives me one. Her eyes widen.

"Joan?"

It's Ursula. She will destroy everything by being here. I hiss and back toward the door. I hope Mildred comes out. Grim-faced Catherine would be better at getting rid of Ursula. Mildred will help me, though. I can't do it alone.

"Jesus, Joan. Are you having quintuplets?" She's walking toward me, staring at my belly, grinning. The smile falls off her face when she meets my eyes.

"What do you want?" I ask.

"Benjamin called me," she says. She's gorgeous, truly a Sharon Tate, so trim and cosmopolitan and out of place in Lilydale. "I'm sorry, Joan. I should have been a better friend. He said he's worried about you, for real worried about you, and that he can't reach you at your old number. He found something out. Something he wanted me to tell you."

I peer over my shoulder again at the clinic. Mildred is laughing with the receptionist. She'll be out any minute. I must get rid of Ursula.

I walk up to her and shove her. "You have to go."

She stumbles back, her expression wounded.

"Joan?" It's Mildred. *Finally.* She's behind me, her voice uncertain.

I turn to reassure her, stepping away from Ursula. I grab Mildred's hand and lead her across the lawn so we can avoid the intruder.

"Minna and Johann Lily were brother and sister, Joan. Their first child was born horribly deformed. Minna went mad and threw it down a well." Ursula's voice starts shaky but grows louder as we walk farther away. "That's not the crazy part, though. She and Johann kept going, having one freakish child after another. Do you hear what I'm saying?" She's yelling now. "That's some Olympic-level incest. This town is haunted. Fucking haunted. You okay? You okay, Joan?"

Mildred wraps her arm around me, and we scurry away.

Clean. Rested. Hydrated. Fed.

I'm ready.

It's time for me to join them.

It's time for me to get my child (*Frances, I will call the baby, boy or girl; God, what my mother sacrificed for me*) and escape Lilydale, for real this time. Forever. This must work out. My plan balances on a pin—so much could go wrong—but I can't think of that.

One way or another, I'm getting out.

Like my mom did. Taking her child, the child of rape, Stanley Lily's daughter, who got his eyes, who recognized a bit of herself in an old newspaper photo of her real father. Changing her name. Always staying on the move.

I pat my pocket. It's in there. My ticket out of Lilydale, the thing I've been meticulously collecting in the weeks since they brought me home from the Saint Cloud police station.

My short hair has already dried. My clothes are clean, all signs of giving birth disguised. My eyes are wide and gaunt. Can't do a thing for that, so I pinch my cheeks, wet my lips, and leave the lemon-yellow bedroom.

I hear the murmurs and clinks of their party.

They're celebrating a new baby.

Mine.

CHAPTER 59

It's August 1.

The weather has grown so scorching that the state weather service issues heat warnings. We sit in front of fans blowing over bowls of rapidly melting ice, but it's no use. The world's on fire.

I'm practicing my crocheting at the dinner table, sweat soaking my shapeless shift. Though I've grown unspeakably huge, Dr. Krause has assured me there's only one baby in there. I am so large that it is difficult to cook, but I still prepare all the meals for Stan and Dorothy.

"You're very good at that."

It's Dorothy. I don't know how long she's been watching me knit. She steps behind me and pulls sticky hair from my neck. I shiver at the human touch. She begins twisting the short bits into tufts. "Catherine says you're pretending."

My needles click. "Pretending what?"

"Pretending to be docile."

I can think of no answer that she will believe, so I keep silent.

She finishes twining my hair and taps my shoulder. "I think you're not. You've always only wanted to make people happy. It was selfish Virginia who made everything so difficult."

I think of Stanley. Dorothy cares for him, moving him from one room to another, bathing him, spoon-feeding him. And sometimes, when she's not looking, I think he grins at me, a wicked, wolfish grin.

"I'm going to walk to Dr. Krause's today," I say. "I need more sleeping pills and Valium. I'd love to have company. I want to make sure the baby is getting everything he needs, and the exercise will be good for me."

"That's my girl," she says. She makes a tsking sound in the back of her throat, as if I've pleased her. "How would you like to become one of the Mothers tonight?"

I turn in the chair as fast as my swollen body will allow. My eyes are full of tears. My emotions have been so close to the surface these last weeks of my pregnancy. "I would love that. I would love that before the baby is born."

She pats my cheek matter-of-factly. "Then you better clean yourself up."

CHAPTER 60

"For God said, 'Honor your father and mother,' and 'Anyone who curses their father or mother is to be put to death,'" Ronald intones, standing on a dais at the rear of the enormous basement.

The basement Dorothy hid me in for five days after she kidnapped me.

This basement once belonged to Johann and Minna Lily, if Rosamund Grant is to be believed. Like my memory of the lemon-yellow room, I recall only flashes of being held down here as a child, impressions of darkness and fear and a cot shoved in the corner of a tiny closet of a room.

Kris was right about the fugue state.

I followed the natural lines of the story Ronald told me, and then Ursula yelled at me. The ancestral poison began with Johann and Minna Lily, brother and sister. Only two of their children survived their deformities, and they concentrated the poison of the incestuous heritage by having kids of their own, and so on down the line. By the time the current Mill Street families came into the picture, all of them, every last one of those rotten, stopped-up Lilys, they couldn't have kids of their own, not normal, healthy ones.

Because they were all, at best, first cousins to one another.

I think of how Becky Swanson described Quill Brody, pointing at her chin and ears, too polite to describe his deformities. Of the woman with the melted face that Deck and I encountered outside the furniture store. How many malformed Lily children—full-blood Lily children—are there, and where are they being kept, these "lifers" as Catherine described her son?

What have the Mill Street families done in the name of purity?

I see a glimpse of their commitment to this ideal in the basement they've taken me to for initiation. Ronald is speaking scripture.

All the Fathers are lined up on the left and Mothers on the right, facing away from him, staring at me. Was it the second or third generation of inbreeding that cemented the inability of descendants of the original settlers to have sound children of their own, that made the Lily husbands seek outside their Lily wives for "vessels"?

It doesn't really matter. There are three times the people here that I've ever seen before. This truly stretches beyond Lilydale. This brittle, rotten old system has its veins threaded through all of Stearns County, maybe farther, and it's fully alive.

That's why Mildred is here with Angel.

Browline Schramel's child, stolen from his mother to be raised in the Lily fold. Mariela had reported Angel missing. She'd paid the Lilydale price, not turning Browline Schramel in, but of course she couldn't keep silent when Mildred demanded her child. Mariela had gone to the police, and I imagine she'd had as much success telling them her story as I had sharing mine. The system would not protect us.

"The Holy Word has taught us that children are a reward from the Lord, and we take that which He offers us," Ronald is saying, his voice reaching the farthest corners of the large room.

I almost blow it, watching Angel's fearful eyes.

I can't bear his pain.

I will do nearly anything to end it, even if it means giving up my one chance of escape with my child.

I am moving toward him when Ronald strides forward, meeting me at the base of the stairs. He's carrying a white Lily pin. The same pin that Deck came home with that first week we moved to Lilydale. The same design as the necklace I stole from Dorothy.

Ronald holds it aloft and faces the men.

"Who sponsors this woman?"

Deck is standing at the rear of the room, near the dais. He's raising his hand, and I believe he is going to speak for me, but then he coughs into it.

"I do," Dorothy says from behind me.

"And I," Barbara seconds.

"And I." Mildred.

"I," Rue agrees.

Catherine is the last familiar voice to speak. She frowns as if she's tasted something sour, but she says, "I."

I duck my head to hide my smirk. I will pay her back for her kindness. Oh yes, I will.

"Very good," Ronald says. He gives me his full attention. "Do you pledge your loyalty to the Mothers, promising to always put the needs of others before your own?"

"I do."

"Do you swear to help those who are suffering, and to never turn a child away from your door? To honor human life above all else, and to honor your sacred duty as a Mother?"

Hypocritical bastards. "I do."

He fastens the pin to my robe. He kisses me on each cheek and then the mouth. "Then let the Fathers welcome you."

He steps back so each man in the room can repeat his gesture: cheek, cheek, mouth. Some of them grip my stomach before they step away, a furtive rub, as if I'm a stone to massage for luck. Stanley—my true father, after all—doesn't seem to recognize me. He's chewing on something he should have swallowed long ago, I think, when I lean down so he can kiss me. He sniffs my neck, or simply twitches, and when he leans back into his wheelchair, I spot a flash of something alert in his eyes. But then they cloud over, and he's gone.

I intend to pay him back, too. For Frances.

When all the Fathers have kissed me, the Mothers are guided to deliver three kisses of their own: cheek, cheek, forehead. Their closeness and breaths and the intimate way they're handling me is starting to take a toll. I fight off waves of dizziness.

When I have been blessed by everyone, Ronald turns me, clasping one of my hands with his and raising them both in the air. "Let's welcome our newest Mother!"

My eyes are dry as everyone cheers.

CHAPTER 61

I'm sprawled on the sofa of Dorothy and Stan's house. Slow Henry is crashed out on his back, feet curled in the air, purring in his sleep. A quilt beneath me soaks up the worst of my perspiration. My engorged belly hides the lower half of my body from my eyes, but I know from the now-constant ache in my swollen calves that they're still down there.

The sky rumbles, and I pray for relief in the form of rain. The heat has been oppressive, unrelenting. The radio tells me people are dying from it all across the Midwest.

It will not be much longer.

Dorothy is helping Stanley into bed. They were pleased with the initiation ceremony. Dorothy was, anyhow. Stanley is too far gone in his senility to know much. I wonder whether his state is reward or punishment for the life he's lived.

The Mothers and Fathers and I celebrated after I was pinned. Initiation is the rare day of the month when the men and women rejoice together. I'm part of something bigger now. I belong to the people who make the rules.

The only way to be safe here is to pretend to be one of them, but it's no life.

My baby is always moving now. Diving and turning and squirming. I can see it ripple my flesh, like a great sea creature roiling just below the surface. I want somebody to share it with, someone who's not a Lily.

A branch scratches my window. There's no breeze, despite the clouds rumbling. So many people have remarked what a good omen it was that the weather was still and cloudless for my initiation.

Heaven can see clearly.

Mildred had said that. Kind, passive, handmaid-of-evil Mildred.

I roll to my side, drop my feet to the floor, and sit up. I am now so big that it's the only way I can stand from a prostrate position.

I lumber to the window.

Kris stands outside.

I shrink back. Dorothy could return to the living room any moment. Before I can decide how to react, I hear the kitchen door open. I hurry to it.

Kris has entered. He has a hard time looking at me, which I think is funny. He's the one who sought me out.

"I'm leaving," he says. His voice is low. He must realize Stan and Dorothy are near.

"Back to Siesta Key?"

He looks at me, surprised. We haven't seen each other in weeks. "That's right. I forgot I told you about that. That was the truth, how pretty it is."

"The rest wasn't."

All his liquid confidence is gone. He seems smaller. His denim jacket is ill fitting and his fingernails dirty.

"No," he says. "The rest wasn't. Except for the part about hearing about Paulie from some army guy who passed through Lilydale in 1944. The story got stuck in the back of my head. When I wanted to check out a new place, I hitched here, and I said I was Paulie. Figured it wouldn't hurt anyone, and it might be fun."

I watch him. The Fathers and Mothers would not approve of him being here.

I *am* a Mother, technically. And I do not approve.

"They knew I wasn't Paulie, all the old guys here, the ones who were at your house when Regina and I stopped by for dinner. I don't know how, but they knew the second I stepped foot in Lilydale. Showed up at my motel room. I thought they were gonna beat the shit out of me, but instead, they told me to spend time with you. Said they'd kill me if I told you the truth, though."

The baby is twisting in my belly. Furious.

"I'm sorry," he says. "I shouldn't have done that. These guys, man, they're dangerous. They run everything here, you know that? Everything in the whole damn county, I think. You're not safe here, Joan."

Has he come to ask me to leave with him?

I'll never know, because I open my mouth and scream as loud as I can.

CHAPTER 62

I am up early so I can apply makeup to walk to the grocery store with Rue.

They were so happy, the Mothers and Fathers, when I screamed. Deck appeared first, Clan on his heels, and they subdued Kris, led him out of the house.

"Dear," Catherine said, coming to me. "It's time for your baby shower. Tomorrow."

I swallowed my smile. I'd passed another test.

I took advantage of it to get permission to shop for all the groceries for the party they'll throw when my baby is born. The Mothers hesitated at first—I'll likely be too tired to even attend the celebration, and the person who shops should always be the person who cooks so they have the right ingredients—but in the end, barely, I got them to agree to me purchasing steak and grilling supplies as well as staples for dessert. All of it will keep in the cupboard or the freezer, and the men can grill.

I'm overjoyed, but I hide it.

Being in charge of groceries was the first hurdle in my plan, and I've overcome it.

I was surprised when Rue volunteered to chaperone me to the grocery store. She's always been so quiet, but I find that I prefer that to Mildred's chattering and Dorothy's doting and Catherine's gloating and Barbara's sighing as we make the slow, ponderous stroll to Wally's. The weather hasn't broken yet, for all last night's rumbling. It's going to, soon. The clouds are black and portentous, the heat so ominous, even at this hour, that it feels like being stalked.

My due date is in four weeks and three days. Soon, I'm going to hold my baby.

"Joan."

I turn toward the quiet voice and see Regina leaning in the Little John's alley, smoking. When did she start smoking?

"Hello, Regina." I should feel guilty for how I treated her. Guilt is so familiar. "How are you?"

Her hair is lank and greasy, her chin a constellation of pimples. She keeps tugging at the hem of her too-short skirt, flashing glances at Rue. "Kris said he was going to spring you. I guess he didn't."

I smile broadly. "I guess not. You're up early."

She looks around as if surprised. "Yeah, got a lot on my mind. Joan—" She steps close to me, hesitates, turns as if to go, then spins back to face me. "I know why you did that, back at the café. Why you turned on me like that. It's because I told Albert, the other bartender, about you seeing your mugger in town. I didn't mean to. He was talking shit about you, is all, saying you were a crazy bitch who should be committed, and I couldn't take it anymore. I told him that if it's crazy to be jumpy when you run into the man who mugged you, then we'd all be insane."

My neck aches to turn toward Rue, to promise her that this is in the past, nothing for her to worry about. I keep my smile pasted to my face, my eyes glued to Regina.

Her chin is quivering. "It got back to you, didn't it? They made you pay, didn't they? I'm so sorry, Joan. Can I ever make it up to you?"

"I'm going to the grocery store with my friend Rue," I say. "We could use a ride home. We need a lot of food, grilling charcoal, and fluid. Can you help us?"

She laughs in disbelief. I keep staring at her. Finally, she shakes her head. "Fine. I'll grab my car and pull it up in front of Wally's."

When Rue and I exit the grocery store twenty minutes later, the bagger following us, wheeling out a dozen boxes of chocolate pudding, eight pints of cream, four tubs of Cool Whip, all the steak in their meat department, two bags of charcoal, and a box of lighter fluid, she's parked at the curb, waiting.

Regina's eyes widen when the groceries are loaded in her back seat and trunk.

"I've never grilled before," I say defensively. "I don't know how many people will be over. I want to be prepared."

Her car's rear drops as the last bag is packed in, but she doesn't say anything. I slide next to her, Rue in the back.

"Thank you," I say when she takes off.

She lights a cigarette. "You want to drive straight to your house?"

She snaps open the ashtray. I think I see a flash of white enamel etched with red inside, the color of a Mother's pin, and my flesh erupts in gooseflesh. I reach for it, frozen but for my hand.

It's the ripped edge of a Marlboro box.

My breathing returns to normal.

"Do you want one?" she asks, opening her purse between us to indicate her cigarettes.

I shake my head, toss Rue a reassuring smile.

She looks distressed in the back seat.

"Hey," Regina says, low and quiet. Her tone is different. For a second, I can almost hear her dimples in it. "It's a wide world, you know. We could go anywhere. Just keep driving. I have five hundred dollars in tips saved up, hidden beneath the spare tire. That's enough to get us far away."

If she's smart—and I think she is—she'll be one of us soon.

"I want to go straight home," I say, turning again to flash Rue a reassuring smile.

Regina continues to smoke as she drives away from the store. Now she's the quiet one. She pulls up to my house, still silent. She stabs out her cigarette.

"Can you wait here while Rue and I go get help?" I ask.

I locate Deck inside the house where I used to live. We are not technically together anymore. It's awkward to be alone in a room with him, this man whose baby I carry, who I slept curled next to for many nights, who I envisioned growing old with. He's a handsome stranger.

"Hello," I say. "Can you help Rue and me unload groceries for the party? For when the baby's born?"

He follows us to the car. "Holy shit!" he says when he sees everything I've bought. "Did you leave anything in the store? There's enough supplies here for a hundred barbecues."

I duck my head. "I've never grilled before," I say.

Regina stays in her car, smoking.

It takes Deck four trips to unload everything.

I have overcome the second hurdle.

CHAPTER 63

I know it's not a baby shower they're inviting me to.

It is their final test. If I pass it, I am free, finally and forever one of them, the watcher, not the watched. I only have to survive this one final test. We pull up in front of the nursing home, me squeezed in the back seat between Dorothy, my "mother," and Barbara, my baby's grandmother.

My baby.

I can feel it pushing, swirling, turning.

Insisting.

My stomach looks like something is constantly wrestling inside it. *If the baby comes early, I am ready. My plan is in place.*

We step out of the car. The cicadas are burring and buzzing, a hypnotic whirr that blends with the kiln-heat of the air. The Mothers are pulling me into the nursing home, Mildred putting her finger over her mouth (*ssshhhh*) and giggling as we pass the nurse in the reception area. They are leading me toward a door, and it feels like it might actually be a surprise party until they open it and I see the stairs leading down and too late I remember Rosamund Grant's warning when I came here to ask what she knew about Paulie Aandeg.

Whatever you do, don't wander into the basement.

We step down the stairs.

The smell reaches me first. I think it's the stench of an animal farm—close bodies, waste—but realize there's something human about it, the smell of meat eaters, of bipeds, of creatures whose clothes are washed sometimes but not often enough.

Then Catherine opens the basement door, her eyes cutting into me, lips pulled back from sharp, strong teeth in an approximation of a smile.

She steps back.

A scream freezes in my mouth.

A dozen people, maybe more, stand inside, each of them terribly deformed, all with the same pin heads and jutting jaws. Some have stumps for arms, nubs of flesh where ears should be, appendages where there should be none.

I recognize the woman from the furniture store, the feral thing with the melting eyes. Mildred walks over to her, tentatively. When she stands behind her, the woman snarls, the sound matched by the two women next to her. They all have the eyes sliding down their faces.

Mildred's three daughters.

The scream breaks free, but it's a sob.

I know what I'm looking at. The cursed full-blood children of Lilydale, doomed to live these half lives because of their parents' commitment to a pure bloodline.

My half siblings.

Dorothy hovers near the door, her hands clasped in front of her. Does she not have children in this basement? Can she not produce even this?

I notice the cots rimming the edges and realize Lilydale's children must live and die in this facility, away from the questioning eyes of the world. Catherine is walking toward the shadowed edge of the cafeteria-size room, her steps mincing, as if she's approaching a caged lion.

That's when I spot him.

A hulking, shirtless man. He's staring at me. His lips are belligerent, but his face disappears just beneath them, perched on a neck that's impossibly wider than his head. What he's missing in chin he makes up for in a slender, towering cranium speckled with bristly hair more animal than human. His ears stick out nearly as far as his sloping shoulders.

"Joan," Catherine says, inching closer to the behemoth lurking in the shadows, not taking her eyes off him. "I'd like you to meet my son. Quill Brody. All the children like to escape, but none of them are as good at it as my boy."

Is that a note of pride in her voice?

"Clan will take him home on occasion, for short visits, if he's good. Isn't that right, Quill?" The man makes no indication he's heard. "Sometimes on those visits, he likes to get out and visit the neighborhood houses—play in the alleys, mess with the garbage, open and close windows. Maybe you've seen him? Clan covers for his son, as any father would."

She's abreast of him. Slowly, she steps back so she can face me while keeping an eye on him.

"Now you see why we need fresh blood. Why we needed you." She points at my belly.

Quill shambles forward. Catherine flinches, but he's not looking at her, only me. That's when I notice his hand-wound music box. He begins to crank it. A hurdy-gurdy lullaby slithers out. When the music begins to slow, he cranks it again, never breaking eye contact. He's so close I can feel his heat.

I look away, but not before I see the figure-eight scar on his left arm, identical to mine and Deck's. *Sometimes certain bloodlines will have a similar adverse reaction to a vaccination. It's uncommon but not unheard of.*

All of us Lily children likely have one. It was Kris whose scar was a coincidence.

Quill is cranking the music box faster and faster.

"He played that for you when you were little," Dorothy is saying from behind me. "Remember? He played with you during your only day at Lilydale kindergarten, visited you in the basement at Dorothy's."

I smile a crazy grin, my eyes spinning. I feel a rupture, and then my underpants grow so wet that moisture runs down my legs.

I drop to my knees.

Not now, baby, not now. Please don't be born down here.

CHAPTER 64

The Mothers hurry me back to the lemon-yellow room. Call Dr. Krause, and then the men. Watch, as he gives me a shot, and then as my sweet baby is born. Cheer like they are watching a football game. Take my child, leaving me behind to drift in and out of consciousness.

As I suspected they would.

But here I am.

Clean. Rested. Hydrated. Fed. Propped up with Geritol and Pop-Tarts.

As strong as I'm going to get.

It's time for me to join them.

It's time for me to get my child (*Frances, I will call the baby, boy or girl; God, what my mother sacrificed for me*) and escape Lilydale, for real this time. Forever.

Barbara is the first person I encounter. She's at the bottom of the stairs, knitting, but hurries to her feet when she spots me. "Oh, no, dear, you need to lie down." She tries to guide me back to bed.

I seize her wrist. "Please tell me my baby's all right."

She pats my cheek. "Well, of course your baby's fine, dear."

I try to smile. "I want to see my child."

"I'm afraid now isn't a good time."

I stagger to the nearest window, the one facing the driveway between this house and Deck's. The neighbors have gathered. All the Mothers and the Fathers. My eyes devour them, hungry for sight of my child. My plan requires me to appear detached and stable, but I can't help it. The desperation to hold my infant, to feed him, is primal.

Laughing gaily, Catherine looks over and spots me. She reaches out to Dorothy, who is holding a cocktail. They whisper and then scurry across the driveway and into the house.

"I tried to get her to lie back down," Barbara says when they appear in the living room.

"I understand the baby isn't mine," I say, pleading. I don't even care about my plan anymore. I didn't account for this passion, for this consuming need to see my child. I'll say anything for the chance to hold him, even just once. "Let me serve, to begin to pay you all back. Please."

Catherine's nose turns up. "I don't think you're strong enough."

I glide across the floor. The movement costs me so much, but I make it appear effortless. "Are you kidding? I'm ready to have *another* baby. Just point me in the right direction." I don't laugh. That would seem too much. I must keep a tight rein.

"She can't hurt anyone," Dorothy says, looking me up and down.

I stand in front of Catherine, staring humbly at my feet. She's the one who will make the decision.

"All right," Catherine finally says, her voice cold. "The doctor said it was an easy birth. You certainly deserve to join us. Come on, then."

I do.

I have crossed the third hurdle.

CHAPTER 65

Clan is the first man at the party to spot me. His face collapses. He turns to find someone, Ronald or Amory, I suspect, so I hurry to him. "Clan," I say, smiling my widest. "I remember you like old-fashioneds. Do I have that right? Let me mix you one."

He smiles, though I sense he's wondering why I've joined the group. I slip into the kitchen and make his drink. I make *everyone's* drinks. I serve them their favorites, one, two, sometimes three. They've never tasted better. I hold the nausea and darkness at bay through force of will. I change my pads every half hour. I'm docile. I *will* see my baby.

The celebration was starting when I came to, dipped at my arrival, and is now back in full swing, everyone talking too loudly, growing drunk and stupid. After the steaks and side dishes are devoured, I bring them chocolate pudding, which I serve up in Deck's kitchen and keep moving, always moving.

Hurdle four.

When Dr. Krause shows up, his round glasses like headlights that pick me out in the crowd, I think it may be over. I don't know if someone called him because they're worried about me, but I'm certain I can't recover from another of his injections, not in time. I don't mix him a drink. He's not a Mill Streeter. I don't know what he favors.

"Hello, Miss Harken."

He isn't calling me Mrs. Schmidt anymore. "Hello, Dr. Krause. My baby is okay?"

"What? Yes, of course. I'm surprised to see you up so soon."

"This is my family," I say, indicating those gathered, their voices loud and animated. "I want to be here for the celebration."

I must escape before he can insist I lie down. I'm pulling away from him, back into Deck's house, when I hear the cry. I moan and lean into the doorjamb.

It's my baby.

The wail comes again, louder. My newborn is in Deck's house. Upstairs. In the bedroom Deck and I shared? I move toward the noise. My swollen breasts are pulsating, the front of my shirt suddenly drenched in milk.

Deck appears. He's been at the party, of course, keeping his distance, not letting me make him a drink, but still, celebrating.

"You can't go up," he says. "Don't worry. Linda has the baby."

I quiet the rage. I don't know Linda. "Please, Deck. Let me see our baby."

Dr. Krause appears with his bag. "I have a shot that will dry up your milk and another that will help you sleep."

I whimper and squeeze my chest.

Barbara appears, wavering slightly. She had only one drink, but she's a lightweight. "It's best if she feeds the baby the first week, isn't that right, doctor? For the colostrum."

Dr. Krause looks confused. "Yes. Breast milk is best for the baby's immunity, and then formula is fine, but you requested I bring these injections."

Dorothy appears behind Barbara, smiling warmly at me. She's as solid as stone. "We've decided to let her nurse, and we'll keep her on the pills rather than the shots for now, Dr. Krause. Thank you for coming. You're not needed anymore."

She turns away from him and takes me by the elbow. I have just seen what she must have been like when she and Stan ruled Lilydale alongside Barbara and Ronald, a woman whose commands were not questioned.

"Come on, Joan. You can meet the baby, but don't get too attached. It wouldn't be good for either of you. I think this is going very well, though, don't you? You should be pleased. Because of you, we won't have to take any more children. We can simply farm the next generation in our own soil. I only wish your father still had his faculties. He'd be delighted to see his plan come to fruition. Now don't be such a crybaby. It's not as if you ever even wanted children. Deck told us everything."

CHAPTER 66

They let me nurse my baby.

It's the purest moment of my life.

I smell my child's hair, sigh with sweet relief as the rosebud lips release the pressure on my breasts, sing a sweet lullaby as he suckles. I marvel at tiny fingers, eyelids the color of seashells. They won't let me change the baby, won't tell me if it's a boy or girl, what they named him, but they can't break my heart, not when I'm holding my child.

It's over too soon. They peel my baby from my arms and herd me back to my lemon-colored bedroom in Stan and Dorothy's house, across the driveway and an ocean away from the only thing that matters to me.

Mildred, obviously woozy and slurring her words, has been assigned as my chaperone. She watches me change the pads in my underpants and step into my nightgown, take a sleeping pill, and lie down. I don't need to fake the relief at being in bed, the trembling in my legs, the exhaustion.

"You're not the only one going to sleep early," she says blurrily, brushing hair from my face. "The party is winding down already. Stanley and Dorothy didn't even make it back over here. They're sleeping in Deck's living room." She yawns, reaches toward the nearest wall for support, misses it, tries again. "I don't know if I'll even be able to stay up long enough to help clean. Oh well! The dirt isn't going anywhere. I can come back tomorrow."

Her eyes are going heavy-lidded. She excuses herself.

I spit the sleeping pill into my palm.

I lie there until I hear garbled goodbyes. Until all the lights are off. Until it is nearly eleven.

I wait, and then I wait some more.

I'm good at waiting.

CHAPTER 67

When I hear no more movement, I change from my nightgown and into loose, dark pants, slipping in a new pad. I leave the empty medicine bottles in my pocket. I'll throw them away when I'm safely out of town. I've been stockpiling and grinding the sleeping pills and Valium since they brought me back from the Saint Cloud police station. I didn't need enough to kill anyone, just to make them all sleep well the next time they'd all be gathered. A time when I would have access to all their food.

The time right after my baby was born.

I don a clean bra and shirt.

I tuck my white gloves into my back pocket, and I sneak next door. I think everyone is out, but I can't be positive. I tiptoe up the stairs. Deck is on our—*his*—bed, and Linda, who turns out to be Miss Colivan, the fourth-grade teacher, is in the spare bedroom. Both Deck and Miss Colivan are fully clothed and on top of their respective covers, passed out. My child lies in a bassinet next to Miss Colivan, sleeping, pink-cheeked and so innocent that I blink back tears.

I kiss my baby's head, then hurry to fill a bag with diapers, pins, clothes, and a purse that I hid in my former bedroom closet, into which I've stuffed all the money I've been stealing from Stan and Deck for the past six weeks. It's only seventy-nine dollars, but it's better than nothing. I toss the bag's strap over my shoulder and scoop up my sweet child.

I turn to leave.

And I run straight into Deck.

"It was the chocolate pudding, wasn't it?" he asks.

I nod—I found the tip not in a cookbook, like I'd expected, but a mothering book (*Want to get your toddler to swallow bitter medicine? No better way to disguise it than chocolate pudding!*)—and try to speak, but my mouth has gone numb. I clutch the baby tighter.

"I thought I was being smart not drinking what you served," he says, swaying in the doorway, "but I ate some of that damn pudding. You knew we wouldn't let you out of town, didn't you? At least one of us has been watching you. Always."

I gauge the space between him and the jamb. Can I push through? Has he ingested enough?

He points at the infant in my arms, closing an eye to focus. "Where are you taking my baby?"

He could have slapped me and gotten less of a reaction. "*Your* baby?"

He nods, his face screwed up in a petulant expression that I used to find charming. "I planted the seed. It's mine."

I come at him with such force that he falls backward. "You forfeited any right to this baby when you put its mother in danger," I snarl. "How could you, Deck? How could you have done this to us?"

He blinks rapidly, stupidly. "It's their rules, Joanie. I didn't make them."

"No, but you followed them."

"You did, too."

I'm crying now, but it's not sadness. It's anger. "I loved you, Deck."

"I loved you, too. Not at first, but eventually. Once I got to know you. I was just like you, Joanie. Taken when I was four. You didn't have to fight it. They give you so much if you just go along. I was hoping I could convince you of that. They wanted me to marry you, you know. I refused. Said I'd only do it once you knew everything, and only if you really wanted to. That was me, Joanie. That's who I am."

I can see he really believes that's good enough. *Shitheel.* My strength is ebbing, the adrenaline that has kept me upright disappearing, leaving pain and bone-deep fatigue in its wake. I need to escape before I collapse.

"I'm leaving, Deck. My mom taught me how to stay on the run. You're never going to find me or this baby."

I dearly hope that's true. I reach for the doorway, grateful to feel the wood beneath my hand. It keeps me upright for another moment. He's still between me and the stairs.

"But Deck, listen to me now." My voice is fading. I cough to bring it back. "Wherever I end up, I'm going to tell the story. You can't stop that. All you can do is let me go without a fight. If you do, I'll make sure your child knows you let us get away to a better life, that you sacrificed for us. What do you say, Deck?"

Only one of his eyes is blinking now. He seems to nod before sliding fully onto his back.

"Thank you," I say to his supine form. I stumble as I step over him, barely catching myself. I'm so close to freedom, but I can't leave, not yet.

I have one more thing I must do.

I grab the locket from the back of the toilet tank, the car keys from the hook in the kitchen, and stagger to the garage, where I find Slow Henry licking the T-bone inside the live trap I set for him. I make the baby as comfortable as I can in the Chevelle's front seat, creating a nest of clean, soft blankets I'd stored in the trunk, and put Slow Henry's cage in the back. This time, I'm not leaving anyone behind.

I back up the Chevelle into the street, parking it at a distance I hope is far enough away. I kiss my sweet baby's head, inhaling the scent of innocence. Leaving the infant feels like ripping my heart out of my chest, but there's one thing more I must do before all my strength is gone. I tug the gloves out of my purse and slide them on before returning to the garage. I gather all the lighter fluid Deck made fun of me for buying. I load it into a bag and return to Johann and Minna Lily's awful basement, flicking on a single light.

I'm grateful Stanley and Dorothy aren't in the house. I'm no murderer. I curse them, though, as I squirt acrid fluid on the dais, across the wood-paneled walls, over the red robes hung on the wall, into the divots of the heavy candleholders, into the closet where Dorothy kept me. I empty one can and then grab another, and then another. The smell is overpowering.

I toss the locket containing the ancestral dirt into the center of the pyre I'm building.

"What the hell are you doing?"

I turn slowly, which is all I can manage. Ronald is wobbling, clutching the doorway for support. I gave him a double dose in his brandy cola knowing he didn't like dessert. It's amazing he can even stand. He looks leathery in the dim light, reptilian. I step closer, because it's important that he hear this.

"I'm burning it all down, Ronald. Destroying your world."

He screeches, his voice part shrill, part slurry. "After all we did for you? All the Mill Street Lilys?"

I'm numb. I have one final question, and I ask it, even though I know the answer. "Why didn't you just adopt? Instead of stealing children?"

His swaying is rhythmic and picking up speed. "They wouldn't have been Lilys."

Exactly as I thought. I've heard more than enough. "I'll give you a better chance than you gave me, Ronald, a running start. You don't have to burn with this house."

"You wouldn't dare." He lunges for me and I step aside, the quick motion costing me. We circle each other, both of us weak. I'm now standing at the base of the steps. He's five feet in front of me, nearer the dais.

I pull out Ursula's rhinestone-encrusted Zippo. I strike the wheel with my thumb, calling a flame to life. "Your last chance, you heartless asshole."

He groans and leans heavily against one of the tables, his hand knocking over a candleholder. I move toward him, the training to help so ingrained that it's automatic. It takes me less than a step before I remember who he really is.

My realization comes too late.

He's holding the heavy brass candleholder in his hand. He flings it at me, aiming for my head. I grunt as it hits my shoulder, knocking the lighter out of my hand. The flame licks the air on the way down, meets the fumes of the lighter fluid, and roars its joy, crackling across the cursed basement.

The force of the ignition forces me back and up. I land on the third stair from the bottom, my skin tingling from the flames. Ronald lies near the dais, a crumpled, motionless figure. The fire is drawing a second breath, preparing to eat this hateful house from the bottom up.

I don't wait for it.

I would have chosen a different ending for Ronald, but I'll be damned if I'll burn with him.

CHAPTER 68

Blood is trickling down my legs, my shoulder is throbbing where the brass candleholder hit it, and the tips of my hair are singed as I limp down the walkway. Part of me knows I can't make it out of Lilydale. I've lost too much blood, exerted too much energy. But I will drive until I pass out, because what choice do I have?

I almost reach the end of the sidewalk before I smell the cigarette, untangle its elegant, gritty smell from the rage of lighter fluid and flame. I stop, frozen. An orange ember burns in the shadows of an oak tree, a flicker compared to the blaze crackling behind me.

Regina steps out. "So, where're you headed?"

We stare at each other. I'm shuddering. The heat of the house is cooking the shirt on my back, but I'm freezing.

Have they made her one of them?

I can't go back.

I won't.

Regina finally speaks. "It's a wide world, sister. We don't have to stay here."

I moan in relief and drop to the ground.

"Jesus," she says, running to me. "You had the baby. You shouldn't be on your feet, you know."

As if on cue, my sweet child wails from the front seat of the nearby car.

Regina's eyes widen. "We have a lot to catch up on."

CHAPTER 69

I'm cocooned in the Chevelle's back seat, a warm breeze kissing my hair.

I am nursing my baby. Slow Henry is sleeping on my lap.

We pass fire trucks screaming into Lilydale.

Regina is driving us south, toward Siesta Key.

She wanted to leave Lilydale immediately until I explained that Angel was being held at the Schramel house. I wanted to be the one to free him, but I didn't have the strength. Fortunately, Regina didn't question me, just ran into the house and came out with a sleeping Angel moments later.

When she leaned over to set him next to me in the back seat, her pearl necklace slipped out of her shirt. I blinked back tears, taking it as a message from my mother, a sign that she was with me now and would keep me safe, just as she had when I was a child.

I caressed Angel's sleeping head as Regina drove us to his mother's house. What monster could steal a child from its mother? How could the Mill Street families have possibly convinced themselves of their righteousness? I could live to be a thousand years old, and I'd never understand it.

It took some convincing for Regina to get Mariela to walk out to a strange car in the middle of the night, but once she did, and laid eyes on her son, she wailed in gratitude. She bundled him in her arms, rocked him, kissed him all over.

He woke up. "Momma?"

She wailed again. He clamped his wiry arms around her neck.

"You have to leave," I said.

Mariela glanced at me, sitting in my own blood, clutching my newborn. She nodded once, her eyes wet and her mouth grim, and strode quickly back to her house.

I knew what her expression meant.

We don't belong here, her and me.

We never did.

And we are going to escape and never return.

Minnesota Town Shaken by Rape, Kidnapping and
Arson Allegations Spanning Decades

By Joan Harken

March 23, 1969

The New York Times

Section A, Page 16

"It's your average small town," declared Ernest
Oleson, the newly elected mayor of Lilydale, Minn.,
population 1,464.

Unlike most small towns, however, 11 Lilydale residents, all direct descendants of the town's founders
and all with homes on once-bucolic Mill Street, are
under indictment for rape, kidnapping and arson in
a scandal that spans generations. The Lilydale police
chief is one of those accused. One of the 11 died as a

result of arson before charges were filed. The surviving Mill Street denizens deny all charges.

The opening trial, that of Barbara Schmidt, is coming to a close. Mrs. Schmidt, 56, is charged with abetting the 1944 kidnapping of Paulie Anna Aandeg, the recently uncovered 1946 kidnapping of Hector Ramirez, whom she raised as her son along with her recently deceased husband, Ronald Schmidt, and the 1968 kidnapping of Angel Gomez.

Ronald Schmidt, who died in a house fire believed to be started by him to gain insurance money, has been posthumously accused of the rape of Hector Ramirez's mother, Maria Ramirez, orchestrating all three kidnappings, as well as insurance fraud. The child he helped abduct and raised as his own child, Deck Schmidt (formerly Hector Ramirez), has also been charged with insurance fraud.

District Judge Stephen L. Miller of Stearns County is presiding over the case. Earlier, the prosecutor, M. Elizabeth Klaphake, rested her case. She had called 13 witnesses, including the town physician, the editor and owner of the *Lilydale Gazette* and Grover Tucker, the now-retired county sheriff who oversaw the search for Paulie Anna Aandeg in 1944. The defense begins its case tomorrow and is expected to conclude within the week.

"A Dark History"

Lilydale was platted by Johann E. Lily and his wife, Minna, in 1857. They were German immigrants as well as brother and sister. Like many early settlers, they created an enclave built around their native language, customs and religion. Fred Munro, director of the Stearns County Historical Society, said Johann and Minna took it even further.

According to church records, the brother and sister had 12 children, only two of whom lived to adulthood, a son and a daughter. The rest were born horribly deformed; those who survived childbirth were kept hidden until their deaths days or weeks later. To guarantee their Germanic bloodline and keep their wealth intact and in the family, Johann impregnated other women in town, and Minna raised the children as her own. In exchange for providing half-Lily children, these women and their families got to live in Lilydale under the patronage of the Lilys.

The town grew and gained a reputation as a safe haven, an escape from the world. Johann and Minna formed a society called the Fathers and Mothers to ensure the town grew in line with their vision.

"Once settled, they only allowed marriage within the immediate family, creating one of the shallowest gene pools in the region. It's a dark history in an otherwise beautiful part of the state," said Munro.

Dr. Sebastian Krause, Lilydale physician and witness for the prosecution at Barbara Schmidt's hearing, testified that intergenerational inbreeding at that level could be responsible for a low fertility rate and a high occurrence of genetic deformity among future generations. He also confirmed that 14 full-blood Lily children live in a facility in Lilydale and are adequately cared for.

"They couldn't have their own children, not healthy ones, not with each other," said Dennis Roth, *Lilydale Gazette* editor, who was offered a plea deal in exchange for his cooperation. "But they wanted to keep the Lily pedigree alive. So the current Lily men looked outside their marriages, just as Johann Lily had."

Paulie Anna Aandeg, now a mother herself, has been informed of her likely provenance. She's chosen not to comment for this article and has requested privacy. Angel Gomez was returned to his family, physically unharmed, less than two months after he first disappeared. The Gomez family has since moved out of Lilydale, and their whereabouts are unknown.

"That's Not Us"

Locals are painfully aware of the town's image on the national stage.

At the Ben Franklin, Kristine Ruprecht said: "Lilydale is a town full of heart, though you'd never know it watching the television or reading the papers. I'm sure the country is wondering if we're all incestuous animals, but believe you me: this was just a few bad apples. Most of us are decent. Those Mill Streeters? That's not us."

Locals are left asking themselves how such a tragedy could have happened under their noses. "You get busy with your life, feeding your family and the like," said William Carstens. "We just figured the people in charge knew what they were doing."

They Kept Records

Several documents seized from Schmidt Insurance indicate a pattern of the Mill Street families, who still called themselves the Fathers and Mothers. While their beneficence ensured no one they approved of ever went hungry, sick or homeless in Lilydale, they also used their influence to control the local population, harass those who stepped out of line and create a culture of fear that had neighbors telling on neighbors. In addition, documents indicate that the Mill Street families forcibly took over the home insurance payments of some locals in the poorer part of town and then burned their houses and chased them out of Lilydale, reaping the payouts for themselves through an elaborate insurance scam.

"I hope they go away for a long time, all of them," said Peggy Warren, a waitress at Tuck's Cafe. "If they did half the things they're accused of, they don't deserve to be free."

When asked if he felt satisfaction to finally find out what happened to Paulie Anna Aandeg, retired Sheriff Grover Tucker had this to say: "I was as pleased as punch when I found out she's alive, and I wish her all the best."

With a lengthy prison sentence likely for all the Mill Street families, there is a palpable feeling of relief in the town to be, finally, free of the Lily influence.

Mayor Oleson said, "We let them run the show for too long. It was easier than any one of us sticking our neck out, we figured. Well, not anymore. We'll survive this. There's good people here, and we'll build something better than what we had."

CHAPTER 70

The sun sparkles across the undulating ocean, dropping toward the water, the surrounding sky lavender and tangerine. The air smells briny and alive, tropical, full of potential. It's nearing nighttime, and the beach is nearly deserted except for the three of us resting beneath a palm tree. "It looks like a goddamned postcard here," Regina says, taking a pull on her beer.

She says this every time we come to the beach, and it makes me smile. Every time.

"Sure does," I say, digging my feet into the sand. My big toe pokes out, and I wiggle it. Frances, now a deliciously chubby toddler, giggles. I drink up the sound. She is healthy and dimpled and *safe*.

We'd driven all night. I don't remember most of it—bits of Regina stopping at gas stations, bringing me sandwiches and water and helping to clean up me and Frances in bathrooms, looking over her shoulder the whole time, and then leading us back to the car and driving some more. I let my baby out of my sight only when I had to—to sleep, to use the bathroom.

When the three of us hit Siesta Key, we rented a cheap room at a long-stay hotel. It had a kitchenette, two beds, a crib, a bathroom. Regina got a bartending job right away. I traded housekeeping services for a used typewriter the motel owner didn't need, made some calls, verified some facts, and hammered out a story for the biggest newspaper in the country.

I've sold two more stories since.

The three of us settled into a routine, one that has carried us for months. I clean rooms and write during the day, never more than a few feet from Frances. Regina slings drinks. We pool our money to pay bills and even started a college fund for Frances. It has only twenty dollars in it, but it's a start.

On Regina's one night off, we stroll two blocks to the beach, chase crabs with good-natured Frances, try to keep her from stuffing sand into her mouth, and splash with her in the ocean.

I love it so much it hurts.

"How long do you want to stay?" Regina asks.

The question gives me a pang. I've been waiting for it, of course. Regina's young, childless. She's been kind to stay as long as she has. Well, Frances Grover Harken and I can make it on our own. My own mother taught me how to live that life.

I'm scared to tell Regina the truth, though, which is that I could stay here forever. Lying might buy me a little more time with her, stretch out the reprieve before I have to do it all alone.

But I'm done lying. I square my shoulders. "I never want to leave," I say.

Frances rolls off my lap and waddles over to inspect a seashell. Her diaper is covered in sand, and her sweet bare feet are filthy. She's the most beautiful thing I've ever seen.

Regina is quiet, and I'm holding my breath, waiting for her response. She doesn't want to hurt me, I'm sure of it. Well, I'm going to let her off the hook. She's already been a better friend than I have any right to expect. She's given up a year of her life and all her savings to get Frances and me on our feet. I didn't even know there were people like that in the world.

I finally get the courage to look at her. "Regina—"

She's smiling so broadly that I momentarily forget what I was about to say.

"What is it?" I ask.

She sweeps the air with her free arm, indicating the sun setting between two palm trees, the jewel-colored sky, the golden sand, the baby. "It's paradise, that's what it is. If you're staying, I'm staying, too."

A warmth grows in my chest, expands until it reaches my eyes. I realize I'm crying. Regina throws her arms around me, and that makes Frances giggle, a rolling melody of pure joy.

I join in the laughter, I can't help it, and then so does Regina.

We're still laughing when the sun drops into the water.

ACKNOWLEDGMENTS

Bloodline is my eighteenth published novel. (I have a couple more, but they're crappers that deserve to live in a drawer.) My kids, friends, family, editors, publicist, agent, and the person who built my computer all helped in this endeavor, but here's the truth: this book wouldn't have been written without you. I would have given up long ago if not for readers who take time out of their busy lives—and often money out of their pockets—to buy and read my books. (If you checked this out from the library, I'm okay with that, too. I love libraries.)

Thank you, particularly those of you who have followed me across genres. It is your attention that turns this pile of words from a doorstop into a book, and for that, you have my gratitude. May your kindness find its way back to you ten times over.

A special thanks to Jessica Tribble, editor extraordinaire, for all the time and talent she dedicated to helping me structure and refine this book. It looked much different when it first landed on her desk, and it's a better book for her efforts. Charlotte Herscher, your patience and guidance took it to the next level; Jon Ford, you are an incredible copyeditor, somehow managing to be surgical, kind, and funny all at once; Kellie Osborne, your sorceress-level proofreading, particularly when it comes to verb tense and continuity, is breathtaking and appreciated; and Sarah Shaw, your support and sunniness make me feel like I'm heard and part of something bigger, and I cannot thank you enough. I am grateful that I get to work with all of you, and everyone at Thomas & Mercer who works hard to get books into the world.

Jill Marsal, thank you for the guidance, both with my stories and my career. I won the lottery when I landed you as an agent. Jessica Morrell, I believe you have freelance edited every single one of my published novels, and your work has made me a better writer. Thank you.

Zoë and Xander, thanks for growing up into amazing humans whom I no longer have to pay to read my books. (That's not true—I still pay you, but at least you follow through on it now.) Carolyn Crane, you are my writing rock. Your wisdom means the world to me, and you're so generous with it. Lori Rader-Day, Susanna Calkins, Catriona McPherson, Shannon Baker, Erica Ruth Neubauer, Johnny Shaw, I love your writing almost as much as I love you; thank you for being on my squad. You too, Terri Bischoff. Cindy, Christine, Tony, and Suzanna, you're the family I choose.

We all come together in story.

FROM *UNSPEAKABLE THINGS*

PROLOGUE

The lonely-scream smell of that dirt basement lived inside me.

Mostly it kept to a shadow corner of my brain, but the second I'd think *Lilydale*, it'd scuttle over and smother me. The smell was a predatory cave stink, the suffocating funk of a great somnolent monster that was all mouth and hunger. It had canning jars for teeth, a single string hanging off a light bulb its uvula. It waited placidly, eternally, for country kids to stumble down its backbone stairs.

It let us swing blindly for that uvula string.

Our fingers would brush against it.

light!

The relief was candy and sun and silver dollars and the last good thing we felt before the beast swallowed us whole, digesting us for a thousand years.

❖

But that's not right.

My imagination, I'd been told, was quite a thing.

The *basement* wasn't the monster.

The man was.

And he wasn't passive. He hunted.

I hadn't returned to Lilydale since that evening. The police and then Mom had asked if I wanted anything from my bedroom, and I'd said no. I'd been thirteen, not stupid, though a lot of people confuse the two.

Now that his funeral had called me home, that cellar stink doubled back with a vengeance, settling like a fishhook way deep in my face where my nose met my brain. The smell crept into my sleep, even, convinced me that I was trapped in that gravedirt basement all over again. I'd thrash and yell, wake up my husband.

He'd hold me. He knew the story.

At least he thought he did.

I'd made it famous in my first novel, shared its inspiration on my cross-country book tour. Except somehow I'd never mentioned the necklace, not to anyone, not even Noah. Maybe that piece felt too precious.

Or maybe it just made me look dumb.

I could close my eyes and picture it. The chain would be considered too heavy now but was the height of fashion in 1983, gold, same metal as the paper airplane charm hanging off it.

I'd believed that airplane necklace was my ticket out of Lilydale.

I didn't actually think I could fly it. *Big duh*, as we said back then. But the boy who wore the necklace? Gabriel? I was convinced he would change everything.

And I guess he did.

CHAPTER 1

"Fifteen two, fifteen four, and a pair for six." Sephie beamed.

Dad matched her smile across the table. "Nice hand. Cass?"

I laid down my cards, trying to keep the gloat off my face and failing. "Fifteen two, fifteen four, fifteen six, and a run for ten!"

Mom moved our peg. "We win."

I shoulder-danced. "I can give you lessons if you want, Sephie."

She rolled her eyes. "In being a poor sport?"

I laughed and dug into the popcorn. Mom had made a huge batch, super salty and doused in brewer's yeast. That had been an hour earlier, when we'd started game night. The bowl was getting down to the old maids. I dug around for the ones showing a peek of white. Part-popped old maids are worth their weight in gold, taste-wise.

"Need a refill?" Dad stood, pointing at Mom's half-full glass sweating in the sticky May air. Summer was coming early this year—at least that's what my biology teacher, Mr. Patterson, had said. Was really going to mess with crops.

He'd seemed bothered by this, but I bet I wasn't the only kid looking forward to a hot break. Sephie and I planned to turn as brown as baked beans and bleach our dark hair blonde. She'd heard from a friend of a friend that baby oil on our skin and vinegar water spritzed in our hair would work as well as those expensive coconut-scented tanning oils and Sun In. We'd even whispered about finding a spot at the edge of our property, where the woods broke for the drainage ditch, to lay out naked. The thought made me shiver. Boys liked no tan lines. I'd learned that watching *Little Darlings*.

Mom lifted her drink and emptied it before offering it to Dad. "Thanks, love."

He strode over to her side of the table, leaning in for a deep kiss before taking her glass. Now I was rolling my eyes right along with Sephie. Mom and Dad, mostly Dad, regularly tried to convince us that we were lucky they were still so in love, but *gross*.

Dad pulled away from kissing Mom and caught our expressions. He laughed his air-only *heh heh* laugh, setting down both glasses so he was free to massage Mom's shoulders. They were an attractive couple, people said it all the time. Mom had been beautiful, every cloudy picture taken of her proved that, and she still had the glossy brown hair and wide eyes, though incubating Sephie and me had padded her hips and belly. Dad was handsome, too, with a Charles Bronson thing going on. You could see how they'd ended up together, especially after Mom downed a glass of wine, and she'd let spill how she'd always been drawn to the bad boys, even back in high school.

My immediate family was small: just Mom and Aunt Jin; my big sister, Persephone (my parents had a thing for Greek names); and Dad. I didn't know my dad's side of the family. They wouldn't be worth sweeping into a dustpan, at least that's what my grandpa on Mom's side swore to my grandma the winter he died of a massive heart attack. My grandma hadn't argued. She'd been a docile lady who always smelled of fresh-baked bread no matter the season. A few weeks after Grandpa passed, she died of a stroke, which sounds like a swim move but is not.

They'd lost a son, my mom's parents, when I was three years old. He'd been a wild one, I guess. Died playing chicken in a '79 Camaro, probably drinking, people said. I could only remember one thing about

Uncle Richard. It was at his funeral. Jin was crying, but Mom was crying louder, and she went up to Grandpa for a hug. He turned away from her, and she stood there, looking sadder than a lost baby.

I asked her about it once, about why Grandpa wouldn't hug her. She said I was too young to remember anything from Rich's funeral, and besides, the past should stay in the past.

"I think your mother is the most beautiful woman in the world," Dad said in the here and now, rubbing Mom's shoulders while she closed her eyes and made a dreamy face.

"Fine by me," I said. "Just get a room."

Dad swept his arm in a wide arc, his smile tipped sideways. "I have a whole house. Maybe *you* should learn to relax. I'll rub your shoulders next."

My eyes cut to Sephie. She was flicking a bent corner of a playing card.

"I'm okay," I said.

"Sephie? Your neck tense?"

She shrugged.

"That's my girl!" He moved to her, laying his hands on her bony shoulders. She was two years older than me but skinny no matter what she ate, all buckeroo teeth and dimples, a dead ringer for Kristy McNichol, though I'd eat my own hair before I'd tell her.

Dad started in on Sephie. "It's good to feel good," he murmured to her.

That made me itch inside. "Can we play another game of cribbage?"

"Soon," Dad said. "First, I want to hear everyone's summer dreams."

I groaned. Dad was big on dreams. He believed you could be whatever you wanted, but you had to "see it" first. Hippie-dippie, but I suppose a person got used to it. Both Sephie and I swapped a look. We knew without saying it that Dad would not approve of our plan to transform ourselves into blondes. *Girls should not try to be anything for anyone,* he'd tell us. We needed to command our own minds and bodies.

Again, *gross*.

"I want to visit Aunt Jin," I offered.

Mom had been going half-lidded, but her eyes popped open at the mention of her sister. "That's a great plan! We can drive to Canada for a week."

"Excellent," Dad agreed.

My heart soared. We hardly ever traveled farther than up the highway to Saint Cloud for co-op groceries, but now that Mom had her full-time teaching job, there'd been talk of road-tripping this summer. Still, I'd been afraid to suggest we visit Aunt Jin. If Mom and Dad were in the wrong mood, they'd kill that idea for eternity, and I really needed some Aunt Jin time. I loved her to death.

She was the only one who didn't pretend I was normal.

She was there when I was born, stayed on for a few weeks after that to help out Mom, but my first actual memory of her was from right after Uncle Richard's funeral. Aunt Jin was a decade younger than Mom, which put her at no more than seventeen at the time. I'd caught her staring at my throat, something a lot of people do.

Rather than look away, she'd smiled and said, "If you'd been born two hundred years ago, they'd have drowned you."

She was referring to the red, ropy scar that circled where my neck met my shoulders, thick as one of Mr. T's gold chains. Apparently, I'd shot out of Mom with the umbilical cord coiled around my throat, my body blue as a Berry Punch Fla-Vor-Ice, eyes wide even though I wasn't breathing. I exited so fast that the doctor dropped me.

Or at least that's the story I was told.

There I hung, a human dingleberry, until one of the nurses swooped in and unwound the cord, uncovering an amniotic band strangling me beneath that. The quick-thinking nurse cut it, then slapped me till I wailed. She'd saved my life, but the band had branded me. Mom said my lesion looked like an angry scarlet snake at first. That seemed dramatic. In any case, I suspect the nurse was a little shaky when she finally handed me over. The whole fiasco wasn't exactly a job well done. Plus, *Rosemary's Baby* had hit theaters a couple years before, and everyone in that room must have been wondering what had propelled me out of the womb with such force.

"It would have been bad luck to keep a baby whose own mother tried to strangle it twice," Aunt Jin finished, chucking me under my chin. I decided on the spot that it was an okay joke because Mom was her sister, and they both loved me.

Here's another nutty saying Aunt Jin liked to toss my way: "Earth. If you know what you're doing, you're in the wrong place." She'd waggle her thick eyebrows and tip an imaginary cigar as she spoke. I didn't know where that gesture was from, but she'd giggle so hard, her laugh like marbles thrown up into the sunshine, that I'd laugh along with her.

That's how every Aunt Jin visit began. The joke about drowning me, some meaty life quotes, and then we'd dance and sing along to her Survivor and Johnny Cougar tapes. She'd spill all about her travels and let me sip the honey-colored liqueur she'd smuggled from Amsterdam or offer me a packet of the biscuits she loved so much and that I'd pretend didn't taste like old saltines. Sephie would want to join in, I'd see her on the sidelines, but she never quite knew how to hop on the ride that was Aunt Jin.

I did.

Aunt Jin and me were *thick as thieves*.

That made it okay that Dad liked Sephie way more than me.

I wrinkled my nose. He was really going to town on that massage. Mom had left to refill her and Dad's drinks even though he'd offered, since it was taking him so long to rub Sephie's shoulders.

"Sephie," I asked, because her eyes were closed and I wanted that to stop, "what's *your* dream for the summer?"

She spoke quietly, almost a whisper. "I want to get a job at the Dairy Queen."

Dad's hands stopped kneading. A look I couldn't name swept across his face, and I thought I'd memorized every twitch of his. He almost immediately swapped out that weird expression for a goofy smile that lifted his beard a half inch. "Great! You can save for college."

Sephie nodded, but she looked so sad all of a sudden. She'd been nothing but moods and mysteries since December. The change in temperament coincided with her getting boobs (*Santa Claus delivered!* I'd teased her), and so I didn't need to be *Remington Steele*'s Laura Holt to understand that one was connected to the other.

Mom returned to the dining room, a fresh drink in each hand, her attention hooked on my dad. "Another game of cribbage?"

I leaned back to peek at the kitchen clock. It was ten thirty. Every kid I told thought it was cool I didn't have a bedtime. I supposed they were right. Tomorrow was the first day of the last week of seventh grade for me, though. "I'm going to sleep. You guys can play three handed."

Mom nodded.

"Don't let the bedbugs bite!" Dad said.

I didn't glance at Sephie as I walked away. I felt a quease about leaving her up with them when they'd been drinking, but I wrote it off as payback for her always falling asleep first the nights we were left alone, back when we'd sometimes sleep together. She'd let me climb in bed with her, which was nice, but then she'd crash out like a light, and there I'd lay agonizing over every sound, and in an old house like ours there was lots of unexplained thumping and creaking in the night. When I'd finally drift off, everything but my mouth and nose covered by the quilt, she'd have a sleep spaz and wake me right back up.

I couldn't remember the last time we'd slept in the same bed, hard as I tried on the walk to the bathroom. I rinsed off my face, then reached for my toothbrush, planning out tomorrow's clothes. If I woke up forty-five minutes early, I could use the hot rollers, but I hadn't okayed it with Sephie, and I'd already excused myself from the table. I brushed my teeth and spit, rinsing with the same metallic well water that turned the ends of my hair orange.

I couldn't reach my upstairs bedroom without walking through a corner of the dining room. I kept my eyes trained on the ground, my shoulders high around my ears, sinking deep in my thoughts. My homework was done, my folders organized inside my garage-sale Trapper Keeper that was as good as new except for the Scotch-taped rip near the seam.

First period tomorrow was supposed to be English, but instead we were to proceed directly to the gym for an all-school presentation. The posters slapped around declared it a Summer Safety Symposium, which some clever eighth graders had shorthanded to Snake Symposium. *SSS.* I'd heard the rumors this week that Lilydale kids were disappearing and then coming back changed. Everyone had. Aliens, the older kids on the bus claimed, were snatching kids and *probing* them.

I knew all about aliens. When I waited in the grocery checkout line, the big-eyed green creatures stared at me from the front cover of the *National Enquirer* right below the shot of Elizabeth Taylor's vampire monkey baby.

Right. *Aliens.*

Probably the symposium was meant to put those rumors to rest, but I didn't think it was a good idea to hold it tomorrow. The break in our routine—combined with it being the last week of school—would make everyone extra squirrelly.

I was halfway up the stairs when I heard a knock that shivered the baby hairs on my neck. It sounded like it came from right below me, from the basement. That was a new sound.

Mom, Dad, and Sephie must have heard it, too, because they'd stopped talking.

"Old house," Dad finally said, a hot edge to his voice.

I shot up the rest of the stairs and across the landing, closed my door tightly, and slipped into my pajamas, tossing my T-shirt and terry cloth shorts into my dirty-clothes hamper before setting my alarm clock. I decided I *would* try the hot rollers. Sephie hadn't called dibs on them, and who knew? I might end up sitting next to Gabriel during the symposium. I should look my best.

I was jelly-bone tired, but my copy of *Nellie Bly's Trust It or Don't* guilted me from the top of my treasure shelves. Aunt Jin had sent it to me as an early birthday present. The book was full of the most fantastical stories and drawings, like the account of Martin J. Spalding, who was a professor of mathematics at age fourteen, or Beautiful Antonia, "the Unhappy Woman to Whom Love Always Brought Death!"

I'd been savoring the stories, reading only one a night so they'd last. I'd confided to Jin that I was going to be a writer someday. Attaining such a goal required practice and discipline. Didn't matter how tired I was. I needed to study the night's Nellie.

I flipped the book open to a random page, drawn instantly to the sketch of a proud German shepherd.

Nellie Bly's — **Trust It or Don't!**

The DOG THAT TRAVELED AROUND THE WORLD IN 30 DAYS!

COACH IS A GERMAN SHEPHERD WHO WAS ACCIDENTALLY LEFT BEHIND WHEN HIS FAMILY HAD TO FLEE WORLD WAR II GERMANY. IMAGINE THE FAMILY'S SURPRISE WHEN COACH APPEARED AT THEIR NEW CALIFORNIA HOME HALF A WORLD AWAY! HE IS BELIEVED TO HAVE SNEAKED ONTO A CARGO BOAT THAT BROUGHT HIM ACROSS THE OCEAN, AND THEN HE MADE HIS WAY TO HIS FAMILY. NOW THAT'S WHAT WE CALL PUPPY LOVE!

I smiled, satisfied. I could write that. My plan was to begin drafting one Nellie a week as soon as school was out. I'd already written a contract, which I'd called Cassie's Summer Writing Duties. It included a plan for getting my portfolio to Nellie Bly International Limited before Labor Day and a penalty (no television for a week) if I did not fulfill the terms of my contract. I'd had Sephie witness me signing it.

I set the huge yellow-covered book on my treasure shelf and stretched, checking my muscles. Did they want to sleep stretched out long underneath my bed or curled up short in my closet?

Long, they said.

All right, then. I grabbed a pillow and the top quilt off my bed and slid the pillow under the box springs first. I followed on my back, dragging the quilt behind. I had to squish to reach the farthest corner. The moon spilled enough light into my room that I could make out the black coils overhead.

They were the last thing I saw before drifting off to sleep.

ABOUT THE AUTHOR

Photo © 2019 Cindy Hager, CK Photography

Jess Lourey is the Amazon Charts bestselling author of *Unspeakable Things*, *The Catalain Book of Secrets*, the Salem's Cipher thrillers, and the Mira James mysteries, among many other works, including young adult, short stories, and nonfiction. An Agatha, Anthony, and Lefty Award nominee, Jess is a tenured professor of creative writing and sociology and a leader of writing retreats. She is also a recipient of The Loft's Excellence in Teaching fellowship, a Psychology Today blogger, and a TEDx presenter. Check out her TEDx Talk for the inspiration behind her first published novel. When she's not leading writing workshops, reading, or spending time with her friends and family, you can find her working on her next story. Discover more at www.jessicalourey.com.